SEDUCED BY A SCOUNDREL

"Has no one told you that a woman is more likely to be persuaded to succumb to your wiles if you refrain from insulting her intelligence?"

He laughed out loud.

"I marveled at first that a lady of your beauty would remain unclaimed at your age, but now I understand."

"Well, that's frank!"

He pushed her backward into the carpet of bluebells.

"Mr. Bourbonnais!" she exclaimed.

"Gabriel," he corrected her as he removed the pins that had been holding her hair in a prim chignon at the nape of her neck. "Such lovely hair. I have longed to see it like this."

He seemed genuinely moved.

Then he kissed her.

She had to admit, he did *that* well too . . .

From "A Breath of Scandal" by Kate Huntington

BOOK YOUR PLACE ON OUR WEBSITE AND MAKE THE READING CONNECTION!

We've created a customized website just for our very special readers, where you can get the inside scoop on everything that's going on with Zebra, Pinnacle and Kensington books.

When you come online, you'll have the exciting opportunity to:

- View covers of upcoming books
- Read sample chapters
- Learn about our future publishing schedule (listed by publication month *and author*)
- Find out when your favorite authors will be visiting a city near you
- Search for and order backlist books from our online catalog
- Check out author bios and background information
- Send e-mail to your favorite authors
- Meet the Kensington staff online
- Join us in weekly chats with authors, readers and other guests
- Get writing guidelines
- AND MUCH MORE!

**Visit our website at
http://www.kensingtonbooks.com**

UNTAMEABLE

Catherine Blair
Kate Huntington
Donna Simpson

ZEBRA BOOKS
KENSINGTON PUBLISHING CORP.

http://www.kensingtonbooks.com

ZEBRA BOOKS are published by

Kensington Publishing Corp.
850 Third Avenue
New York, NY 10022

All Kensington titles, imprints and distributed lines are available
at special quantity discounts for bulk purchases for sales promotion,
premiums, fund-raising, educational or institutional use.

Special book excerpts or customized printings can also be created
to fit specific needs. For details, write or phone the office of the
Kensington Special Sales Manager: Kensington Publishing Corp.,
850 Third Avenue, New York, NY 10022. Attn. Special Sales
Department. Phone: 1-800-221-2647.

Zebra and the Z logo Reg. U.S. Pat. & TM Off.

First Printing: October 2002
10 9 8 7 6 5 4 3 2 1

Printed in the United States of America

CONTENTS

THE ROGUE'S WIFE
Catherine Blair

Chapter One

Charlotte stared at the snow as it whirled past the drawing room window in dizzying swirls and eddies. She suppressed a shudder and braced herself as though she were facing that cutting January wind instead of sitting cozily wrapped in fully three layers of wool. Four, if one counted the dowdy, drab-colored shawl she'd tucked tightly around her shoulders.

It wasn't as though she was cold. On the contrary, she felt rather uncomfortably overwarm. Somehow, though, she felt as if she needed the protection.

"Yes, Lord Sinclair," she murmured, practicing the correct tone that combined polite pleasure with genteel restraint. "I would be delighted to accept your offer of marriage."

What she truly felt, of course, was relief. After four Seasons, a plain young lady, even one with an entirely respectable dowry like her own, couldn't really hold much hope of making a good match. Or even, really, a bad one.

Until recently, Charlotte hadn't allowed her thoughts to run in the direction of matrimony at all. Upon the death of her parents, she'd come to live in London with her sister, Lady Binghamton, and the Seasons were incidental.

But now, just when her situation with the Binghamtons had become unbearable, Sinclair had stepped in and asked for her hand.

It didn't matter why. It didn't matter that it was utterly inexplicable. It only mattered that he had.

The wind roared at the windows, rattling the casings and scratching at the panes like a live, hungry thing. She pulled the curtains closed to shut out its wildness.

"Yes," she said firmly. "I would be delighted."

She knew Sinclair, of course. Though it was primarily for his reputed ability to juggle a spectacular number of vices while still retaining the looks, charm, and vitality of a young Adonis. He was handsome, yes. And he possessed the kind of charm that made a woman's heart pound harder when he chose to turn his full attention upon her. At least she had heard that it did. Sinclair had never chosen to charm her.

He had, however, chosen to marry her.

"Who are you talking to?"

Charlotte turned around to see her brother-in-law standing in the doorway. He was a tall man, imposing, perhaps handsome, though there was a vague air of dissipation about him. Her sister had assured her, however, that he'd been the catch of the Season when she'd married him. A bit wild in his day, but then reformed rakes made the best husbands, didn't they? Charlotte had never been able to tell Amanda that she had grave doubts as to the man's reformation.

"Only talking to myself," she replied. She tucked the shawl more tightly around her shoulders.

"My poor dear," he said, his sandy brows coming together in an expression of deep concern. "I really believe we should talk about this more seriously. I told Sinclair you would consider his suit because you had instructed me to do so. But I am beginning to think I should have yielded to my better judgment.

"The married state can provide benefits of course, but it should not be taken lightly," he went on sternly. "And as for Sinclair wishing to marry you? To be honest, I believe I thought the man was joking." He laughed and then gave her a tight squeeze about the waist to show that he was merely funning.

"Really, my dear," he went on, "you belong with your family. What would we do without our little Charlotte?"

He dragged out the syllables of her name as though she were a pet dog or his favorite downstairs maid. She extracted herself from his overfriendly embrace.

"I wish to marry," she said staunchly, going back to the window to peer out again through the curtains. "And I wish to marry Sinclair."

Her brother-in-law gave a dismissive snort. "Sinclair is an unprincipled scoundrel. A wastrel with no morals to speak of. He's accepted by the *ton* on sufferance, but he is a man of no reputation. Not the kind of man a woman of breeding wants to wed."

Charlotte's resolution faltered. Could things really be worse than her life here? She knew they could. Here she was merely humiliated. After all, Binghamton confined himself to looks and squeezes. The man would never stoop to actually seducing someone so plain as herself. But a husband owned his wife, body and soul.

Perhaps, if she waited just a little longer, she'd have an offer from someone else. Someone closer to the kind of man a girl, even one who isn't a beauty, invents for her marriage dreams.

She felt Binghamton's eyes upon her back and girded herself with resolution. Lord Sinclair it would be. It was patently impossible that the rakish lord had conceived a sudden *tendre* for her. She'd met the man at precisely two musicales, a gala ball, and four nodding passes in the park. And she knew well enough that with her unremarkable face, pale brows, colorless hair, and stick-thin figure, she was hardly likely to attract the attention of an experienced connoisseur of beautiful women.

Binghamton's thoughts must have followed the same lines, for he gave a heavy sigh. "Charlotte, you're not the first young lady he's asked to marry. Girls with less breeding than you have had the sense to turn him down. He wants a wife now, for whatever reason. Do not believe that he has asked because he cares for you. He has asked because he thinks you'll accept, and because he thinks you would not interfere with his mad, dangerous, immoral lifestyle once you were married."

Again his arm slid around her waist. "Don't leave us

little Charlotte.'' He pulled on one of her mousy ringlets, destroying what little curl her maid had been able to coax into it. ''And certainly not for the likes of him.''

No, she would do it. Whether she was Sinclair's last choice or not, she would accept him.

As Binghamton said, she could only offer Sinclair a life of placid comforts and an absolute lack of interference in his life. But she would be free.

The door opened and she felt Binghamton release her quickly and step away. Behind the butler was the tall form of Lord Sinclair, his eyes upon her, his face unsmiling.

''Lord Sinclair,'' she said, in what she hoped was a polite, easy tone. ''How kind of you to visit us, particularly in such dreadful weather. Are you quite frozen through? Do sit down. May I ring for tea?''

''Lady Charlotte,'' he said, coming to her and bowing deeply over her hand just as though he had always treated her with such warmth. ''I am pleased to find you at home.''

Merciful heavens, but he was handsome. She'd met him before, of course, but never as a man she could possibly consider sharing . . . well, all those things married people shared. He stood up and smiled at her, the picture of dangerous sensuality and promise. She could see now why ladies tended to blush and giggle when he turned the full heat of his dark eyes upon them.

''Lady Binghamton was requesting your presence, sir,'' the butler said, bowing to her brother-in-law. Charlotte wasn't sure if her invalid sister was merely feeling left out of the party or was doing her the favor of giving her time alone with Sinclair. Either way, she was glad. Best to get this over with quickly.

Binghamton was obviously trying to send her a silent message via raised brows and subtle hand gestures, but she turned her back on him. ''Browning,'' she said to the butler, ''will you bring up some tea, please?''

Her brother-in-law was ushered reluctantly out of the room, and with the close of the door, she and Sinclair were alone.

For a moment or two they merely looked at each other.

Likely he was wondering just how much she knew of him and therefore how much charm weaving would be required.

"I believe," she said at last, "it's traditional that you should begin with an extravagant and highly unbelievable compliment. Not too personal, of course. Perhaps regarding my dress, or my skill at speaking in complete sentences."

For a moment, she regretted her sarcasm. After all, the deal was not yet made. To have the only proposal she was ever likely to receive come crashing around her ears would be a disaster indeed. But then she saw a spark of humor in Lord Sinclair's eyes.

"May I say how very much that gown becomes you," he began gravely. "Putty is your color."

Charlotte pinched her lips together to keep from laughing. Touché. It would take more than a modiste's skills to make her into a beauty. But a small part of her swore that she would stop wearing such dull colors once she was married.

"And your grasp of the English language is altogether admirable," he continued. He led her to the settee and then sat down beside her. His buff-colored pantaloons were nearly touching the drab wool of her gown. It was the closest they'd ever been. "Now," he said, "you're to giggle a little and perhaps blush, so that I don't get discouraged."

She did feel a telltale warmth creeping up her cheeks, but she ignored it. There was no point in pretending this was a normal courtship. Why couldn't he have been ordinary-looking? It would have made things far less awkward. "Let us say that I have done so and that you may consider yourself encouraged."

"Very well," he said, dragging out the words as though he were slightly uncomfortable as well. "Now, I will embark on a rather difficult and delicate subject, during which, at the height of my emotional outpouring, the tea tray will arrive."

At that moment, Browning rattled at the door, cleared his throat explosively, and after a discreet pause, entered the room. A man of his experience and training was perfectly adept at pretending he did not see that his mistress's sister and one of London's most notorious rakes were sitting together in what might be vulgarly termed a fit of giggles.

"Lord Sinclair," Charlotte said, once the door closed on the butler's heels. "Let us both speak plainly. I believe you are here to ask me something?" She tried not to remember what the gossipmongers said: that he had asked at least three other young ladies the same question but had been coolly rebuffed.

Sinclair looked taken aback for a moment, but quickly recovered his polished manners. "I admire your directness," he said with a faint smile. He seemed to hesitate for a moment, gathering his thoughts. Charlotte watched his long, elegant hands as they folded together, opened, then folded again.

She fixed her eyes on his face and tried to recall that this was a business arrangement. Sinclair wanted a pliable wife, and she wanted a husband. Any husband.

"I know we do not know each other well, Charlotte, but I feel as though we do." There was something in the use of her given name that seemed even more intimate than the way her hand was suddenly pressed between his own. "I've been watching you for a long time."

"You have?" She stared at those hands. They were perfect—hands a sculptor would cry to see—and they were holding her own with a perfect imitation of sincerity.

"I have," he said with a little shrug. He smiled his quizzical smile again, as though he wasn't at all sure what he had gotten himself into. But then he sobered. "I know that you dance very well, though never with the same man more than once. You are the only lady in all of London who actually listens to the opera, you prefer piquet to whist, and your mare is too short in the back for perfection, but you had a hand in training her and refuse to give her up."

His eyes, so dark they seemed to be lacking even pupils, were watching her with a laughing expression. Though if he was mocking her or himself, it was impossible to tell. It didn't matter, she reminded herself. It only mattered that they made the deal.

"You know me very well indeed, then," she murmured with only the faintest trace of facetiousness. She was flattered though. She'd had no idea Sinclair had noticed her enough to even be certain of her name. She felt her cheeks heat with a pleasure she did not wish to feel.

Sinclair apparently chose not to hear her dismissive tone. He looked at her as though she'd told him she loved him. "I'd like to know you better," he said softly.

She meant to say something cutting, to let him know she wasn't taken in by his silver-tongued charm, but somehow there was nothing in her head but a faint ringing. She tried to recall her sister Amanda and how Binghamton had duped her.

"Really, Charlotte," Lord Sinclair said, "I know I am neither clever nor charming, but at this critical moment it is imperative you pretend I am. Any more of this agony, and I shall be obliged to resort to telling very unamusing anecdotes, or do something utterly desperate, like commenting on the thinness of company in town or the unpleasantness of the weather."

"Yes," she said, wildly hoping that that was the proposal.

"Yes," he repeated. "Do keep thinking that. Now"— he took her other hand alongside the first, effectively forcing her to look at him—"I am going to ask you to go driving in the park with me Wednesday." He gave her a look as though prompting a child. "And what are you going to reply?"

"Yes," she said, unable to stop a laugh.

She'd seen him driving in the park on several occasions. Always with a different beautiful woman by his side. How very odd the *ton* would think it when they saw plain, silent Lady Charlotte Fawnhope by his side. But, she wouldn't think about that. She would only think about what it felt like now, as he held both her hands in his and looked entirely pleased.

"Excellent. We're making headway. And now I am going to ask you to dance with me, twice, at the Graves's ball Thursday. Despite the fact that it will be about as exciting as playing cards with no suits, and there will not be a waltz to be heard." He grinned. "And your reply will be—"

"Yes." Good God, no wonder this man got everything he wanted. It was impossible to refuse him when he looked so boyishly delighted.

"And now, since things are going so well," his voice dropped to a note of complete seriousness, "I am going to ask you to be my wife." His lips twitched into a smile that tightened quickly into a nervous line. He drew a breath in the silence. "And what are you going to say?"

She smiled at him, relief and joy singing harmony within her. "Yes," she said. "Oh, yes."

It was a glorious moment in which the choir should have sung, the violins played, and the audience risen to their feet in thunderous applause. Instead, two people who still didn't know each other at all found themselves staring at each other, both grinning with a mixture of sheepishness and terror.

"Excellent," Sinclair said at last, rubbing his hands on the knees of his pantaloons. "Excellent."

Charlotte, her hands feeling quite light now that he had released them, twisted her fingers together and contemplated them. "Would you like some tea?" she hazarded, wondering if they should shake hands or some such thing to seal the bargain.

"No, no." He stood. "I should be off. Thank you, Charlotte. You've relieved my mind a great deal. Your brother-in-law made it most obvious that he was reluctant to countenance the match. Not that I—well, anyway. I'm delighted, yes. Really delighted. I like you. No nonsense about you. You'll make an exceedingly amiable companion, I'm certain. I think we will deal very well together."

"I hope so," she replied, suddenly aware of the enormity of what she'd just done. This man would be her husband forever. She'd just bound herself irrevocably to a man she hardly knew. And worse, one about whom the things she knew were highly suspect.

To her surprise, he stepped closer to her and took her chin in his hand. "Let's marry soon. I see little point in waiting."

She knew he was thinking the same as she: *Let's get this over and done with. Before we have the chance to think about it overmuch.*

"Shall we do it by special license? You plan whatever you'd like. Just tell me when and where, and I'll turn up."

He'd turn up. Just as though it was any other party he was obliged to attend. It wasn't how she'd pictured it, but it would have to do.

"Tomorrow?" she suggested. Then, seeing his look of alarm, asked, "Is that too soon?"

He stared at her, a bemused expression on his face. Perhaps, like her, he wasn't sure this was really happening. "I'm busy tomorrow," he said hesitantly. "The day after?"

"Very well. The day after tomorrow."

"Where?"

She thought for a moment, then shrugged. "We may as well do it here. No sense in making a big fuss."

He began to say something, then stopped, let out a breath, and started again. "You're a remarkable woman. I think this may work out very well indeed."

"I'm certain it will."

He looked at her intently. "Are you certain this is what you want? There is no need to make up your mind right away if you are unsure. I mean, I am sincere in my offer, but I want you to be positive you want to accept it."

She must have nodded because he smiled. "Thank you, Charlotte," he said. And then he leaned down and kissed her.

She'd never been kissed by anyone, much less by an excruciatingly handsome dark-eyed man who knew exactly what he was doing. His mouth was warm and insistent. Before she knew what he was about, she found that his arms were around her, one hand on her waist, the other disentangling the shawl wound around her shoulders.

Then, just when she thought she would be crushed under the weight of so many clashing emotions and sensations, he pulled away. "That's what I like about you, Charlotte," he said with a smile. "No romantic folderol." He stepped back and straightened his coat. "Once we're married, we won't get in each other's way in the least. No bother or nonsense." He bowed cheerfully over her hand. "I'll come by for you Wednesday for our drive."

He was unaffected. The horrid man was absolutely unaffected. Her head was swimming and her knees had turned to trembling aspic. Her life had been changed with a touch, and with that touch, Sinclair had aroused a passion that she assumed had not existed. But for him it was all in a day's work.

"Yes," she said, knowing she was making a poor show of calm. "I will see you tomorrow."

Once he was gone, she sank down on the settee and stared absently into space while the wind shook the windowpanes. There, it was over. They'd made a civilized arrangement with the explicit understanding that they would not interfere with each other's pursuits. She would be free of Binghamton's increasingly inappropriate attentions at last. But somehow she had the impression she'd just leaped from the frying pan into the fire.

Chapter Two

Lord John Sinclair was drunk. And having spent the last several hours attempting to attain this desirable state, he was delighted to find his head slightly muzzy and his spirits soaring. Everything was right in the world. Particularly here in the stinking, dark cavern that was his favorite gaming house.

"Care for a hand, Sinclair?" Richard Palmer asked. His friend waved a pack of rather greasy cards at him and gestured toward a scarred gaming table. John digested this idea for a moment, considering whether he'd rather gamble or continue in his pursuit of fermented bliss. He was experienced enough to know one couldn't do both, and generally was wise enough to know he was better at the former. The odds were better.

His hesitation lost them the table, however, and two rather grizzled campaigners slid in and began an intent game of ecarte. Reif's was crowded tonight, and not with the very best company. It was mostly the usual crowd: the gamblers and gamesters who lived on the fringes of good society, the Corinthians who came here after their clubs threw them out for drunkenness, and the occasional cutpurse. The place was well known for its mixed crowd, its late hours, and high stakes.

Not, Sinclair reflected, for the quality of its spirits. He

took another swallow of indifferent brandy and shrugged. "Couldn't play anyway. I'm celebrating." He took Palmer by the elbow. "Let me buy you a drink. I just got married."

The boyish young man looked at him as though he'd grown a second head. Then he shook himself. "Oh. Ha, ha. I thought you said you just got married."

"Married," Sinclair confirmed.

Palmer gave him a look of suspicion, which then relaxed into relief. "You mean you have picked another pigeon to *ask*. Asking isn't the same thing as actually receiving the affirmative, you know."

Sinclair laughed and gave a shrug. After all, it was common knowledge several protective papas had given him a resounding no to his inquiries into the matrimonial receptiveness of their daughters. A man with a cultivated reputation for recklessness, perhaps even rakishness, should be proud that he had well-bred families locking up their daughters. He certainly shouldn't feel humiliated.

He put on his most wolfish smile. "Oh, no, this is signed, sealed, and delivered. Did the deed yesterday morning out of her sister's drawing room. Didn't want to give her a chance to change her mind, you know." He signaled to a waiter for a drink for his friend. "Don't look so slack-jawed, Richard. Someone was bound to be desperate enough to accept me at some point."

His friend looked slightly put out. "Why didn't you warn us? You might have let us get used to the idea first." He grabbed a tall man by the sleeve and dragged him into the conversation. "Vaughn, Sinclair just got buckled the other day, did you hear? Someone finally said yes." He shook his head in disgust. "Why is everyone suddenly married at once? Iverley here just got leg shackled to my sister last spring, you know."

Iverley gave a helpless and pleased shrug. John couldn't imagine what the man was so delighted about. But then again, Iverley was more of a sporting man; perhaps he didn't feel as though marriage was much of a sacrifice.

"All this marrying will give my family ideas," Palmer went on. "It doesn't look right for a man not to have any bachelor friends. And your new wife isn't likely to want you to keep up your current circle of associates." Palmer gave a knowing look around the gaming establishment.

John thought about his friend's comment for a moment and then shrugged. He hadn't given it much consideration. Yes, there were certain acquaintances that he was certain the new Lady Sinclair wouldn't want running tame in her house, but it wasn't as though he would be entertaining at home much anyway.

It had been understood from the first: Charlotte would have her life and he would have his. All marriages were that way. His would merely be more so.

"Who is the fortunate one?" asked Palmer. "And why all the secretiveness? She isn't—"

"No," John said quickly. "Of course she isn't with child. It wasn't as though it was a secret. There merely didn't seem to be a reason to make a scene about getting married. It's a necessary evil, but I refuse to let it change things."

Iverley regarded him with a long, considering look. "Marriage always changes things," he said in his quiet, rational way, "whether you mean for it to or not."

John felt unaccountably irritated. He hadn't had any desire to marry, of course. But it had to be done at some point, and he had promised himself that he would take care of that duty this Season. He would be five-and-thirty in the spring. By that age his own father had had four children in the nursery. Of course the man hadn't lived to see them grow up, but that was the way of the Sinclair men. Rakehells every one. They died young, but with a smile on their faces.

So the time to marry had come and he had done his duty. It hadn't been easy; yes, prim, moral fate had had a good laugh in his face for a while. Four refusals in the last Season alone. He hadn't anticipated how much damage he'd done to his own reputation. Not much left on the market to a man of his past but plain, dull little things with no hope of something better.

"Marriage changed things for you, perhaps," he said shortly, downing the rest of his brandy in a gulp. Iverley had been a well-known Corinthian no one had expected would marry. But to everyone's surprise he'd wound up shackled to a little bookish chit from the country. "But it's well known that you are an anomaly in good Society. You married for love. For the rest of us, marriage is something best gotten over with and forgotten about.'' He gave his friends a thin smile. ''As to my lady wife, I have married Lady Charlotte Fawnhope.''

He felt as though the entire room had suddenly fallen silent. Both Iverley and Palmer were staring at him in slightly openmouthed surprise.

''Lady Charlotte Fawnhope?'' Palmer echoed incredulously.

Iverley raised one russet brow. ''The little dab of a thing who came out four Seasons ago?''

''Yes,'' he growled. ''And what of that?''

''Nothing,'' Iverley said quickly. ''I hardly know the woman. We danced once last year, and she didn't speak a word to me. But,'' he added, ''there is often something fascinating about a quiet woman. They can be the most interesting. My wife is very shy with strangers.''

''But at least Georgie is pretty,'' Palmer interjected.

It was true. Charlotte's plainness was undisputed. He himself had likely commented on it in the past. But he'd asked her because he knew she'd be undemanding, and likely pleasant enough company when interaction was necessary. And because she likely had as few choices as he.

They were, effectively, the last man and woman on earth.

He knew the correct thing to do would be to plant Richard a facer for daring to insinuate that his new wife was not the most lovely creature to walk the earth. Instead he found that he was laughing. ''Yes, she's not much to look at, is she? I suppose our children will be absolute frights. But who cares of that? At least she said yes.''

''I wish you happiness,'' Iverley said with a smile. ''Despite what you may think, marriage can be a comfort and a pleasure.''

Sinclair was about to retort with his usual skepticism when he realized that Charlotte wasn't likely to interfere with his current comforts and pleasures. He smiled, feeling rather clever.

''Well, if it isn't Sinclair the Sinner,'' Blynesmith shouted across the room. ''I've a friend at *The Times* who says there's to be an announcement tomorrow that you're married. Once you found someone willing to take up your offer, you lost no time! Dash it all, man, I had twenty bob on the books at White's that this spring you'd beat last Season's rejections by two.''

He laughed heartily and came over to slap John violently on the back to assure everyone he meant no harm. ''Don't you know that a pretty face like yours ain't enough to make up for the fact that you're a right rotter? You should have married some pretty cit and been done with it. It's what I'll do when the time comes. Not some whey-faced spinster who's been on the shelf for Seasons altogether.''

He jammed his elbow into John's ribs. ''But don't feel bad about the twenty pounds. Won thirty since Harrison bet me that the Binghamtons would actually have the gall to trot Lady Charlotte out again.'' Blynesmith allowed Sinclair to make the appropriate acknowledgment of his superior wit, then gave a roar as he saw Harrison stagger into the room and took himself off to share the excellent news.

John shrugged and grinned. He felt a prickle of annoyance at hearing his new wife disparaged, and an accompanying stab of guilt that he'd let the comments pass. But after all, he'd thought the same things himself. And if he didn't take his own marriage terribly seriously, he could hardly expect anyone else to.

He did feel sorry for Charlotte, though. She'd shown an unexpectedly wry sense of humor during this whole process, starting with his ridiculous farce of a proposal. She'd made it very easy for him. The wedding and bedding had been accomplished with businesslike efficiency, and he had every reason to think the matter quite handily done.

And she wasn't so very unattractive. In fact, when she wasn't wearing that perpetual expression of mousy panic, she was rather pretty. Even that trait seemed to have improved since she left the Binghamtons' household.

''Where were we?'' he said, turning his attention from the ripples of Blynesmith's gossip spreading across the room. ''Ah, the lamentable lack of passion between myself and the new Lady Sinclair. Well, we can't all be as bourgeois as you, Iverley, and fall in love with our wives. Nonetheless,

I've done my duty to the family, my mother will be convinced I'm entirely redeemed, I'll beget dozens of hatchet-faced little heirs, and I'll be entirely respectable without the bother of actually having to change my ways.''

"It never actually seems to happen that way," Iverley mused.

"Nonsense. Lady Sinclair and I are of one mind. She is everything sensible. Nothing silly and romantic about her. That's why I chose her. We shall rub on very well with no inconvenience to either of us."

"To the new Lady Sinclair, then," Palmer said, raising his glass. "The perfect wife."

"Yes," Sinclair echoed, taking a long drink from his glass. "The perfect wife."

Chapter Three

Charlotte could admit now, as they bowled down the snowy track, that she had been looking forward to her first drive in the park with her new husband. She had dressed herself with special care, and though she knew the ginger silk pelisse trimmed in black fur didn't transform her into a diamond of the first water, it did bring out the gold and red highlights in her hair and didn't make her look quite such a monochromatic dun color.

Sinclair, however, was splendid. In the bright, clear afternoon, made dazzling by the snow, he stood out like a dark jewel. His many-caped driving coat was cut to perfection and the black wool emphasized the striking depth of his dark hair and eyes.

"You look like a raven in the snow," she said before she realized how entirely ridiculous her words would sound when said aloud.

"What?" He looked at her as though he'd been thinking of something else entirely. "I look like a raven?" He gave her a quizzical grin. "I don't believe I've ever been told that before." He looked down at himself and grimaced. "Not very dashing, ravens. Scavengers, really."

Charlotte realized it had been the wrong thing to say. She shouldn't have said anything at all. But it felt so unbearably awkward to be sitting next to him in his fashionable carriage with nothing to say between them.

Lord and Lady Iverley drove by, bundled to the teeth against the cold. Lady Iverley held the ribbons, while her husband sat back and looked delighted.

Charlotte was not well acquainted with the couple, but by their warm greeting she knew they were aware of her recent marriage. Since the announcement was made in the paper, the whole town must know. She could only imagine the speculation. What could such a comically mismatched pair possibly see in each other?

"Where will we live now that we are married?" she asked suddenly. "We cannot live in the Pulteney Hotel forever."

He looked surprised—he always seemed to look surprised when she spoke. "I hadn't thought of it too much. We could let something in town if you like. There's the family town house on Clarges Street, of course, but it isn't fit to live in at the moment. Didn't seem much point in pouring money into the repairs and decorating when I was a bachelor." He made a wry face. "I should have thought about providing for a wife before I proposed to you, Charlotte. I'm sorry. Though I suppose I thought you would prefer to live at Bellamy Hall."

With you? she almost asked. But she knew he had no desire to live the quiet life at his ancestral home. He rarely went there, and though it was deemed a fine estate, the prospect of such isolation was not inviting. "I don't know," she said quietly.

She didn't know. What had she expected, the slavish attention of her husband? Nonsense. Two days ago she'd wanted nothing more than to be free of male attention forever. Now she was cross that her husband meant to grant that to her.

They would live together until he got her with child, and then she would retire respectably into the country. It was what she had wanted all along, wasn't it? She'd accepted his proposal because it promised stability, respectability, and children. That was really all one could want out of life.

She was about to cast her vote that they give the Clarges Street house a try, when Lady Champhill rode up on a beautiful black saddle horse. She must have known that the animal stood out in high relief against the snow and that its overlarge stature made its rider look all the more petite and fragile.

"Lord Sinclair!" she exclaimed, as though he was the very last man on earth she expected to see. "How charming to find you. I hardly thought you would be one for driving out on a cold day like this. I rather thought you would be curled up somewhere warm and cozy." There was an expression on her face that suggested her own house on Regent Street provided all the warm and cozy amenities a gentleman could wish for.

Charlotte knew Sinclair's name had been linked with the widow's, but somehow she'd assumed that that was in the past. After all, he wouldn't have married her if his heart was otherwise engaged. But of course, it wasn't his heart that was involved, in either case.

Sinclair had the grace to look uncomfortable for an instant, but he quickly covered it with his easy smile. "Lady Champhill," he said. "I have decided to brave the elements today in order to show the world my new wife. Lady Champhill, may I introduce you to Lady Sinclair?"

Lady Champhill looked at Charlotte with an admirably feigned start of surprise, as though she simply hadn't noticed the woman sitting at Sinclair's side. "Why, of course," she said with the brightest of smiles. "We met years ago. Back in your first Season, was it not?" She put her limerick glove up in front of her lips. "Oh, and you are married to John! What a delightful surprise. Everyone in London was wondering who would finally have the pleasure of being Lady Sinclair. How pleased you must be."

Sinclair was twitching the reins, obviously anxious to remove himself from the conversation. "Good heavens, Arabella," he said in some irritation. "You'd think no one ever decided to marry before."

Charlotte could feel the tension crackling between her husband and the woman before them. She hadn't missed the fact that he had used Lady Champhill's given name or the fact that that lady was baring her teeth in a smile that looked as though her face might crack.

"On the contrary," that woman said in a voice that was too loud and too high. "I think it will make your life a great deal easier. Good day, Lady Sinclair; my heartfelt congratulations to you. How pretty you look in that pelisse. I never wear brown, but now I will just have to have my mantua maker do one up just like it." She reached out her hand to Lord Sinclair. "Good day to you, sir."

Charlotte caught sight of a brief flash of white paper as it passed from her hand to his.

They continued on, nodding and bowing to people, all of whom seemed to have already heard the news of their marriage. Charlotte smiled and accepted their slightly bewildered congratulations, but inside she was wounded. Did Sinclair think she was a fool? Of course she had little illusion of his future faithfulness, but she had expected his full attention for at least a little while. Until she was with child. Until she was packed off to the country.

"What does Lady Champhill have to say?" she asked, once they had extricated themselves from the congratulations of a knot of men on horseback.

Sinclair looked nonplussed. "We met Lady Champhill only minutes ago," he reminded her.

"Oh, I mean in her note," she replied pleasantly.

She had the satisfaction of seeing a faint blush rise up the man's cheeks. "You mean the note she handed me?" he asked, obviously deciding there was no point in pretending he didn't understand what she was saying. "She often writes to me to ask for advice on business matters. Since her husband died."

"Since she is your mistress," Charlotte corrected him.

He sighed, his annoyance tangible, like the white cloud of vapor he exhaled. "This is not a fit topic for us to discuss."

"On the contrary, I think it is an excellent topic, and it's an excellent time to discuss it. Oh, don't look so worried, Sinclair. I am not going to ask you to give her up or anything so foolish. You'll only find someone else when you tire of her. I am not widgeon enough to think you're in love with me. But we will rub along better if you do not humiliate me by allowing the entire *ton* to know of your affairs."

To her surprise, he pulled up the horses and took both of

her hands in his. For the first time that day, she felt as though his attention was fully upon her. "No, Charlotte, I don't love you. And I know you don't love me. But you are right. I should not have let Lady Champhill make a spectacle of herself, and I'm sorry that she embarrassed you.

"Come now, my sensible Charlotte," he continued with a faint smile of self-mockery. "You seem to know me better than I know myself. I'm an irredeemably rag-mannered bounder, and I've no intention of reforming. I have every intention of continuing to game, womanize, and waste my time and fortune on pleasure as I always have. All men are that way, but most of them wrap it up in a tissue of lies. I won't reform, but I won't lie to you." He smiled again, more warmly this time. "And I'll make certain you aren't embarrassed like that again. I am sorry for that."

She thought for a moment he might kiss her, and was surprised to find she would have welcomed it. But reason reasserted itself, and she was glad he merely turned back to the horses and urged them on toward home.

There was no reason she should feel deflated, and even less reason she should feel angry. After all, she had known all along that Sinclair had no plans to reform. He wanted nothing more than a wife who wouldn't interfere.

Did she really want Sinclair to fall in love with her? That was a rather laughable notion. Neither she nor he had any experience of love. He'd taken her from an unpleasant situation and provided her with a safe, albeit somewhat lonely, home. And that was that.

They pulled up in front of the hotel, and she realized she had spent the entire drive back wrapped in silent thought. Sinclair was looking at her with a slightly worried expression.

"You're a very hard woman to charm, lady wife," he said ruefully. "I always knew you were a sight too good for me, but now I'm afraid you've found that out for yourself." He looked at her for a long moment, his face solemn. "I'm sorry, Charlotte."

"Nonsense," she said firmly. "We shall rub along together very well. Now I know you are off to your club, so there is no need to walk me in. Here is a footman to help me down. I won't expect you until quite late tonight.''

Sinclair had been right. There were men she could marry who would live the same rakehell life he did, but they would hide it. What she saw in her husband was exactly what she would get. No less, and certainly no more.

She saw the man as soon as she entered the dimness of the hotel's foyer. Binghamton must have been waiting for her; he rose to his feet as soon as he saw her.

"Charlotte," he said affectionately. "How are you my dear?" He gave her a moist kiss on the cheek. "I was in the neighborhood, and I thought I would see how you were getting on."

"Very well. Thank you." As a married lady, she could reasonably be expected to invite him, a near relation, upstairs for tea, but the idea revolted her. Instead, she stood in silence, cursing herself for leaving Sinclair's protective company.

"I haven't seen you since the wedding. Sinclair is treating you well?"

"Yes, of course."

Binghamton took her hand and patted it. "Well, I must say, married life suits you. I had my reservations about Sinclair, but I see now that it needn't be the end of our friendship. And we always were friends, weren't we, Charlotte?"

She gave him a thin smile.

"Now, my dear." Binghamton squeezed the hand he retained. "Aren't you going to invite your old friend to take tea?"

Charlotte shot a glance at the door. "I'm afraid I cannot, sir. I am only here to pick up a parcel I must return to my modiste. I can only stay a moment myself." She extricated her hand and pulled the collar of her pelisse closer together.

"No sign of your husband," Binghamton noted, looking around. "I would hate to think of what devilment he might be up to." He looked at her with an intent expression that made a shiver of alarm dance down her spine. "If you ever need anything, Charlotte——'' He let the invitation hang in the air.

''You and Amanda have been very kind.'' She deliberately pretended to misunderstand him. ''Now, I'm afraid——''

''You're too good for Sinclair,'' he said, putting on the sympathy face again. ''Ladies often think they can change a man. But I must tell you most honestly, you can never change a man like him.''

Her husband had said those two very things himself only a few minutes before. When Sinclair said it, she'd only given a fatalistic shrug. When Binghamton said it, she wanted to slap him.

''No,'' she said cheerfully. ''I cannot change him. But rather than try to reform him, I'll just have to give him what he wants.''

Chapter Four

It was ten o'clock. Rather late to be arriving at the ball meant to celebrate one's own marriage, but not too awful. John pulled off his greatcoat as he mounted the steps of the town house Charlotte had miraculously rendered livable. The place he'd always thought of as big, dark, and uninviting now seemed gracious and welcoming. Strange, though, to think of it as home.

He let himself in, hoping he could slip into the crowd of guests without anyone noting that he'd only just arrived. Breaking things off with Lady Champhill had taken longer than he'd expected, but it was worth it to get that piece of business out of the way.

He tried to convince himself that he was only ending the affair because he was tired of the beautiful widow, but truth to be told, it was the memory of Charlotte's stoic face that had spurred him on. She was a good woman, certainly one who deserved better than the likes of him. As she said, she didn't deserve the humiliation of knowing he had a mistress while he was married to her. He mentally swore to stay away from the muslin company until Charlotte was safely breeding and ensconced at Bellamy Hall.

He quickly changed his coat and was halfway back down the stairs to the ballroom before he noticed the noise. There was the usual stringy squalkings of the musicians and the sounds of voices engaged in conversation, but there was also something different. The party seemed much louder than it should be, and involved much more laughter than the typical Society affair.

Emma Holyoak impaled him with a sharp finger as soon as he entered the room. "You are late, Sinclair," she said, prodding his shoulder. He saw quickly enough that the punch served this evening must be rather strong.

"But no matter," the woman continued, waving a limp hand. Her lined face was flushed with more than just cosmetics. "That gel of yours knows what she's about. Not one of those milk-and-water affairs. The dancing, the ratafia, the inevitable damned lobster patties . . ."

She pressed her finger into his flesh again, this time pleased. "This is a proper party. Nothing vulgar, mind you. Proper and jolly. And she didn't put the card players back in some stuffy little room and force everyone to play for chicken stakes. I like that."

He smiled, slightly taken aback. "I'm delighted. I'm certain Lady Sinclair knows how to best please her guests. Our guests." Speaking of it, he looked around at the guests. They were mostly the people he expected to see, the staid dowagers of the *ton*, overly excited young girls in town for their first Season, the polished gentlemen who apparently needed the aid of quizzing glasses to gaze down from heights of their aristocratic noses. The usual, dull crowd.

But there were others he knew as well, however, and had certainly not expected to see. There was Señora Balducci, the opera singer who was very fashionable, though not quite respectable. There was Captain Beltwhistle and several of his regiment, all shocking gamblers. Near the punch bowl he saw Mr. Hodskins together with his wife, a woman everyone knew used to be an actress. In short, they were the kind of people he expected to see at his favorite gaming hell, not his ballroom.

"Hello," Lady Binghamton called out, languidly wending her way through the crowd. "How charming to see you here at last. Even my husband arrived before you. My poor dear man, I've hardly had a word with you since you married Charlotte. But you know, I hardly ever leave my chambers.

It's only for dear Charlotte's sake that I'm on my feet now. And I expect I look quite hagged indeed."

She waited for Sinclair's protests, then looked around the room with satisfaction. "Quite a good turn out, particularly for this time of year." There was another loud burst of laughter from the direction of the card room. "I never knew Charlotte had such lively friends. Of course we rarely entertain ourselves. I'm so often unwell, and Binghamton has so many other pursuits." She smiled blandly, looking for a moment very like her sister. "I know Charlotte was looking for you to start the dancing. The last time I saw her she was routing them all at vingt-et-un."

Was that Mrs. Waterford-Jones wearing one of her famously transparent gowns? Had his wife been mad when she sent out invitations? John recovered himself enough to follow his sister-in-law as she led him through the crowd toward the card room.

Good God, even Lord Lambrook was here, a blackguard if ever there was one. He was recently back from a prudently timed trip to Jamaica after attempting to run off with some young miss. Was there a rake in London who had not secured an invitation?

John resolved to have a serious discussion with Charlotte regarding the propriety of the guest list. Her sister might be a bit too self-absorbed to properly guide her, but Charlotte, after four Seasons, should know well enough who was good *ton* and who was not.

"There she is," Lady Binghamton said, waving a hand toward the smoky room. "Do go on to her. I simply must sit down with a glass of ratafia."

The card room, if anything, was more crowded than the ballroom. John resisted the urge to check his watch. It was late, but not overly so. Nonetheless, everyone seemed to be in excessively high spirits. Normally he would be pleased to find himself in the midst of such a lively party, but he hadn't been prepared for it. He'd set his mind on a quiet, ordinary, genteel evening, and in truth had been looking forward to it to a degree.

Instead, it looked like his first ball as a married man could very well end up a wild melee.

Then he saw Charlotte. She looked like an angel, almost luminous in the dark room. Her gown was silver, threaded with midnight blue, and the smoke in the room seemed to wreathe her like a halo. Though, he noted with slight disapproval, the bodice was cut a bit low, even for a married lady.

"Much improved, ain't she?" he heard a voice say by his side. He looked down and saw that Lady Holyoak had followed him. She'd somehow managed to refresh her glass along the way. "Never will be too much to look at, but marriage seems to suit her." She cackled and stuck her finger into his bicep. "She'll be a dashing wife, I daresay. Who knew she had it in her? Always thought she was a bit of a milksop miss myself. But she's invited all the highfliers tonight. She'll lead you on a merry dance, Sinclair, mind my words."

John did not want to mind her words. He wanted to tell her it would be better if she minded her own business. The Charlotte Fawnhope he'd proposed to was quiet and well behaved. She promised a life that would be comfortable and ordinary, a safe haven from the indulgences he knew were a part of his nature.

Was she instead the kind of woman who wore revealing gowns and threw balls attended by London's most fashionably scandalous sinners? Charlotte, dashing? It was a very peculiar thought.

As though she felt his eyes upon her, she looked up and saw him, then leaned over to murmur something to those who played at the table with her. Since when had she a figure to display? Instead of the stick-thin form he'd always thought she possessed, Charlotte seemed to have been secreting a wealth in subtle and appealing curves. He found his thoughts roving pleasurably toward the bedroom.

She rose and smiled at him. "Lord Sinclair," she said, holding out both hands. "You're shockingly late. People were beginning to think I'd been abandoned by you already."

To his relief she sounded calm and pleasant as she always did. "Forgive me, my dear. My business took me longer than I thought." He took her arm and guided her from the

room. "You are looking well. Very well." He tried to think
of a compliment that would not sound like one he had used
a thousand times. She really did deserve better than that.
"Very well," he found himself repeating.

"Thank you," she said with an indulgent smile that indicated she didn't believe him in the least. "Would you like
something to drink or eat? I would not wish to rush you,
but I believe our guests are anxious to begin the dancing."
She cast a mild glance to where two very exuberant misses
were already making up a set with a pair of Beltwhistle's
young officers.

"Charlotte," he said with a slight frown. "How do you
know Lambrook?"

She looked up at him with an expression of faint surprise.
"Oh, well, I don't. Not very well, anyway. We've been
introduced. I invited him because I thought he was a friend
of yours."

"Hardly," he growled. But he looked around more
closely. It was true, all of the more shocking guests were
well known to him. But just because he gambled with them
and enjoyed going to their parties didn't mean he meant to
continue an acquaintance with them after he married. Just
then, a small voice in his head reminded him that he'd
chosen Charlotte precisely so he wouldn't have to change
anything after he married.

"Oh, dear," she was saying. "Then I suppose I must
disinvite him from the house party I was planning."

"What?" he fairly shouted.

She laughed then, a surprisingly low and sensual sound
he hadn't heard before. "I am joking, Lord Sinclair. I would
certainly consult you as to whom you would wish to attend
before I invited anyone."

He entertained momentary nightmares of a house party
made up of all the lecherous men and loose women he
generally consorted with.

"Yes," he said, feeling rather uncomfortable. "Let us
open the dancing."

He need not have worried that Charlotte would make a
show of herself or act in any way other than a lady of
impeccable breeding and manners. As the musicians minced

through the dance, she smiled pleasantly and made easy conversation. He'd half expected this new, unknown woman to flirt with him, cling to him, or make some kind of a scene. But no, she was her ordinary self, calm and composed in the middle of the raucous set they found themselves in.

"Charlotte"—he tried again to resolve the niggling worry that plagued him—"this is not the guest list I would have expected for our first party."

She completed the figure and came back to partner him. They were well matched for dancing, really. She was a good height for him, and responded with ease and skill to his lead. "I showed you the guest list," she reminded him. "But you said you'd no interest in it, and I should do as I thought best. The ball is meant to celebrate our marriage. I thought it would be nicest if we invited your friends as well as mine." Her blue eyes were guileless. "I didn't invite anyone who was truly ineligible."

He recalled with a stab of conscience that there were indeed quite a number of shocking characters she might have invited.

"It's a lovely party," he said, not wanting to scold her in front of anyone. "As long as you are happy, I am happy."

She smiled her distant smile and did not laugh again.

Charlotte felt a pang of regret as the music ended. Her husband was a fine dancer. He made her feel as though the complicated steps were as simple and natural as walking. It was pleasant to reflect that he would be expected to dance with her at least once at all of the balls they would attend together from now on.

She looked at Sinclair's frown and wondered if she'd made a mistake in not consulting him further with respect to the invitations. There was no doubt from his comments and the worried glances he kept shooting toward the squealing party at the punch bowl that he was still annoyed about the guest list.

No, she told herself, standing up straighter. This was her grand statement as to how she would handle their marriage. This proved she wouldn't restrain his life once they were together. If Sinclair wanted to continue leading his wild bachelor life after he married, why shouldn't he? She would cheerfully provide him with all the vices he'd indulged in before he'd become her husband.

She allowed Sinclair to bow over her hand and escort her back where her slightly bored-looking sister was reclining on a settee. It was plain that his original intention had been to abandon her with Amanda, but he apparently recalled himself in time, and, retaining her hand by covering it with his own, stood chatting with her sister as though he'd never entertained the idea of escaping to the card room.

Perhaps she would never be the dashing kind of wife he wanted, but at least she would give him the kind of life that he wanted, and he would not come to resent her for domesticating him. Perhaps she would learn to like the high-flier's life of gambling, indulgence, and adultery. In that event, then, she would not care whether her husband liked her or not.

Lieutenant Fox came to claim his dance with her, and Sinclair relinquished his hold on her hand, though she noted a small frown formed between his eyes as the handsome lieutenant bowed elegantly over her glove.

"A very lovely party, Lady Sinclair," Fox said, making an admirable pretense of sobriety. "You are looking absolutely stunning."

She forced a smile and took her place in the set. "I trust you have found enough young ladies willing to dance, Lieutenant?" she asked when the figure brought them together.

She saw him give a wink to a pretty girl in cherry ribbons who had been partnering him earlier. "Oh, you throw a grand ball, Lady Sinclair. Just like one should be. Pretty girls and strong punch." He gave a loud laugh. "Sinclair is a lucky man. Must be pleased to pieces to discover you've a knack for throwing a party."

He didn't look too pleased at the moment, she thought, glancing across the room to where her husband stood, still talking with her sister. In fact, he looked quite pale. She followed the direction of his startled gaze. Oh, dear, had she gone too far in her enthusiasm to prove her openmindedness with her guest list?

She looked over her shoulder and smiled cheerfully at the new arrival who stood in the doorway. Lady Champhill was looking absolutely stunning in a crimson gown embellished with gold rouleaux and the merest hand's width of bodice. Every head in the room had turned to gape at the woman. Charlotte felt a moment's disappointment. She'd expected Sinclair to look surprised to see Lady Champhill, not horrified. And she'd expected triumph, perhaps even smugness from Lady Champhill. Instead, that lady, too, looked absolutely furious.

Chapter Five

The evening was going from bad to worse. No, from worse to absolutely hellish. John shot a quick look from Arabella to Charlotte. His former mistress was still standing in the doorway, gowned in that vulgar dress and glaring daggers at him. His wife continued innocently in her dance with Lieutenant Fox.

Perhaps there was still time. He excused himself rather precipitously from Lady Binghamton and elbowed his way across the room. Arabella looked somewhat gratified at his hasty response.

"What are you doing here?" he hissed.

She gave him a heavy-lidded stare. "I was invited."

"Charlotte invited you?"

Arabella gave a shrug that very nearly served to dislodge her from her bodice entirely. "Sweet of her, wasn't it?" She concealed her catlike smile with her fan. "Now which one is she? I can never recognize her. Ah, yes, there she is. How charmingly she dances. She even manages to make Fox look as though he isn't jug-bitten."

She took his arm and began a leisurely promenade of the ballroom, but he stopped her. "I don't want you here. You have to leave."

The woman's arched brows rose higher up her forehead. "But, my dear, I already told you, I was invited."

"Not by me." Dear God, did no one in the world have any sense? What was Charlotte thinking, inviting the woman she knew very well was his mistress? And what was Lady Champhill doing, appearing here only a few hours after he'd announced their affair was at an end? "Arabella," he said in a low, dangerous voice, "this party is mine as well as Charlotte's, and I don't want you here. I will have you forcibly removed if need be. You are in the mood to make a scene, and I won't have you upsetting my wife."

"Lady Champhill," Charlotte said, appearing at his side, "how good of you to come. That gown is absolutely stunning. How very brave you are."

His wife's arrival was greeted with stunned silence. He heard a gurgling in Lady Champhill's throat. He made an effort to leap into the conversation himself and ended up only standing with his mouth open.

"I believe you know almost everyone here." Charlotte gestured around the room. "In fact, I believe several of the gentlemen here are particular friends of yours."

John stared at Charlotte. He'd almost forgotten what a quick, dry wit she had. Rather than sounding jealous of the woman she knew to be his mistress, his wife merely seemed amused. He felt an uncomfortable mixture of shame and annoyance. "Lady Champhill cannot stay. In fact, she was just leaving," he managed at last.

Charlotte's face fell. "Oh, that can't be so. Look how she is glaring at you, Sinclair. She doesn't want to leave, I'm sure of it. Not when you haven't even had a dance together."

At this unexpected remark, he saw Arabella jerk in surprise. Whatever approach she'd planned, either to humiliate or seduce him, Charlotte had taken the wind from her sails.

"No, I—" He was suddenly repulsed by the idea. Lady Champhill was lovely, of course, but she looked quite tawdry here in Charlotte's elegant ballroom. Even among the raffish company, Lady Champhill, standing next to the slim, silvery figure of his wife, seemed gauche. And heaven knew the woman had only her looks to recommend her.

"Really, my lord, I insist," Charlotte said. "Listen, here

is a waltz. I'm certain Lady Champhill knows how to waltz
very well.''

And before he knew what he was about, Charlotte had
pushed the two of them toward the dancers. The talk in the
room seemed to have quieted. The word appeared to have
gone around that Sinclair's mistress had turned up at his
new wife's first ball, and he had had the audacity to dance
with the woman.

He felt every eye in the room upon him as he reluctantly
took Arabella into his arms and began a sedate waltz. From
the back of the room, near the punch bowl, he heard Lieutenant Fox begin to titter.

Arabella seemed to have regained her wits. She smiled up
at him, pushing slightly against the arm's length he forcefully
maintained between them. "See, my dear," she said. "There
was no need for your attack of conscience. Your wife is
either too foolish to know that I am your lover, or she does
not care. She practically ordered you to dance with me. I
like her better and better. Now we can continue on as we
have been and be comfortable.''

John was not comfortable. He was not certain who he
was more annoyed with, Arabella for her ridiculous, vulgar
display, or Charlotte, for forcing him to embarrass himself
in front of the *ton*.

Or perhaps he was just angry with himself for bringing
this down on his head in the first place.

"Is that Lord Lambrook?" Lady Champhill asked in
astonishment. "I never expected to see him at a party like
this. The man is a disgrace." She looked at the crowd of
guests. "And the Holyoaks. And Captain Beltwhistle. Good
heavens, a fast crowd indeed.''

He refrained from reminding her that she herself was one
of the barely genteel guests everyone was shocked to see.

He took a cue from Charlotte and smiled placidly as
he whirled Lady Champhill around the room. The crowd
continued to watch him, openly speculating whether Lady
Sinclair knew the truth. A few of the more rakish men looked
slightly admiring. To dance with his mistress under his new
wife's nose. How bold he was, how well he had chosen the
most compliant of wives.

He vowed that those were the men who would never be welcome in his house again.

"John?" Arabella said, in a tone that indicated this was not the first time she'd tried to attract his attention.

"Yes?" He looked over her shoulder, trying to see Charlotte. She was talking with the elderly Lord Harrow, playing the part of the perfect hostess. Good God, if anyone could pull off this strange mix of genteel and not-so-genteel guests, it was her.

"Will you come to the house tonight? I believe we have a great deal to discuss."

"I believe we already discussed everything I had in mind," he said coldly.

Lady Champhill's beautiful face was marred with a look of annoyance. "You cannot still wish to end things? Not when you have your new wife's blessing."

The last strains of the waltz faded away, and he dropped his hand from her waist. "Yes," he said. "I'm afraid things stand exactly where they did before this unfortunate meeting."

He bowed over her hand, and then turned to find Charlotte.

She was standing in the corner, quietly directing one of the servants to replace the candles that had burned too low.

"May I speak with you, madam?" he said, sounding rather more forceful than he had intended.

"Of course, my lord." She quickly completed her instructions, then held out her hand to him. "What can I do for you?"

"Well, for a start, you can stop calling me 'my lord.' John, please, or Sinclair if you can't bear that," he said irritably.

She smiled. "Of course. John it shall be. Would you like some punch?"

He stepped closer. "No, dash it all. It's too strong for a party like this. Everyone's half in the bag."

"I'll ask Stafford to dilute it. I apologize, my—John. I was warned by Mr. Palmer that you detested weak punch."

Palmer! What did Palmer know about social niceties? "Let us go somewhere private; I would like a word with you."

Always accommodating, Charlotte led him to a small reception room that was unoccupied. She stoked the fire to life and then indicated that he should seat himself on the brocade settee. "You are upset," she said, seating herself beside him. "What can I do?"

"Yes, I'm upset," he sputtered. Was the woman always a cold, calm icicle? Did she never feel irritation or joy or passion? "Why did you invite Lady Champhill?"

Her pale brows drew together. "I thought it would please you."

Oh, Charlotte. She'd thought all of this would please him. Loud, low company, high-stakes gambling, strong drink. Was that how she saw him?

How could he explain that he'd been expecting, even looking forward to, an evening of genteel entertainment that was vastly different than the fare he normally pursued? "I am pleased," he said, forcing control on himself. "And you were thoughtful to invite people who are my acquaintances as well as yours."

In the ruddy light of the fire, her face looked as though it had more color, her hair more highlights. She looked almost pretty.

He felt an unexpected rush of something like tenderness. "Let's do something together tomorrow. Just the two of us." He was rather surprised to hear the words come out of his mouth.

"We could go to Tattersall's," she suggested.

He was taken aback. He'd been about to suggest they go to an art gallery or to the opera in the evening. Though, to be frank, he found both activities excruciatingly dull.

"Tatt's would be good fun," he said hesitantly, wondering if this idea was put forth only to please him. "Or we could go skating on the Serpentine. Iverley and his wife were out today, and they said it is quite safe. Then afterward perhaps we could go to the theater."

Her face fell. "Amanda and I always have dinner in on Wednesday, and then we read aloud and play piquet. Lord Binghamton is out, so it is our special time together. Besides, I thought you would be going to Lord Hudsbeth's club dinner."

Had he really agreed to go to that? It was likely to be rowdy. Ah, well, he always enjoyed it. "What about Thursday night?"

"I'm promised to Madame Solage's political salon. I'm sorry, I thought you were going to Lady Well's party. I heard Lord Lambrook mention that you'd been invited."

"I'm not going," he said firmly. But she did not invite him to join her and her sister.

"Well," she said cheerfully, "skating will have to do, then. Besides, it is my special intention that I do not interfere with your life. I don't want your marrying me to inconvenience you one bit."

It was a rather adorable thing to say. He grinned and put an arm around her waist. "You're a good girl, Charlotte. I knew you'd be the one to marry. You're not at all what I expected, but I think this will do very well." Swept up in the warmth of the moment, he leaned in and kissed her.

He'd meant it to be the kind of kiss they always shared. Chaste, sweet, affectionate. A mark of esteem shared between two people. He realized now that he hardly ever kissed her when he came to her chambers at night. But somehow this time his mouth stayed upon hers for longer than he intended and his arms tightened around her slender form. And, she was responsive this time, not merely a recipient.

John had kissed many women in his time, and he fancied he knew what he was doing. Certainly he knew what he was doing more than his chilly, reserved wife. But she surprised him. She was passionate, giving, eager. And yet, beneath it all was restraint. Even when he took her in his arms, exploring the feel of her body in a remarkably bold way, she was distant. It was strangely alluring. And utterly frustrating.

"You're very good to me," he said again, breathing in the scent of her that lingered behind her ears.

"Of course," she said. She drew a breath and seemed to collect herself even more. "Now, I think we should rejoin our guests. They will wonder what has become of us."

She stood and smoothed out her skirts. Though her lips

were slightly reddened, and her mousy hair ever so slightly out of place, it was as though the kiss had never happened.

He stood up and followed her out of the room. He should feel triumphant. He should be delighted to have found himself a wife who would not mind—in fact, practically fostered—his vices. She'd excused him from dull evenings and made no complaint that he planned to continue bachelor events without her. She'd made him dance with his mistress, for God's sake.

But instead of feeling smug at having discovered a man's ideal wife in plain, ordinary Lady Charlotte Fawnhope, he only felt slightly bewildered.

Chapter Six

"So, my dear," Lord Binghamton said, drawing her arm through his. "Did you enjoy the evening?"

Charlotte detached him and pretended there was an urgent necessity to direct Stafford as he marshaled the battalion of servants cleaning the wax, scuffs, and spilled punch from the ballroom floor. "Yes," she said from a safe distance. "I enjoyed myself very much."

"Well, you certainly look a picture. Amanda was just saying how very becoming you looked. I'm so sorry she had the headache and had to go home early. You know how frail she is."

Charlotte pursed her lips. Her sister had always sought refuge in illness; she hoped tonight's headache didn't precede a full-blown fit of the vapors tomorrow.

She felt her brother-in-law's appreciative gaze on her bosom and wished she'd worn the kind of sensible gown she usually wore. It was vain of her to wish to appear her best for Lord Sinclair. After all, they were already married; he was stuck with her whether he liked the look of her or not.

But then she remembered that kiss. That kiss which had superceded even the marvelous kiss he'd given her upon becoming betrothed to her. And this time she'd been an eager participant. The memory of her momentary loss of control made her blush to her fingertips. Perhaps the gown was worth Binghamton's rude stares.

"Your husband didn't seem to pay very much attention to you," Binghamton said, raising his eyes to her face at last. "In fact, there were few people here tonight who spent less time together."

"We are hardly going to live in each other's pockets," Charlotte said tartly. She picked up the handle of a broken punch cup and sighed. Poor Lady Holyoak would have the devil of a head tomorrow.

"He spent most of his time with Lady Champhill," he went on. He laid his hand on her arm in the solicitous manner she most hated. "I would not pollute your fair ears with gossip not fit for a young lady, but I must say"—he raised his brows in an expression meant to convey the idea that the worst sin she could conceive of was by far the least of it—"I have heard rumors regarding your husband. He is somewhat wild in his manners and loose in his morals."

Charlotte drew herself up. "He is my husband, sir. And as you have always said, most gossip is not fit for anyone's ears."

At least with Lord Sinclair—John, she reminded herself—she knew what she was getting up front. There would be no nasty surprises. No closeted peccadilloes or hypocritical talk of love and honor. She turned her back on her brother-in-law. Unlike Amanda, she would not need to be protected from John's true nature by careful relations and her own determined blindness.

Lord Binghamton came up behind her and took her elbow. "Very well, I won't speak of it." He took the broken cup handle from her and then pressed her fingers. He had the avaricious look in his eye she'd come to fear. "I just want you to know that I am always here for you. If you need anything, anything at all, come to me."

How foolish she'd been to think she'd be safe once she was married. Now the challenge just rose to a different level.

"Well," she said brightly, "I believe everything is well in hand here. Good heavens, is that really the time? How quickly it went. I believe everyone else is gone."

His arm came around her waist. "Now I hope you don't

think I'm being critical, but I know Amanda will say the same. There were quite a few people here who I believe were not quite the thing. If your husband told you to invite those people, I'm certain he shouldn't have. I think perhaps you'd better let me take a look at the guest list for your next party. I'm sure Amanda would do it, but poor creature, reading wearies her out so. I think it might be best if you and I did the next list together, what?'' He gave her one of his best squeezes.

"I'm sure Sinclair and I can manage," she said coolly.

"Furthermore, dear"—he leaned closer—"I have the suspicion that some people were a bit intoxicated. You'll have to speak with Stafford. He should not have made the punch so strong."

"I'll have a word with him," she promised, edging him toward the door. "Thank you for coming tonight, Lord Binghamton. Please tell my sister that I will call on her tomorrow evening for our night of piquet."

"You're a good girl," he said with another squeeze. "We miss you. But I bet you're finding that being a married lady gives you a great deal more freedom, eh?" He pinched her cheek.

She murmured her good night and indicated that the butler should show him out, but not before he'd had a good look down her décolleté and murmured "lovely dress," again.

She fairly ran to her room. Poor Amanda. Was she wrong not to tell her sister of her husband's behavior? The few times she'd tentatively broached the subject, Amanda had turned the topic quite adeptly.

Charlotte sat down at her dressing table and began pulling pins from her hair. Would she herself end up that way? She tried to imagine how she would feel if she caught John bedding the chambermaid or ogling someone's wife.

She looked at her reflection in the mirror and smoothed her expression into placid lines. She wouldn't care. She was braced for it; she expected it, and she didn't care. Her primary concern in marrying John had been that she would become an object of the *ton's* smug pity. But if she made it clear that she knew and didn't care, they could not feel pity. Confusion perhaps, but not pity.

Her maid entered and began unbuttoning the tiny pearl buttons that fastened the back of Charlotte's gown. She stood still while the yards of silk and gauze buckled and came loose around her. The night air was uncomfortably cold on her skin.

It really did seem like the perfect approach. If one had the ill fortune to be married to a rake, one must establish, from the very beginning, that one fostered—even encouraged—his vices and didn't give a rap that he caroused, drank, and gamed. People would likely think her enlightened, open-minded, Continental. No one would think she wished for attention, affection, fidelity, or even kisses on the settee in the back room. No, no one would think it at all.

In the end, they went to the art gallery. Charlotte had been rather looking forward to doing something new, but the weather the next day was sleety and miserable as only a February in London can be. Charlotte half expected John to change his mind about their outing, but he came down to the breakfast table appearing to have every intention of spending the day with his wife.

Unfortunately, Amanda picked today to decide that she was expiring from boredom and must be amused. She sent around a note demanding her sister's presence, and since John was determined not to be foisted off, it was not long before the two of them found themselves sitting in the same yellow drawing room where they had been married not but three weeks before. They sat side by side on the same settee, taking a sedate cup of tea and listening to Lady Binghamton's newest self-diagnosis of impending death.

Sinclair proved the very tonic to Amanda's malaise, and in a short time she was laughing and chattering with vivacity. Since the weather was so inclement, Charlotte suggested they go to the art gallery, and since it seemed a good enough idea, there was no way not to invite the Binghamtons to make up the party. So in the end the foursome bundled up and drove to the Royal Gallery.

"I'm sorry to hear that Lady Binghamton's health is not

good. I did not realize she was practically an invalid,'' John said quietly as they walked along one of the long hallways.

Charlotte resisted the urge to respond shrewishly that her sister was only an invalid when she found herself faced with things she did not wish to do. ''She and my brother-in-law have been very kind to me,'' she said instead. ''They have hosted me every Season''—she gave him a smile—''which, as you recall, have been too numerous to mention.''

He laughed and drew her arm through his. ''Nonsense. I only wish I had not wasted my time. I could have married you years ago.''

''Gallantly said, sir. But I believe you kept yourself well occupied.'' She stopped to examine a small pencil sketch of a country house set in a pastoral landscape. It reminded her of her future at Bellamy Hall. ''Besides,'' she murmured after a moment, ''I believe there is plenty of time in the future that we may spend in each other's company.''

He laughed, a laugh so loud and genuine, it made others in the gallery look over at them. ''Yes, I suppose there is. And trust you to make my every compliment sound like utter fustian.''

''Well, it usually is.''

He stepped closer to her and took her chin in his hand. ''Sometimes,'' he admitted. ''But I'm getting better. I want us to get along. I want you to like me, Charlotte.''

She refrained from telling him that she did not wish to like him.

''I believe I like this one best,'' she said, stepping back and examining a small Dutch still life. ''I have tried forever to paint flowers and they always look quite flat and stiff. I've no talent for it.''

''Why didn't you tell me this before, woman?'' he demanded in shocked accents, evidently willing to let her change the subject. ''I must protest. I am beginning to believe that I was lured into this marriage under false pretenses.''

She could not help but laugh. Perhaps there was nothing wrong with enjoying his company when he chose to spend it with her. She shouldn't expect it, of course, but there was no need to freeze him out with rudeness. ''I'm afraid there are a great many things about me you should be forewarned about," she said.

"Please don't say you play the harp."

"I'm afraid I don't."

"Excellent. I am astonished and delighted that I have found the one gentlewoman in all of England who hasn't rotted her intellect mastering useless skills like painting and playing the harp."

"I do sing a little."

"We all have our faults."

"And I'm afraid I'm considered quite proficient at embroidery."

He drew a sharp breath and closed his eyes. "Ah. Well, I'm certain we can arrange for your discreet admittance to the Reformatorium for Ladies of Quality who have Lapsed into Needlework."

Was she giggling? She actually thought she could hear herself giggling. "You're very good, sir. But I must confess all. I occasionally indulge in whitework."

His lips thinned in mock concern but there was a twinkle in his eyes. "Very serious indeed. I believe I will have to reconsider this venture. If I wanted a woman who did whitework, madam, I would have visited my aunt."

"There you are," Lord Binghamton said in a censorious voice as he led his wife up to them. "We thought we'd lost you entirely."

They both ducked their heads in meek acquiescence. Charlotte could hear John stifle a laugh.

"There now, isn't that pretty?" Amanda pointed across the room toward a large canvas. "A woman at the harp. I do so love the harp." Lady Binghamton looked slightly wounded when her sister and brother-in-law burst into a fit of laughter.

Chapter Seven

As his wife had planned to spend the evening with her sister, John could have politely left her and the Binghamtons at their door after the outing. Instead, however, he allowed himself to be invited in for tea. And when he'd curdled his stomach with enough of that vile brew to float an East India man, he could easily have excused himself. But he decided that a slice of cake sounded appealing, and then Lady Binghamton was quite keen to show him her large collection of medical texts. Afterward, Lord Binghamton required an audience as he recalled some of the more off-color escapades of his younger days.

So, somehow the early darkness of February crept on, the candles were lit, and the drawing room took on the cozy glow of a winter evening.

"I should go," he said reluctantly at last, putting the dainty, doll-sized cake plate back onto the tea table. "I know this is the evening you and Amanda guard jealously for piquet."

"Nonsense," said Amanda. "We are four now and could play whist."

He tried to catch his wife's eye. She was scrupulously careful of invading on his pastimes; he should offer her the same courtesy. Besides, an evening of whist—possibly the dullest game on earth—should hardly be tempting to him.

"We would love to have you of course," Charlotte said, with a polite smile. "But I know you are promised to Lord Hudsbeth."

"I don't think I'll attend," he replied with a shrug. "After your strong punch last night, I've little desire for another night of indulgence. Getting up in years, you know." He laughed, privately wondering what had possessed him to speak those words. Until he'd said them, he'd had every intention of going.

"Well, then, you must stay for dinner," Lady Binghamton said, settling the question.

He protested a little, just to be polite, but found, much to his own surprise, that the idea of spending an evening at home, *en famille*, was rather appealing.

He tried to recall the last time he'd had dinner with a small group of people who were not in the least bit fashionable, powerful, or scandalous. Likely when he was still at Eton.

The conversation through dinner was hardly remarkable, but it was still a novelty to eat somewhere besides his club. He vowed he would spend more evenings at home. In the time he'd been married, he hadn't dined with his wife above twice.

"Lord Sinclair, my sister tells me that you will be retiring to the country?" Lady Binghamton asked mildly as she picked at her roast beef.

"No," Charlotte corrected quietly, "I said that I will likely retire to the country. John will stay here. He has many business affairs to keep up with," she added, to be certain no one thought he would be so callous as to abandon his new bride so quickly.

"Is that what you wish, Charlotte?" he asked, slightly wounded that she said the words so confidently. Either she had no desire to live in the same house as her scoundrel of a husband, or she thought he meant to send her away as soon as could be conveniently arranged. Neither was particularly flattering. "I didn't know you'd decided. Wouldn't you rather stay in town for the spring?"

He could not read her face as she answered demurely, "I'll do whatever you wish, John."

He was disappointed. He'd felt like he'd made some headway today. After their laughter in the gallery, he'd thought she was warming up to him. He thought he was finally breaking through that cold reserve.

Then he wondered in bewilderment where that goal had come from. After all, he admitted to himself, once she was breeding he'd had every intention of suggesting she stay at Bellamy Hall. Why was he suddenly all solicitude that she choose where she would spend the spring?

"The country," Amanda said with a sigh. "Yes, Charlotte, I think that would suit you very well." Her blue eyes, pale and inexpressive like her sister's, were steady on her husband's face. John felt a prickle of danger on his neck.

He didn't like Binghamton, and he didn't like the way the man looked at Charlotte. But he hadn't realized that perhaps the trouble ran deeper.

"Indeed," Charlotte said quietly. John thought he saw an infusion of color in her cheeks, but then she turned to him, her face in its usual pleasant, calm lines. "Regardless, I don't know that the matter is decided. I hear Bellamy Hall is lovely. Is it pleasantly situated, John? I know Amanda would love to hear all about it."

"Now Charlotte, don't bury yourself in the country," Lord Binghamton said with a hearty laugh. "I know how much you love life in London. The opera, the theater ... You can't have all that even on the finest country estate. Surely there's no reason for you to leave, since, as you say, Sinclair has business here in town." He reached out and patted her hand in a way John did not like.

Charlotte, if anything, was more remote than before. "We shall see," she said, moving her hand out of Binghamton's reach.

"We'll take a trip up to see the place next month," John said, just as though he had been thinking of this all along. "Then we can make a decision."

His hand found Charlotte's under the tablecloth. It was balled into a cold little fist. Did she despise his touch as much as Binghamton's? Did she think all men were lecherous bores?

She smiled up at him, her countenance unfreezing just a

little. "Yes," she said. "Let's do that." Her hand did not relax into his.

"I'll send word to Bellamy Hall to prepare for their new mistress." Good God, could they do it in a month? The place hadn't had a mistress in nearly twenty years. He himself couldn't have seen it above five times since he'd inherited the title.

In his father's day it had been a fine place, practically gracious, but now? The roof was likely leaking like a sieve and the Holland covers crumbling to dust over the furniture. He began feeling a little overwhelmed when he realized how much was to be done before his life was really ready to receive a wife.

He stood as the ladies rose to leave, and drew Charlotte aside, pretending to help her with her shawl. "Honestly, my dear, I wish for you to be happy. Do not be afraid that you cannot tell me what you want." He wondered if she knew he liked the violet scent she wore. And that he preferred her hair arranged in loose ringlets as it was now. "I hope you don't think me an ogre."

Her eyes flicked to Binghamton and then to her sister. "Really, John, there is no need to be so solicitous. Though I do thank you. There is no need to pretend with me that we married each other for any reason other than convenience. I know my duty is to provide you with heirs, and I would prefer to do so in private and not while hearing the whole of the *beau monde* snickering up their sleeves at the other women you're bedding."

He stared at her, shocked, then angry. Perhaps more angry than he ought to be, since it was true.

"I'm sorry," she said, drawing the shawl very tightly around her shoulders. "I should not have spoken so plainly. I beg your pardon."

Lady Binghamton came to them and Charlotte followed her sister out of the room. She did not give John a backward glance.

He exhaled a sigh of frustration. Why did she have to explode the pleasant fantasy they'd been weaving? She'd stated things just as they were, and he saw himself now as the rest of the world saw him: ugly, selfish. This afternoon things had seemed to be going splendidly. He'd been enjoying her company far more than he'd expected to. Remarkably, he'd started to look on the married state with complacency, and perhaps even pleasure. Now, he saw it as she must see it, nothing but escape for her and convenience for him.

He looked up from his brown study to see that Lord Binghamton's eyes were fixed upon him.

"Port, Sinclair?" the man asked pleasantly, gesturing to the servant who held the decanter. He'd had quite a large quantity of wine over dinner and it had evidently dulled the edge of his usual hostility toward John. Now, the man's thin lips curled into a smile. "So you have taken our little Charlotte from us," he said at last. His jovial laugh went on far too long.

"I am honored that she accepted my proposal," John replied.

"You'd best be good to her," he said, playfully shaking a finger in his face. "She is young and clever, but very unworldly." He steepled his hands, his handsome face almost petulant. "We were loath to let her go. After all, she has lived with us for so long. She's such a support to Amanda. Of course, we've grown very fond of her."

John wondered if Binghamton considered him such a fellow lecher that he wouldn't mind if the man continued to ogle his wife.

"When did Charlotte come to live with you?" he asked. He sipped carefully from his glass, watching Binghamton. He thought of Charlotte's clenched fists, and how he had failed to soothe her.

Binghamton blew out a breath, considering. "Well, she came to us nearly five years ago. The girl's mother died shortly after Amanda and I were wed, and there was nowhere else for Charlotte to go. You should have seen her then. Ha! She was a scrawny, rabbity little thing. No brows, no lashes, no bosom—nothing to recommend her. She's hardly a beauty now, of course, but she's vastly improved."

The man drank from his glass, remembering. "There is something appealing about her, don't you think? You must, or you wouldn't have offered for her. A man like you could have any woman he wanted. And likely does, if rumors are to be believed. And of course, Charlotte's got a tidy little dowry, I don't deny it. But there were certainly heiresses with a great deal more to offer.''

Binghamton leaned back, his eyes narrowed at the ceiling. "No, you chose Charlotte because you see that something I see. All that passion that must have been building up for years in that plain little package. Oh, she hides it well enough, but she reads poetry, novels. She burns with passion. I'd have offered for her myself if I'd had any sense. Of course she was fifteen at the time, but I should have waited. The plain ones are always the lusty ones, you know.'' He grinned. "Suppose it stands to reason. They get little enough attention and are oh, so eager to please when they do get it.''

John regarded the man with ill-disguised loathing. "I married Charlotte because I had come to care a great deal for her,'' he said, rising to his feet. His insistent conscience reminded him that he had married Charlotte not because he cared for her, or even because he saw some great passion in her. He had married her because it seemed easy. Because she was the only woman who'd said yes.

He felt a weight settle over his shoulders. For all his cold pronouncement and elevated tone, he was no better than the aged roué before him. So, standing aside to let the older man precede him, he followed his host up the stairs to the drawing room.

Charlotte sat at the pianoforte, more to ensure that she didn't have to speak to John than anything. She was proficient at the instrument, but not inspired. The memory of their ridiculous conversation this afternoon in the gallery made her want to smile. That charming man seemed like a different person than the wicked seducer the gossips had branded him. She felt a wave of shame for the crass way she'd accused him of philandering.

Why was she so irritable? After all, things were going exactly as she wished. She was married to John and safely out of the Binghamtons' household. She did not find the married state onerous, and her husband appeared pleased enough with his choice. Unexpectedly, she found the man to be far more interesting and pleasant company than she had anticipated.

Perhaps that was the problem.

She annoyed herself further by stumbling over the keys when he came to stand beside her. "I'm sorry I was rude to you," she said. "It was inexcusable that I should have spoken to you that way." She wished her heart would not beat quite so hard.

"What I find upsetting is not that you said it," he said in a low voice, "but that you believe it."

She looked up at him to find his eyes looking intently into hers. Her fingers limped to a stop. "I do not know what to say," she whispered at last. The way he was looking at her did the strangest things to her insides.

"Let us start again," he said. "Let us forget any notions we had of each other before we met." He smiled slightly, but it was warm and genuine. "I want to get to know you for who you really are. And though I know it is likely that the less of my past one knows the better, I would like for you to know me, the real me, a bit better as well."

It was too much. Too tempting. Too doomed for heartbreak. She stood, stammering something about asking her sister to play instead. At John's look of hurt, she stilled. "Thank you for your kind offer, my lord," she said quietly. "But I'm afraid that it is one I cannot accept."

Chapter Eight

For the next several weeks everything seemed to be going perfectly. John showed no further interest in invading Charlotte's psyche and accepted with gracious alacrity every invitation to any vice she chose to provide for him.

While he did not appear to be interested in reviving his public relationship with Lady Champhill, he began to frequent the more notorious gaming hells, losing and winning fortunes in the course of a night. When he did come home, it was generally just as Charlotte was getting up. They passed each other on the stairs, he with a cocky drunken grin, she forcing a pleasant smile as she reminded herself this was part of the bargain.

He generally made a short appearance, at the beginning of his night's agenda, to dance attendance on Charlotte at whatever evening event she had chosen, and then he would take himself off to the card room to play and drink as deeply as the hostess would allow. What he did after those tame amusements, she chose not to contemplate.

She noted, however, that he was as good as his word and not a breath of scandal regarding any exploits in the feminine arena reached her ears.

Yes, Charlotte congratulated herself, she was the model wife. She accepted his presence or his absence with equal equanimity. She never asked where he had been or what he had done. She allowed him to accompany her to the opera, but discreetly disappeared during the interval so he could smoke a cigar and talk with his friends. She made certain he was among acquaintances more sober than himself when he left whatever prim party he'd deigned to attend for her sake, and she smiled serenely when he turned his considerable charm on every other woman in the room besides herself.

In short, she was utterly miserable.

Why had she been so adamant in refusing his offer of friendship? Did she really intend to keep him a stranger for the rest of her life? There were times, now, when she made an effort to open up to him. But somehow her confidences came in fits and starts, and they always seemed to come out sounding cold and stilted. It was better to let things go on the way they had originally planned.

The better they knew each other, the more she would feel she had a right to demand things of him. Things he would never give her.

The only way to make their marriage work was to let him have a free rein, she reminded herself. She couldn't reform him; it would be futile to attempt it. Their future happiness depended on each of them learning to live with the foibles of the other.

Though she wondered sometimes, as he appeared at the doorway of her private sitting room for their occasional afternoon drive looking wan and peaky, if she wasn't pushing him too hard to indulge himself.

He looked pale today as he took up the ribbons and drove her toward the park. She almost asked if he felt well, but decided that if it was, as she suspected, merely a result of his overindulgence, she really didn't want to know.

"We are invited to the Yarboroughs' house party in Richmond," she said cheerfully. "That will be a nice way to spend a few days."

"The Yarboroughs are notorious for throwing house parties that border on the vulgar," John said in a testy tone.

"Yes," she agreed, "but nonetheless, it is an honor to be invited." She paused, looking at his scowl. "Do you wish me to refuse the invitation?" After all, she recalled,

Yarborough himself had gone to school with John. The fact that the man was a notorious drinker, gambler, and womanizer would seem to recommend him to her husband rather than otherwise.

"I do," he said, then softened. "Charlotte, you must trust me. They're a good deal too loose in their morals. You'd be shocked to the core if you knew half the rowdy goings on at their parties. Bad *ton*, for all their money and breeding."

She looked at her gloves in her lap for a moment. "If you would prefer to go without me, I'm certain we can put out a story such that—"

"Dash it all, Charlotte!" he exploded. "I don't want to go without you. I don't want to go at all."

She shot a glance at him, but he looked so fierce, so utterly unlike himself that she turned away and watched the glossy backs of the horses as they swept around the curve at the entrance to the park.

It was quiet today, the noises of the city muffled by the fresh powdering of snow. There hadn't been much last night, but it had sifted straight down and stood piled in small, pointed ridges on every tree branch and broken blade of grass. It was as still and quiet as if they were driving through a painted winter landscape.

The town was certainly very thin of company. She'd noticed it more recently. The parties they'd been invited to had been most often termed intimate affairs to excuse the fact that there were hardly enough couples to make up two sets. Everyone but the most inveterate town dwellers had gone off to their country estates to indulge in wholesome country pursuits and rest up for the excesses of the spring Season.

With so little company, even at the fashionable hour, the park itself appeared more like a country estate than anything else. Charlotte could practically imagine what it would be like if they were driving in the countryside, perhaps on their way to see a neighbor or merely for the pleasure of a winter outing. Then she remembered there was very little likelihood she would ever spend time in the country with John. Her pastoral fantasies would have to be solitary.

"Very well," she said pleasantly, returning to the subject of the Yarborough party. "I will write with our regrets."

He was silent, almost contemplative. Strange, she thought as she looked at his profile, it was as though he were tired. As though his charm was wearing thin. Though of course he was as handsome as ever, his dark hair blown back from his broad forehead and the solid strength of his lower jaw emphasized by the tight muscles that bespoke clenched teeth. At the moment he appeared even more devastatingly appealing than when she'd first accepted his proposal of marriage. Perhaps dissolution improved him. Or perhaps, despite her best efforts, she had grown attached to his looks.

When he turned to her, she could see that his eyes were bloodshot and the skin beneath them was dark to the point of appearing bruised. "You have won," he said in a grim voice. "I'm enough of a gamester to be able to admit when I am done in, and you have won."

"Won?" she repeated stupidly.

"You meant to let me enjoy myself, indulge myself until I was heartily sick of it. You meant to show me the error of my wild ways by fostering every vice and weakness until I sickened myself with it. Instead of begging and pleading with me to leave off the folly of my bachelor days, you have treated me like a child who cares too much for sweetmeats. I have eaten myself sick and now heartily wish never to see another again." There was a flat, dull look in his eyes, as though he would loathe her if he only had the energy.

She stared at him. "I believe I had no such plan."

He gave a rough bark of laughter that held no joy. "Ah, you play the innocent so well. Can you honestly say you had no idea Lady Champhill was my mistress when you forced us to dance? That the contrast of your innocent sweetness with her candied debauchery would not give me a disgust of her? Can you say you did not push me in the way of known gamblers at every card room we entered together? That you did not pour me a glass with a heavy hand, abandon me at the opera, and pretend you had other engagements nearly every day I asked to you spend time with me?"

She meant to be indignant but could not help laughing. And once she had started laughing, she found it difficult to stop. "So it is my fault?" she gasped, when she saw he did not share in her mirth. "You have indulged yourself to sickness, and it is my fault for allowing you to do so?"

She laughed again, but found it had grown bitter. "If I had plotted to give you a disgust of yourself, which I assure you I did not, it would have been easy enough to foil me."

It was irritating to have to speak to his profile as he drove. She knew he heard her though, for she could see the blood and anger rising up his tanned cheeks. "I knew from the start that I could not *make* you do anything," she said. "I have only let you do what you wished, which you would doubtless have done anyway. If you are disgusted with yourself, if you see yourself now as others see you, that is your own fault."

She realized with a shock that this was the first time she'd ever raised her voice to anyone. This was the first time in her adult life she'd ever had what could be termed an argument. But any emotions she might feel upon this discovery were quickly dampened when John did not respond. As the silence lengthened until it stung her ears more than the cold, she wondered if the reason she did not argue was because she was not good at it. Just as John claimed she had done to him, her actions were reflected back to her. She saw herself as he must see her: cold, pious, smugly superior. And one must not forget a heavy-handed dash of martyrdom for being shackled to such a rakehell.

"I'm sorry, John, I—"

"Hello Lord and Lady Westhaven," John called out cheerfully, though the couple was quite far enough away that a friendly wave would have sufficed. "Back from Crownhaven, are you? I'm delighted to see it. We'd heard you'd planned to stay there until spring. Though the city can rival the country when it's freshly dusted with snow. Will you be attending the Montbello masquerade tonight?"

There was nothing Charlotte could do but smile and nod and make the proper replies. It was likely a mercy; she'd already put her foot in it by saying too much—perhaps things that could never be repaired.

The Westhavens, looking cozy and loving under their snug fur blanket, replied in the affirmative and continued their blissfully harmonious drive through the park. She and John, two snowbanks on the carriage seat, drove on in silence.

Charlotte felt a mingled sense of relief and dread as they at last drove down the street toward the town house. The drive had been agony, but there had at least been the lingering hope that she would have a flash of insight, say the right thing, and everything would be comfortable again.

The carriage rolled to a stop, and John threw the reins to the groom as he got down to help her out. "I didn't mean to anger you, John," she said in a rush. "I only meant to show you that I wasn't the kind of woman who would keep you from the things you enjoy."

He looked at her, his dark eyes blank of any emotion. "I have no idea of the kind of woman you are, Charlotte," he said quietly, with what sounded like a thread of tired sadness in his voice. "You never trusted me enough to let me see inside you at all."

And with a low, polite bow, he handed her over to the butler, climbed back into the carriage, and drove off in the direction of his St. James Street club.

Chapter Nine

She was right, of course. It was ridiculous to pretend that he had any right to feel wounded. His indulgences, which truly had been exorbitant of late, could be blamed on no one but himself. There was little wonder she thought him a wastrel.

He dragged a cravat out of the linen drawer and slammed the drawer back into the dresser.

Ever since their marriage, they'd been rattling around the town house like two dice in a box. He kept to his own, dissolute hours and amusements and she her quiet ordinary ones. When they passed on the stairs or went on their occasional drives, he found himself battling not only an irrational sense of guilt but a strangely unexpected sense of longing.

He'd now made six attempts to tie his cravat and at last was forced to admit defeat and ring for his man.

Charlotte didn't give a rap what he did. That should have freed him. Instead he found himself sitting in his club indulging in lurid fantasies that he was at home, reading some nice dull book while his wife did whitework.

His valet came in, concealing a triumphant smile and began his expert ministrations. John obediently held up his chin and tried to work a way out of this coil. What kind of a man, particularly one with a wife who didn't mind his excesses, forsook those excesses and went and fell in love with his wife?

It was true; he loved her.

"Sims," he said with a rueful grin, "you work marvels. Don't know why I ever do it myself."

"Because you generally don't care how you look, my lord," Sims replied grimly.

"True," John admitted, examining the quality of his shave in the mirror. "But I am turning over a new leaf. I shall stand up straight, as my mother always admonished me, eat my vegetables, smile more, and I shall even go so far as to wear that claret-colored waistcoat you are always trying to talk me into."

"Very good, my lord," the valet replied with the utmost impassivity. But John noted with a grin that the man ran his hand down the brocade fabric with something that bordered on reverence.

He did not bother telling Sims his new leaf also involved a severe reining in of nearly all the pastimes he generally indulged in.

"Ah, well," he said lightly. "All good things must come to an end. And all bad things, too."

He allowed Sims to ease him into the waistcoat and then examined himself in the mirror with more attention than he generally did. He wasn't hideous-looking, had plenty of the ready, had often been accused of possessing charm, and, good God, now sported a claret waistcoat. What more did the woman want?

Plenty, a voice in his head reminded.

Charlotte didn't care a snap for all those trappings. She looked at a man as though those clear blue eyes could see straight into his soul. And there wasn't a waistcoat in the world that could conceal his black heart.

"Where is my wife, Sims?" he asked, carefully neutral.

"I believe she's already left for the evening, my lord."

"The opera?"

"The Montbello masquerade, sir."

"Ah." He pushed back the frustration that had been dogging him for days. Why did it matter? Why did he care for her good opinion? After all, she was married to him whether she liked him or not. She'd never given any indication that she regretted her choice. But somehow, he found that he very much cared if his wife liked him.

He thought of how she'd looked in his arms the night of their first ball, when he'd taken her into the back parlor and kissed her. At that moment he'd realized there was something beautiful about her. And he wanted her to wear that expression of pleased surprise and admiration forever.

Strange how someone who generally got everything he wanted could want something so badly.

He hummed a tuneless tune as he went downstairs to prove that he was completely relaxed and had not a care in the world.

"Are you all right, Lord Sinclair?" the groom who held the waiting carriage door asked, surprised into speech.

"Of course. Why?"

The man blushed to the roots of his hair and began stammering. "Oh, well, you look very well indeed, my lord. I just— I'm sorry, sir. I just thought you looked anxious."

John stared him down. "It's the waistcoat," he said calmly. "It makes me look anxious."

He waited until he arrived at the house to don his cape and black domino. In general, he rather liked masquerades. They were always jolly, occasionally ribald, and lent one an excellent excuse to behave entirely badly. Tonight, however, he wanted Charlotte to see him in the best light, not as some loutish fool.

He wanted to be someone else, someone better. But a cape and mask weren't likely to help.

Still, it must be done, so he climbed from the carriage and ascended the steps, marveling at how many people were arriving along with him. Peculiar thing, arriving on time. He made his way up to the ballroom, graciously pretending to be deceived as to who people were, as though a cape and a bit of silk over the eyes could possibly conceal anyone.

He bowed over Lady Montbello's hand and complimented her on gathering so many tonight, no small feat this time of year. It seemed as though everyone was tired of winter, tired of the usual musical evenings, opera, and theater. Vauxhall would not open for months, and there was little but the most tame entertainment to be had if one were the more respectable sort. So the *beau monde* had little choice but to delve into amusements—such as a masquerade—that were, perhaps, not quite as respectable.

He half listened to Lord Montbello's effusive and hilarious comments as to his surprise at seeing John so early, so sober, and so finely dressed, but John's eyes darted around the room, looking for Charlotte.

At last, frustrated, he removed himself from his host's clutches, and began to prowl the room. Charlotte must be here; she'd said she was coming. He wondered if his idiotic behavior in the park had given her such a disgust of him that she had decided not to attend. Or perhaps, he thought wryly, she had decided to take a page from his own book and would not arrive until long after supper.

He caught sight of Lady Champhill glaring at him from across the punch bowl. She was wearing peacock blue with a fantastic headdress meant most likely to represent that bird. The male of the species, of course. Lady Champhill would never identify herself with a peahen.

Perhaps most people only looked into their acquaintances' faces. Certainly, a mask made things less obvious, but people always gave themselves away by their figures, their gestures, the way they held a glass, wore their cuffs. There was only a handful of people in the room he didn't know, and those were likely so moral he hadn't met them anyway.

"Hello, John," Lord Iverley said, coming up to him. The man was dressed as a baker, covered with a fair explosion of flour. The woman on his arm wore a silver domino and was evidently supposed to represent a star. "Didn't make much effort with your costume, did you?" Iverley chided. "Or are you one of the other six dozen gentlemen highwaymen?"

"Nonsense," John said, "I'm wearing a claret-colored waistcoat."

His friend failed to look properly impressed, so he turned to the woman on Iverley's arm. "And how are you, Lady Westhaven?"

The woman visibly deflated. "Oh, you recognized me. I

thought it was so clever of me to come to you with Iverley instead of Georgiana.''

He wished he had played along with her game, but he had been distracted, still looking for Charlotte. "Your costume is lovely," he said truthfully. "Silver suits you very well. Is that Lord Westhaven there, dressed as the sun?''

"Yes. I told him a rain cloud would have suited him better; the man can find the dark lining in any situation.'' She looked after him affectionately. "And there is Georgiana dressed as a butterfly. Oh!'' she said with a start of surprise, "and there is Lady Sinclair.''

John suppressed an exclamation of surprise as well. The woman in the deep green gown, a leafy mask, and orange blossoms twined in her hair did not look like his wife. "So it is," he said, still not really certain. "Please excuse me.''

He saw her gracefully reach out her hand to allow Westhaven to bow over it and knew Lady Westhaven had been correct as to the woman's identity. But he continued to stare at her, bewildered, as though he had never really looked at her before.

He forced himself to go to her, wondering if she was so angry with him that she would be cool to him in front of everyone. She was too well bred to actually cut him, but then again, his accusations during their drive in the park had been as rude as they were ridiculous.

"Hello, John," she said, her voice calm and pleasant as always. "I didn't know you'd planned to attend. If I had, I would have waited for you.''

"I decided at the last minute to come." He bowed over her hand. Why had he never before noticed that her hands were perfectly formed? They were bisque white, the fingers long and tapered, each nail smooth and pale as an almond. He forced himself to release her. "Are you a dryad? A tree nymph?''

To his surprise, she laughed, and looking more unlike herself than ever. "You are the first to guess it. I'm relieved. Lord Montbello asked me if I was a hedgerow.''

"I thought she was spring," Lord Westhaven admitted with a sigh. "Though now, of course, I see dryad." The man evidently read John's mind at last and murmured a few more polite comments before going off in search of his celestial wife.

They were surrounded by people, but they were alone. John cleared his throat and wished the dancing would start. At least then he would have the chance to take her in his arms.

She really did look remarkable. Unrecognizably so. The gown, now that he saw it up close, was many shades of green. Each one lay in diaphanous layers over the other, so that her movements shifted and changed the colors like light and shadows in a glade. The rich greens brought out the reds and golds in her normally colorless hair, and the mask of leaves left temptingly bare a mouth so full and well shaped, he marveled he'd ever had the audacity to kiss it.

"I like your waistcoat," she said at last.

"Charlotte, I was abominably rude to you this afternoon in the park. I beg your pardon for everything I said. I have only myself to blame for my actions and anything they've brought on me is less than I deserve."

She was looking up at him, her expression behind the mask impossible to read.

He drew her into a corner, pulling off his mask so she could see his expression and know he was sincere. But he found he didn't know what to say. Facing her own mask was like talking to a wall. Dash it all, even without a mask she always kept up that wretched wall of reserve. He felt the words sputter and die in his mouth. "You were right. I've been self-indulgent and it's entirely my fault."

She didn't respond, so he plowed onward. "You deserve better. So I shall try to behave."

She smiled then, a tremulous smile, but one that for the first time seemed vulnerable. "I've hardly given you the chance, have I? I was so anxious to give you what I thought you wanted, I never stopped to find out if you really wanted it."

He reached out and carefully loosened the ribbons that held her mask. When he removed it, she was looking at him with an expression he had never seen before.

"Charlotte," he said quietly, "I know what I want. A month ago, it was something entirely different, but you must allow me license to learn something, no matter how I resist learning it. I know what I want, and it isn't that life. I want a home, and comfort, and a wife who respects me. One who perhaps even cares for me. But don't give me that life because you are dutiful. Give it to me because I have earned it.''

He did not know what she would have said then. Those perfect lips had only just opened, to condemn him or forgive him, when Lady Montbello fluttered over and swept her away. Charlotte looked over her shoulder with an apologetic smile, but whether it was for the interruption or for the answer she had yet to give, he couldn't tell.

The night seemed to drag on forever. While he'd always before seen a masquerade as license for innocent fun, he seemed to have developed new, puritanical eyes along with his new leaf. Everyone seemed to be comporting themselves most inappropriately.

There was a milkmaid who was plainly Miss Haverstead showing off far more ankle and bosom than any self-respecting milkmaid—or even a cow—would allow. Lady Champhill was making it very obvious that her new protector was Lord Meterford, though it might have been only that his armor best reflected Lady Champhill's own beauty. And apparently John was the only one aware that Mrs. Ramsbottom was deep in flirtation with none other than Mr. Ramsbottom, who in normal circumstances, she detested.

He was not at all certain that things were patched up with Charlotte. It was impossible to tell with her. There were a few times, in the art gallery and in that little room at their marriage ball, where he felt as though they understood each other, where he imagined there was some modicum of real human warmth behind those impossibly pale blue eyes. Now, however, with the added layer of her mask, she was as impenetrable as dark ice.

She danced more than usual tonight. Occasionally he saw her teeth flash in a laugh, though it was rare. And while she didn't ignore him, she did not seek him out, either. He realized it was the way she had always treated him: with respect, cordiality, and utter remoteness.

"Sulking, are you?" asked a voice. John turned to see

Richard Palmer leaning on the other side of the pillar where John had chosen to prop himself. "Or cultivating a new, brooding look? I hear it is all the rage since Byron was set loose on the *ton*."

John stood up and uncrossed his arms, realizing he had indeed fallen into a most melodramatic gloom. "Indeed. I'm just watching things. Much more interesting than being a part of it, really."

The bells on Palmer's jester hat jangled with his silent laugh. "I'm sorry, I mistook you for my friend Sinclair."

"Dash it all—look at that," John interrupted, his eyes narrowing. "He takes a good deal too many liberties with her."

His friend followed the direction of his gaze. "Now, Sinclair, don't be a prude. He's just having a bit of fun. It's a masquerade after all. He likely doesn't even know who she is."

"He knows," John said in a low growl. "He's always been prowling after her. I fancy she only married me to be out of his house."

"What? Is that Binghamton? Must be a lot of padding. Can't deny he makes a capital Henry VIII. Ah, well, it was only a kiss, and it *is* a masquerade. Most ladies here will be cross if they don't get one anonymous kiss. Entitled to some— Oh, well that is beyond!"

John looked around and realized practically no one in the room had any idea who the woman in green or the man dressed as Henry were. And with the rest of the flirtations going on tonight, it was hardly likely anyone would notice the fat monarch was pulling the woman out on the balcony.

"You'd better go and get her," Palmer said grimly. "Want help?"

John grinned for the first time that night. "Absolutely not. Lady Sinclair will never let me rescue her willingly. If I am to play the role of knight errant, I should like to have all the credit."

He wasn't certain what he expected. It was possible Charlotte might even rebuff him. After all, she'd never accepted anything, bar his offer of marriage. And he was hardly the type of knight errant who could go about armed with morality.

The cold night air hit him forcibly as he stepped through the French doors onto the balcony. And then something else hit him, square in the chest. It was Charlotte.

"Are you all right?" he asked, his arms going around her. He recovered and tried to step back so he could see her expression, but she refused, her arms going tightly around his back.

He looked from the top of Charlotte's head to the ponderous form of Henry VIII. "What's going on?" he demanded.

"Sir!" the man exclaimed. "You interrupt a private conversation."

"My dear sir," John exclaimed in mock surprise, "I believe you must have mistaken Lady Sinclair for someone else. I'm sure you would not have dreamed of forcing your attentions on my wife."

"We were speaking of matters that don't concern you," the man said coldly.

He'd liked to have planted the man a facer, but Charlotte still clung to him, and frankly, the feeling of her arms around him was far too precious to risk any kind of movement. He turned his head down to speak close to her ear. "I know you can take care of things for yourself, Charlotte," he said. "Say the word and I'll be gone."

"No"—her voice was muffled in his cravat—"I need you."

She needed him.

He leveled a stare at the man. "Let us presume you *did* mistake my wife for someone else," he said coldly. "And then I shall be spared the trouble of calling you out."

"You're hardly one who can claim the moral high ground," the man said daringly, though he backed up a pace, his eyes under his mask darting toward the French doors. "I fancy you came out here for an assignation of your own. Lady Sinclair's married the most notorious rake in London. Would you deny her the right to enjoy herself as you do?"

Charlotte turned around, suddenly fierce. "I believe it is my sister who is married to the most notorious rake in

London. My husband is a good and generous man. A kind
man. I count myself fortunate to have married him, and I
will never have need to look elsewhere.''

John stared at her. It was the kindest thing she'd ever
said. For a moment he forgot his fury and stood there smiling
like an idiot.

Binghamton made a noise in his throat. John recalled the
notion that Charlotte had only accepted his proposal to
escape this man before him. She'd married him for protection. Damn it all, if he did nothing else for her, he would
do that.

He lunged at Binghamton, intent on nothing but punishing
the man for every insult to his wife. But Binghamton, poised
for flight, took to his heels and sprinted clumsily through
the ballroom, his large false belly wagging wildly.

John turned to Charlotte, a searing possessiveness tingling
through his tense limbs. ''I'm going after him.''

''No,'' she said.

''No,'' a voice echoed in the darkness. The sound stopped
him and he watched in surprise as a woman dressed as
Boadicea stepped out of the shadows. ''I'll take care of
him,'' she said in a grim voice.

And with that, Lady Amanda Binghamton turned on her
heel and stalked after her husband.

Chapter Ten

John stared at her for so long, Charlotte began to think he might scold her for being so foolish as to leave the ballroom with a man like Binghamton. She wanted to blurt out the whole story, explain how frightened she'd been. She wanted to feel the rough linen of his starched cravat against her cheek again.

John looked back to where Binghamton had fled and drew a deep breath to dispel his evident frustration. "Are you all right?" he asked in a gentle voice she'd never heard him use.

"Yes." Though they were no longer touching, they were still standing far too close. Charlotte clenched her hands to keep from reaching out for him again.

"Did you know it was him?" Again, that quiet, caressing voice.

"No, not at first. I thought he was just some man who'd had too much to drink and didn't know who I was." She saw with dismay that her fingers had indeed reached out to clutch his sleeve.

Before she could release him, he caught up her hand between his own. "I know he hasn't always behaved as a brother-in-law should," he began hesitantly, "but, has he done this to you before?"

"No," she said quickly. "He's . . . he'd been given lately

to treat me . . . improperly. But only in word and in look. It was bad enough at my sister's house; I thought when I married and left the household he would cease to pursue me.'' She could not look him in the face. It seemed ridiculous that a woman as plain as she would claim to have a man chasing her. ''Instead, he seemed to look upon my married state as further license. He never touched me until this evening,'' she clarified, seeing the muscles tighten in her husband's jaw.

''If your sister doesn't set him very *very* straight on this matter, *I* certainly will,'' he said in a grim voice. He was looking down at her with an expression she had never seen him wear before. It was so wounded, so worried, that her heart gave a strange jerk.

How could she explain to him how afraid she'd been, how terrified that he would think she encouraged Binghamton's advances? She'd been so cold to him recently; she knew it. Even this evening she'd been unable to tell him how much she'd missed his company. Could she explain that her reserve had only been fear that she had grown to love him too much?

''Why didn't you tell me?'' he asked. His arm went around her waist, the other hand touching her face as though he'd never seen her before. He touched her as though she were beautiful. ''I know I've been a good-for-nothing rattle. I know it's hard to believe I'd do anything honorable, knowing me as you do, but I would have.''

''I know.''

''If I'd known the whole of it—''

''I know.'' She leaned her head against his shoulder and inhaled deeply. It felt as though it was the first full breath she'd ever taken. ''I'm sorry, John. I should have told you. I just thought I could take care of everything on my own. I'm not used to depending on other people, you see.''

''I'm not used to being dependable,'' he admitted.

They stood in silence for a long time. The warm comfort of his arms made her feel calmer, but the strange thrill of his closeness, the vague, sensual promise that hung in the air made her blood sing faster.

''I think I could learn to be dependable. Solid, even,'' he said with a ghost of a smile in his voice. He pressed a kiss to her forehead. "I think I'd even like giving respectability a try."

"And I will try to be what you want," she said, bewildered at all the emotions that chased through her. Could she open up to him without risking heartbreak? She must. If he could reform, so could she.

"What I want?" he echoed. "Why are you always trying to provide what *I* want? What do *you* want?"

"Why . . . I . . ." She felt her face growing warm. Her desires were not the kinds of things that could be spoken aloud.

"What do you want?" he asked again.

"I don't want to be shut up alone at Bellamy Hall," she said at last, blurting the first coherent thing that came into her mind.

He nodded gravely. "If we live there, it will be together. I have no desire to send you away, Charlotte."

Her heart was pounding loudly in her ears. He didn't wish for separate lives after all. Perhaps . . . She wound her arms around his neck, suddenly bold. "I want to live with you, wherever you are," she said. "I want you to be a father to our children, I want you to be a companion to me—"

"A companion?" he interrupted, making a face of distaste.

"A . . . a friend," she amended. Would he let his wife be his friend?

"Friend?" He drew out the word coaxingly, as though he already knew what was hiding in the secret corner of her heart.

"More than a friend," she admitted at last. She drew a breath and looked him in the face. Did he know how hard this was for her? "You asked what I wanted, and I will tell you. I want you. All of you. Now that I know you, I cannot go back to feeling nothing."

He stared at her in stunned bewilderment. "I didn't think you even liked me."

"Yes," she said hoarsely, her eyes dropping to his cravat, "I like you." He said nothing for so long that her heart began to sink within her. "I will not allow my feelings to become a nuisance for you," she said, raising her chin.

He cupped that defiant chin in his hands and looked down at her, his eyes dark with passion. "They certainly will," he said in a low voice. "I *want* your feelings for me to become a nuisance. I want you to forbid me to stay out late at night. I want you to be jealous of any woman who even looks at me." He leaned over and kissed her behind the ear, then continued, his voice low and insistent, "I want you to refuse to be packed off to the country. I want you to live in my pocket in the most bourgeois way."

"Are we back to your wants?" she breathed, her blood racing.

"You married an unprincipled, selfish rogue, my dear," he said with a faint smile. He took her face between his hands and kissed her deeply. "Charlotte, I more than like you," he said at last. "I've grown to love you. Could you ever learn to love your scoundrel of a husband in return?"

She steadied herself against his chest, feeling his own heart pounding as hard as hers. "I believe I could," she whispered, "given the proper enticements."

"I'll be everything you want, my love," he said. "I will specialize in enticements. After my last wild weeks on the town, I'm a reformed man."

She smiled then, a wicked smile. "But you must promise me not to reform too much. I've begun to love you very much, my rogue, the way you are."

A BREATH OF
SCANDAL

Kate Huntington

Chapter One

May 1821
London

Abigail Pennington was willing to indulge her high-spirited, eighteen-year-old niece, Violetta, in almost anything—particularly now that the girl was about to be married and Abby's tenure as her guardian was nearly over—but her freakish start of insisting upon having live doves as part of the bridal bouquet was the outside of enough!

"Think of the botheration," the ever-practical Abigail said in what probably was a vain effort to dissuade the girl from her latest flight of fancy. "We cannot have the poor, frightened things loose in church to do what frightened animals invariably *will* do all over the ladies' hats and gowns."

"Foolish Abby," Violetta said sweetly in that superior tone she had adopted since the age of sixteen, when she realized her guardian was a hopelessly old-fashioned creature who hadn't the least knowledge of how fashionable, worldly people such as Violetta go on. "Did you think I meant to release them in St. Paul's?" She gave a little trill of laughter to emphasize her aunt's naiveté.

"They will be held quite securely in a pretty cage of gold draped with lavender-throated orchids, of course. How charming it will be to hear their song during the ceremony. And once the vows are pronounced and the procession moves outdoors, I will open the cage and release the doves to freedom.''

''By tradition, the bride's bouquet is the gift of the bridegroom, and perhaps Mr. Whittaker has already made other arrangements,'' Abby replied as she tried, without much hope, to catch the eye of the gentleman in question.

Violetta turned a melting look on her fiancé, and Abby watched that otherwise sensible young gentleman's lips relax into what could only be described as a besotted simper.

''Do you not agree, William?'' Violetta asked with a flutter of long, dusky eyelashes. ''What could be more suitable than the release of a pair of doves into the sunshine to symbolize the joining of our souls and their flight into freedom?''

''A charming thought, my sweet,'' said Mr. Whittaker, which was exactly what he said to all of Violetta's mad suggestions.

Personally, Abigail rather thought marriage and freedom contradictory terms.

''I knew you would agree, dearest,'' Violetta said with a triumphant toss of her glossy dark curls at Abigail, the insignificant entity who was merely the paymaster for this increasingly extravagant wedding.

Resigned to the inevitable, Abby wondered if it would be fatal to dose the doves with laudanum before their journey up the aisle of St. Paul's.

She knew of few married couples—feathered or otherwise—who could endure close confinement under such circumstances without pecking one another's eyes out, especially when their domicile was swinging to and fro in the hands of an excited young bride.

''Why should they peck each other?'' Violetta asked in surprise when Abby voiced this thought aloud. ''They will be a mated pair, of course.''

Abigail had to smile at such innocence.

Unlike her niece, Abby had few illusions about the married state, having endured her father's less-than-benevolent dictatorship over his wife and children until his death, and seeing during her adult life that the marriages of her acquaintances differed very little from her parents'.

But Violetta, Abigail devoutly hoped, might actually find happiness in marriage, united, as she was to be, with a gentleman who worshiped the ground she trod upon, lived to shower his beloved with extravagant gifts, and—most importantly—possessed the purse to do so. His background and expectations had been investigated most thoroughly by Violetta's trustees practically before their first dance together was over, as it would not do for Violetta's wealth to fall into the hands of a handsome fortune hunter. Abby, herself, had been untiringly vigilant in preventing this catastrophe.

But Mr. Whittaker's credentials were perfect. His breeding was impeccable, his expectations were almost as princely as Violetta's own, and he was handsome enough to melt any maiden's heart.

This paragon greeted each of Violetta's most insane proposals with admiration and immediate agreement. Not possessed of an imagination himself, Mr. Whittaker sincerely admired his future bride's vision.

Violetta just as easily could have persuaded the gentleman to go to his wedding in the wake of a matched pair of trained bears with diamond collars doing somersaults the entire length of St. Paul's.

Abigail should be grateful, she supposed, that Violetta's fancy merely settled on doves.

She wondered again about the effect of laudanum on the birds' constitution. She hardly thought the spectacle of two doves cocking up their toes and expiring during the ceremony would be perceived as a good omen for the success of the marriage, as she pointed out to the betrothed couple.

"Darling Abby," Violetta said indulgently when her aunt suggested this possibility to her as an argument against the doves. "You worry too much."

Violetta had no fear she would be otherwise than deliriously happy with the adoring William. She would rule the roost, of course. Abigail had every expectation of that. Otherwise, she could not view with equanimity the thought of entrusting her precious girl's happiness to an institution as flawed as marriage. William couldn't have been more perfect for Violetta if Abigail had chosen him for the girl herself.

Actually, Violetta had chosen him, but it was Abby who had to draw upon all her skills of diplomacy to dissuade Violetta's stodgy and exacting trustees from foisting an aging peer of ancient name and magnificent fortune upon the poor girl instead. It was they who made Abby's life a trial with their constant sniping and criticism. No breath of scandal must attach to the precious heiress. Therefore, no breath of scandal must attach to Abby, either, or they would find a way to overturn her brother's will and its unusual stipulation that his sister be entrusted with the guardianship of the little heiress. This threat was enough to guarantee her compliance with their strict dictates for the past five years.

But the resourceful Abigail always, somehow, found a way to get Violetta what she wanted and needed. And she would continue to do so with the last breath in her body.

Laudanum, Abigail noted on her ever-expanding mental list, with a question mark after.

She must go to Violetta's country house soon to put her niece's affairs in order for the couple's honeymoon, for the newlyweds would take residence there for a brief time after their tour of the Continent before they returned to London in time for the Coronation celebrations. Never mind that King George III had died over a year ago. The ascension of his son, the former Prince Regent, to the throne would be observed with all the extravagance that had marked that gentleman's notorious career, and Violetta was unwilling to miss a single moment of the spectacle merely to languish in the country with her new husband.

But back to the subject at hand.

Abby would ask her ward's land steward for his opinion on how to keep doves tranquil yet alive for a period of several hours. The heat of summer in London and a noisy crowd of wellwishers would be certain to terrify them. On the other hand, it would not do for the creatures to be so docile that they merely blinked in confusion at the dramatic moment when Violetta opened the clasp of the cage and gave them their cue to spiral upward into the cloudless blue sky Violetta had ordered from the Almighty for her wedding day.

Even as Abby puzzled over the details, she suspected that Violetta's will somehow would impose itself upon the creatures and they would perform to the girl's expectations.

Violetta's life was just that way. Heaven knew Abigail had done her best to make it so.

"What *is* all that clatter?" William exclaimed. "A fellow can hardly hear himself think!"

Abigail came to attention with a start and gave a sigh of exasperation. Indeed, she had gotten so accustomed to the cacophany of banging doors, the plodding of horses and job carts, and the shouting of orders next door that it had assumed a dull roar of background noise in the back of her mind. But she had to admit it was most distracting.

"That has been going on all morning," she said. "Violetta, do stop gawking out the window. What will our new neighbors think if they see you?"

"Don't be fusty, Abby, dear," said Violetta. "What charming furniture! It came from France or Italy, I am persuaded."

Since her tour of the Continent with a friend and her parents the previous summer, Violetta had become a self-proclaimed authority on all things European. Thank heaven the girl eventually had tired of inserting such exclamations as *mon dieu* and *qué lastima* into every sentence.

"William, darling, only come and see these elegant side tables," Violetta called to her fiancé, who went at once to stand behind her and put his gloved hands on her slim shoulders.

"You shall have a similar pair for your boudoir, my love," he promised. "And a gilded mirror decorated with cherubs to frame your pretty face each day."

"William, you are so sweet to me," Violetta said warmly.

Then the girl's rosebud-shaped mouth dropped open and her eyes widened.

He must have appeared, Abigail thought wryly.

Violetta had still been in bed, sipping her morning hot chocolate and nibbling on sweet biscuits as she contemplated which one of her many morning gowns was most likely to stun poor Mr. Whittaker into incoherent stammering when Abby stepped outside her front door to determine the source of the racket that disrupted the serenity of the neighborhood. She was just in time to see a horseman bring his magnificent white stallion to a halt before the house next door and dismount with athletic grace to solicitously hand a tall, veiled lady out of the traveling carriage he was escorting.

Once the lady had alighted, he turned toward Abby as if he could feel her gaze upon him.

Abigail was vexed to have been caught spying on the new neighbors. It was too late for retreat, however, like the most vulgar of housemaids.

The gentleman had a wide forehead framed by windblown chestnut hair, large, luminous blue-gray eyes of grave expression, and a beautifully sculpted jaw. He was splendidly dressed in what Violetta no doubt would pronounce the European style. Abigail herself paid little attention to male fashion, but even she recognized at once that the coat molded to his magnificent shoulders had been created by a tailor of the first stare.

Those solemn eyes leisurely perused Abby's appearance from her neatly pinned blonde hair to the tips of her sensibly shod feet.

Abigail's breath caught and she had stared back, mesmerized by him.

Then his sensual lips quirked up in a smile and he gave her a slight bow.

Released from his spell, Abigail's breath whooshed out all at once. She forced herself to make a dignified retreat inside the house, where she leaned against the door until her foolish heart stopped its frantic beating. Thank heaven none of the servants were about to see her composure come all undone. How embarrassing!

Violetta, however, knew her own worth, and it was hardly a source of embarrassment to *her* that the magnificent man caught her staring at him. She moved closer to the window, in fact, so the stranger would have a clear view of her pretty face and charming, pin-tucked white gown with the pale blue sash.

Why would she spend so much time primping, after all, if she did not intend for her efforts to be seen and appreciated?

"Who is he?" Violetta breathed. "Abby, do you know?"

The question was answered from an unexpected source.

"A Mr. Bourbonnais and his mother," Mr. Whittaker said with a shrug as he drew his betrothed back from the window, although whether it was to prevent Mr. Bourbonnais from ogling Violetta or to prevent Violetta from ogling Mr. Bourbonnais, Abby couldn't say. Both, most likely. "They have been living in high style the past few weeks at the Clarendon Hotel while the house has been readied for them. They are lately arrived from the Continent, one assumes."

"Is this Mr. Bourbonnais married?" Violetta asked.

Abby waited for the answer with equal eagerness, even though she would not have asked the question herself.

Undue inquisitiveness, she felt, was a sign of low breeding. She had endeavored to instill this lesson into her young charge with only qualified success.

"No," Mr. Whittaker answered. He smiled teasingly at Abby. "Perhaps he will be the answer to a certain maiden's prayers. He appears to be of an appropriate age."

"One wedding at a time, if you please," Abby said, uncomfortably aware she might be blushing. How vexatious! She was no schoolroom miss to be flustered by a handsome face.

"There is no time to be lost, if you fancy him, Miss Pennington," Mr. Whittaker said with a chuckle. "They are hiring the house for a few months only, with an option to buy. It is said one resourceful lady actually scaled the wall of the Clarendon in an attempt to surprise the gentleman in his bedroom. Fortunately—or unfortunately, depending on one's point of view—she was discovered before she achieved her purpose and escorted off the property in disgrace."

Abby, remembering those hypnotic eyes and that handsome face, had no difficulty in believing this.

"You are certainly a fountain of information today, Mr. Whittaker," Abby remarked with a disapproving frown at the gentleman. She did not care to hear such things repeated in Violetta's presence.

"There appears to be quite a bit of gossip about the pair of them," he said, unabashed. "The mother, one hears, is born of some royal European house, a duchess, I believe, although she is traveling incognito. The gentleman's position in society is . . . somewhat vague."

"Vague?" Violetta questioned. "Come now, William. Do not leave us in suspense. I can see you are perishing to tell all."

Mr. Whittaker pursed his lips, as if considering. "Perhaps I should not," he said teasingly. "I know how Miss Pennington eschews idle gossip."

Thus put on her mettle, Abby considered it beneath her to betray an unbecoming inquisitiveness. Happily, Violetta had no such scruples.

"Do tell, William, darling," she said with her most impish smile. "Is Mr. Bourbonnais's secret very dreadful?"

"Well," Mr. Whittaker said, "Mr. Bourbonnais is said to be the natural son of a certain prominent gentleman, and this connection may well mean that Mr. Bourbonnais will soon receive a dukedom or a cabinet post due to this highly placed gentleman's influence."

"What utter nonsense," Abby scoffed. "The only person in England capable of bestowing such a position is . . ." Mr. Whittaker was looking at her with an expression of such expectation on his face that Abby sputtered to silence.

"The king?" she exclaimed after a moment. "Mr. Whittaker, you *cannot* be serious."

He held up both hands as if absolving himself of blame. "That is the rumor. Personally, I don't believe a word of it, and I know you and Violetta are far too intelligent to be taken in by such flummery."

"Abby, we should call on Mrs. Bourbonnais without delay," said Violetta. "It is the neighborly thing to do."

"But, dearest, with the wedding only a month away, I don't see how we are to find the time."

"It is our duty," Violetta insisted as she stole another glance out the window. "As neighbors."

Abby's heart nearly stopped with horror.

Violetta was an intelligent girl, and Abby felt sure she valued Mr. Whittaker's good qualities as she ought. But she was only eighteen, and Abby had not missed the gleam of girlish infatuation in her eye when she first beheld the mysterious Mr. Bourbonnais.

Her sense of uneasiness increased when Mr. Whittaker took his leave and Violetta was so preoccupied with her own thoughts that she barely roused herself sufficiently to wish him a pleasant day.

"You will not forget you are to dine with us tomorrow, Mr. Whittaker," Abby said to cover the awkwardness of his bride-to-be's inattention.

"You may depend upon me, Miss Pennington," he said gallantly.

Chapter Two

"Such a pity sons grow up to have whiskers and minds of their own," the duchess—or so she always thought of herself—said soulfully as she patted her son's clean-shaven jaw. "You made such a charming dauphin, my dearest. Ah, that lovely summer in Naples! I was the toast of the city— the tragic young queen who had miraculously escaped the guillotine with her child in her arms while her loyal maidservant died in her place. The rumors about us were particularly entertaining that year."

She gave her son a fatuous smile.

"The Italians are such welcoming, *generous* people," she said with a reminiscent sigh.

Gabriel Bourbonnais, for that was the name he had assumed shortly after he debarked from Dover, rolled his eyes. To use his own name would be decidedly awkward.

"Mother—"

"*Maman,* darling, if you please," the lady said in a pained tone. "The more you use it in private, the less likely you are to get it wrong in public. Remember, we have not set foot in England before now."

"*Maman,*" he said dutifully. "You did not tell me the girl is to be married soon."

"Yes. How very fortunate we have arrived in time. She is absolutely perfect for our scheme. Rich, pretty, and connected by birth to the first families in London, although few of her relatives remain alive, which is especially fortunate. She can be the key to acceptance in all the right circles. You must do your best to captivate her.''

"If I must,'' he said with a marked lack of enthusiasm.

His mother raised her eyebrows at him. "Since when do you object to making love to a pretty girl?'' she asked.

"A jealous betrothed is a tedious complication that too often leads to grass before breakfast,'' he said with a sigh.

"That is why I paid for all those frightfully expensive lessons in fencing and marksmanship, darling. It will not come to that if you use good judgment. You need not compromise the girl. Just charm her into introducing us to all her very-well-connected friends and get us invited to their parties. I trust that isn't too much to ask.''

"Not at all.'' A bit too casually, he asked, "What do you know about the aunt?''

He had been disappointed to learn that the solemn, willowy, fair-haired woman staring at him from next door when he and his mother arrived was not the heiress. It would be no inconvenience for him to charm *her*.

His mother made an airy gesture of dismissal. "A nonentity,'' she said. "An old maid. She does not go out much in Society except to chaperon the girl. We need not be concerned about her.''

"She did not seem very old to me,'' he observed.

His mother gave him a straight look. "I know you have a weakness for blondes, my son, but trifling with this one could be our undoing. She has a reputation for shrewdness, and we cannot risk having our objective discovered until the proper time. Concentrate on the heiress—*only* the heiress—and all will be well.''

"As you wish,'' he said with a slight bow.

"Very good,'' the duchess said. "I adore the way your eyes frost over with disdain when you are displeased. It is most ... regal. Now all you have to do is look imposing and practice your compliments.'' She frowned at him suddenly. "It is unfortunate that you lack a tendency to put on flesh. It would heighten your resemblance to the Hanovers, although it is already quite close. And you are in rather more robust health than one could wish, for one knows that the Hanovers, as a rule, are a sickly lot.''

Gabriel shook his head. ''You are an unnatural mother,'' he said ruefully.

''Thank you, my angel,'' she said with a becoming smirk, for all the world as if he had meant it as a compliment.

''Shall I go outside and give the heiress an opportunity to admire me some more from her window?'' he asked.

''Certainly not! You must cultivate an air of mystery. Make the girl come to you.''

Which she did, not two days later.

Violetta would have come sooner if Abby had not pointed out that it was the height of bad manners to appear on one's neighbor's doorstep within a quarter hour of the last carter's departure.

Mrs. Bourbonnais received them alone, much to Violetta's obvious, and Abby's more subtle—she hoped—disappointment.

Their hostess was a faded beauty of middle years. Her morning gown was simple but of elegant fabric and workmanship. A cashmere shawl in warm, muted tones of mulberry and russet was thrown over her shoulders. Her long, fair hair was tinged with silver and arranged in a coronet on top of her head. She may as well have worn a tiara and been done with it, so regal was her appearance.

The lady graciously extended one aristocratically slender, gloved hand toward her visitors. ''How kind of you to come,'' she said in a rich contralto. ''My son was afraid I would be lonely today in his absence, and here I have two lovely young ladies to brighten my afternoon.''

Now that she knew Mr. Bourbonnais was not going to appear, Violetta stopped glancing at the door and settled down to a comfortable cose with hands demurely folded in her lap. She was obviously entranced by the lady, who pleasantly discussed the sights in various capital cities that Violetta had so recently toured.

''There is a certain charming restaurant on the Rue de St. Germain,'' Violetta said with all the blasé casualness of the most seasoned traveler. ''Do you know it?''

''Ah, Paris,'' murmured their hostess with a sad, sweet

smile of reminiscence on her face. "I have not been there for many years. I *could* not return after . . . I could not bear to see it so changed."

An emigré, Abby decided, albeit one of means from the look of her furnishings, her gown, her jewelry, and her expensively groomed person.

"Now, Vienna," the lady said brightly. "*There* is the place to eat pastry, my child. Dear Vienna, my haven after a cruel fate altered my destiny forever." She gave them a small, rueful smile. "Mustn't dwell on the past," she said. "Here I am in a bustling new city with charming young neighbors to greet me. I am certain my son and I will be very happy here. It was sad to leave Vienna, but a son's interests must always come first in a mother's heart." She smiled impartially at both ladies. "Someday you will understand."

"Mr. Bourbonnais is your only child, then?" Violetta asked.

"Yes, he is," the lady said fondly, "and quite a handful was my precious boy as a child. I am convinced that an intelligent child is much more challenging to rear than an unintelligent one. Willful, my boy was, so sure that he knew better than his *maman* and all the finest tutors who could be hired for his education. Having a child so gifted is a grave responsibility, and my Gabriel has been blessed with the same formidable intellect and artistic acuity as his—" She broke off with a cough. "But I am boring you young ladies with this unseemly boasting of my son's good qualities. You are sweet girls to indulge me so."

"Not at all," Abby said politely. "Will you stay in London for the Coronation ceremonies? It will be an exciting time to be in the city."

"I am sure it will be," she said with a short, mirthless laugh. "However, I fear my son and I would hardly be welcome guests."

"More welcome than the king's wife, I daresay," Violetta said sagely.

Abigail frowned. Regardless of the fact that all of polite—and impolite—Society was tittering over the king's machinations to avoid having his estranged wife, Queen Caroline, participate in the Coronation ceremonies that would take place in July, Abby considered it indelicate for a maiden of tender years to allude to the king's domestic difficulties.

"Violetta," she said in gentle reproof.

"But everyone knows he can't abide the queen," the girl replied.

"That woman," their hostess said through gritted teeth, "is *not* the rightful queen."

Abigail and Violetta both stared at her in astonishment. She seemed so . . . angry.

"Do you know her?" Violetta asked before Abby could catch her eye to indicate she should be silent.

"No," she said vehemently. "Never would I allow that woman in my presence. Her behavior is scandalous. And she aspires to honors that are not hers."

"But she is his wife. None can deny it," Violetta said in confusion.

"True. But that does *not* make her the rightful queen," Mrs. Bourbonnais snapped at Violetta. "Do *not* call her that while you are a guest in my house." Her mouth was a harsh, angry line.

"I . . . I beg your pardon," Violetta said. Her eyes were wide with dismay. "I had no wish to offend you."

Mrs. Bourbonnais blinked and passed a frail hand over her eyes. "Forgive me, my dear young lady. It is I who must apologize. If you will excuse me, I . . . I am not well." She started to stand but half fell back into her chair.

"Mrs. Bourbonnais," Abby exclaimed. She rushed forward at once to aid their swooning hostess. Violetta jumped to her feet and wrung her hands in distress.

"Violetta," Abby said as she chafed the lady's wrists. "Tug the bell pull. Mrs. Bourbonnais needs her maid."

"Of course," the girl said, obviously glad to be of use.

"What is the meaning of this?" a haughty masculine voice said from the doorway.

It was Mr. Bourbonnais, but although Violetta stumbled to a stop and stared, Abby was much too concerned about his mother to do more than glance over her shoulder at him. "She is feeling faint," Abby told him. He went at once to go down on one knee by his mother's chair.

"I am all right, my son," the elder lady said weakly. "So silly."

"I will assist you to your room, *Maman*," he said solicitously as he gently helped his mother stand.

"I am so sorry, Mrs. Bourbonnais," Violetta blurted out. "I had no wish to distress you. I do not know what I said to cause such trouble."

The elder lady smiled bravely at the girl. "I forgive you, my dear child. You could not have known," she told her.

"Known what?" Violetta asked, all at sea.

"Violetta," Abigail said repressively. She was uncomfortably aware of the way Mr. Bourbonnais's eyes narrowed suspiciously at Violetta, and then at Abigail.

"I am so sorry," Violetta repeated softly.

"We will take our leave now, Mrs. Bourbonnais," Abby said, thinking they had caused enough damage for one day.

Mr. Bourbonnais made an imperious gesture that caused her to stop at once in her retreat for the door. "You will wait, if you please," he said curtly. It was not a request, but a command. It did not occur to Abby to disobey. "I will return as soon as I have seen my mother to her room."

"Yes. Of course," Abby said at once. Violetta was positively quivering with anxiety.

He gave an abrupt nod and guided his mother's faltering steps from the room. He was back within minutes.

Abby and Violetta had remained standing. To be seated somehow seemed presumptuous under the circumstances. "How is your mother?" Abby asked him.

"I thank you for your concern," he said. "She is resting now, and seems to be much improved."

"I am so glad," Violetta said. Her eyes were moist and her lips trembled. Abby supposed Mr. Bourbonnais would have to be made of wood if he didn't notice how lovely Violetta was in her distress. "I would not have had this happen for the world."

Predictably, his grave expression softened. "I believe you," he said, "but I must know. What did you say to my mother?"

"I merely observed that the king was eager to keep the queen away from the Coronation ceremonies," the bewildered Violetta said. "Everyone is saying so. I cannot imagine why Mrs. Bourbonnais became so angry."

"Ah," he said with a sigh. "I begin to understand. It is a source of some bitterness to my mother that—but her secret is not mine to tell. I can only assure you she is justified in her grievance and beg you not to mention the subject again in her presence."

"The subject of the queen?" Violetta asked.

"She is *not* the queen," he snapped.

"That is what *she* said," Abby said slowly. "I do not understand."

"Please," Mr. Bourbonnais said with a charming smile. "It is a bad host who dwells on sad past history on such a lovely day. Forgive me, but I do not believe we have been introduced, although I understand you live in the white house next door, do you not?"

"How rude of me," Abby said at once. "I am Miss Pennington, and this is my niece, Miss Violetta Pennington."

He bowed. "Charmed," he said. "It is kind of you to call on us. My mother's health does not permit her to go out much."

"Will she be all right?" Violetta asked anxiously.

"Perfectly, I assure you, Miss Violetta," he said warmly. "No harm was done."

"We are relieved to hear it," Abigail said, rising. "My niece and I must make our departure. We have taken up enough of your time."

"Not at all," he said with another of those charming smiles, but he rose at once. "I hope you will call again soon. I promise you my mother will be delighted to see you."

"You are very kind," Abby said. To her dismay, her voice quavered when Mr. Bourbonnais took her hand in his large, warm one, even though there was nothing personal about his touch or expression.

"Nonsense," he said. "Miss Violetta," he added as he pressed that young lady's hand. The girl nearly tripped over her own feet. Her eyes were shining with shy admiration as Mr. Bourbonnais steadied her elbow and smiled at her.

Poor Mr. Whittaker, Abby thought with an inward sigh.

* * *

"You mark my words," Lady Letitia Logan said with fire in her eyes. "She is an actress, if not something even more disreputable! They are penniless fortune hunters, the pair of them. If I were you, my dears, I would use caution in befriending them."

Abigail and Violetta had been acquainted with Lady Letitia for years, for Violetta's mother had moved in the highest circles both before and after her marriage to Abby's brother, a match many considered far beneath her. But until now, that august leader of fashionable society had not deigned to pay them a visit. Her whole purpose now seemed to be to put them on their guard against that scheming baggage who called herself Mrs. Bourbonnais and her son. She had questioned them quite urgently on anything they might have seen or heard from next door.

"My brother, who is usually awake on every suit, seems to be quite captivated by the creature," Lady Letitia said, sounding quite put out. "He visited her several times at the Clarendon Hotel, and with my own eyes I saw him driving her in the park in his carriage."

"Lord Stoneham has been a widower for a long time," Abby said comfortably. "Is it not wonderful that he might seek the company of an attractive lady?"

"No one has greater respect for my brother's intelligence than I," Lady Letitia said, "but I will *not* stand by while some dreadful harpy gets her hooks into him!"

"Surely it is not as bad as all that," Abby said in a vain attempt to calm the lady, whose face was turning an alarming shade of purple. "Your brother is still a very handsome man. He could have had his choice of any woman in England these past thirty years if he wished to remarry."

"When I ask him what he knows of the woman, after all, he is silent."

"It could be," Abby suggested, "that there is nothing to tell."

"Or," Lady Letitia said, "that there is *everything* to tell. Promise me if you learn anything to the point about that woman and her rogue of a son, you will inform me at once."

"Of course," Abby said with raised eyebrows. "But I do not know what it is you hope to learn."

"Just keep an eye on them," Lady Letitia snapped, rising to go now that her purpose in coming had been accomplished. She favored them both with a smile that did not quite reach her eyes. "Good day, Miss Pennington. Miss Violetta. I wish you a pleasant afternoon."

"Good day," Abigail said, returning the lady's slight valedictory inclination of the head.

"I cannot believe he is a rogue," Violetta said defiantly once the lady was gone. "He is much too . . ."

"Handsome?" Abby finished for her. "My dear, that is the most dangerous kind."

"Now you sound just like Lady Letitia," Violetta said, looking mulish. "I meant to say he is much too gentlemanly. Lady Letitia seems determined to have us snub Mrs. Bourbonnais and her son, and I, for one, will do nothing of the kind!" And so was foiled Lady Letitia's unsubtle attempt to discredit Mrs. Bourbonnais and her son in the eyes of polite Society.

Chapter Three

Abigail gave a long sigh when she looked out her bedroom window the following day to see the unedifying spectacle of Violetta's friend, Emily Branshaw, perched upon the garden wall and spying on Mr. Bourbonnais as he read aloud from a book in his own garden to his mother.

Violetta, she could see, was laughing up at her friend and shaking her head when Emily tried to coax her onto the wall by pantomime. Violetta pantomimed to Emily that she should come down instead.

Abby permitted herself a smile of satisfaction, pleased to observe that Violetta obviously had benefited from Abby's instruction enough to put an end to Emily's naughtiness.

The smile was quite wiped from her face when she saw Violetta give in to her friend's blandishments and use the chair Emily had dragged over to join her on the wall.

Lips compressed, Abby was just about to go downstairs to put an end to this impropriety when Violetta lost her balance and fell off the wall.

By the time Abby, her heart in her throat, had rushed to the scene, Mr. Bourbonnais had gathered Violetta into his arms and carried her through the gate in the wall. Her young face was twisted in pain.

"My ankle," Violetta said, bravely suppressing a sob.

"My poor dear," Abby exclaimed. "Please bring her

inside, Mr. Bourbonnais.'' She turned to the other girl, who was making a dreadful din. ''Emily, there is no cause for all this shrieking. Violetta is hardly at death's door.''

Emily scowled at her, and Abby noted her eyes were perfectly dry. The little minx merely wanted to attract Mr. Bourbonnais's attention to herself, and failed dismally, for the gentleman paid her no heed at all.

No. He was too busy whispering soothing words to Violetta in a gentle tone of voice that had her smiling tremulously at him. He carried her all the way up to her bedroom, where he carefully lowered her into a chair.

''Send one of the footmen for a doctor at once,'' Abby said to Violetta's startled maid, who had been in the process of putting away some linen.

''It *hurts*,'' Violetta fretted. ''If it is broken, what will I do? The wedding is only a month away, and I will *not* hobble down the aisle on a crutch.''

''Oh, surely not,'' Abby said in horror.

Mr. Bourbonnais gracefully lowered himself to one knee in front of Violetta.

''If you will permit, Miss Violetta,'' he said, ''I have had some experience in caring for broken bones.''

Abby realized with horror that he meant to put his large, muscular hands on her vulnerable ward's slender limb. ''Do not!'' she blurted out.

Mr. Bourbonnais did not look at her. ''I will be very careful, I promise you,'' he said softly to Violetta as he loosened her shoe and removed it. The injured ankle was already swollen to twice the size of the other.

The girl bit her lip and Abby could see a pulse beat in her throat.

''Of course,'' Violetta said, blushing as the man took her dainty foot in one hand and gently probed her ankle with the other.

''It is sprained, not broken,'' he pronounced at last. ''The bone is intact.''

''It looks *dreadful*,'' Violetta exclaimed. ''I will not be able to wear my new, white satin shoes for the wedding.''

''The swelling will soon go down,'' Mr. Bourbonnais told her. ''Your white satin shoes will fit to perfection.'' To

Abby's indignation, he touched one of Violetta's dusky curls with a lazy finger and allowed it to trail down her pink, dewy cheek. "But even if your ankle is still swollen a month from now, I promise you your fiancé will not care. No man would." His gaze was so intimate, his eyes so full of admiration that Abby could see both Violetta and Emily just melt. Abby's own insides quivered, heaven help her!

Her duty was plain. She must separate this dangerous man from her ward. At once.

"Thank you so much, Mr. Bourbonnais, for coming to Violetta's rescue," Abby said coolly as she moved toward the door. Both Violetta and Emily looked at her in surprise, but she ignored them.

Mr. Bourbonnais rose at once and followed her.

At least the man had the good manners to take the hint. He also had refrained from exhibiting any curiosity as to why the young ladies were on the garden wall spying on him. But then, he already knew. The smug creature was no doubt well accustomed to having females make fools of themselves over him. Thank heaven Violetta was going to be married in a month. Otherwise, she might be quite susceptible to the rogue's blandishments.

When they got to the ground floor, the doctor had just been shown in. He gave Abby a respectful nod and proceeded to go up the steps. He was the doctor who had taken care of Abby's and Violetta's health for the past three years, and he knew this house as well as his own.

"May I offer you a cup of tea, Mr. Bourbonnais?" Abby felt compelled to ask for politeness' sake, even though she wished he would just go away.

His well-shaped lips quirked up at the corners and his eyes were alight with humor, for all the world as if he could read her mind perfectly. "Yes, you may," he said.

"Very well," she said, leading the way to the parlor. Once there, she tugged the bellpull and sent the maid who answered for refreshments.

"My dear Miss Pennington," he said archly when they were seated across from one another. "You do not like me very much, do you?"

She could have said that, in perfect truth, she didn't know

him well enough to either like or dislike him, but that would be a lie. Abby might not know *him*, but she was intimately acquainted with his kind. She had not spent the past two years since Violetta's come-out chasing away fortune hunters for nothing. "As a matter of fact, Mr. Bourbonnais," she said bluntly, "I do not like you at all."

"No, I believe you do not," he said, looking amused. "May I ask why?"

"My niece is to be married in a month," she said crisply. "She is a young, impressionable innocent, and I will thank you to stop trying to turn her head with your attentions."

"Come now, my dear lady," he said. "She fell off the garden wall like a ripe apple, practically into my arms. Of course I caught her. What else could I do? But I was very respectful of her person, I promise you."

"Let me speak plainly, Mr. Bourbonnais," Abby snapped. "I will not have my niece trifled with."

"Do not be distressed. Your pretty niece is perfectly safe from me."

"Thank you," she said as she let out all her breath at once. He seemed perfectly sincere, and she felt like a complete fool.

Abby was about to apologize for jumping to conclusions when the gentleman leaned forward and captured both her hands in his. "You, however, are another matter," he said, turning the full force of his compelling blue-gray eyes upon her. "I have this unfortunate weakness for beautiful blonde ladies who know their own minds. No doubt any number of gentlemen have told you how magnificent you look when you are angry, so I will not annoy you by adding to their number."

She snatched her hands away. He was making sport of her, of course. Beautiful? Hardly. Magnificent? Hah! She was a spinster far past her prime to give the branch with no bark on it. He must think her a complete fool.

"Forgive me," he said, looking chastened. "I have forgotten myself."

Abby blinked at him. Was it her imagination, or did his slight foreign accent suddenly seem more pronounced? She tried to remember if he had used it when he told her she was beautiful. He hadn't, she realized. A man who assumes a false foreign accent can only be up to no good. "Stay away from my niece," she warned him.

"And you, Miss Pennington?" he asked softly. "Am I to stay away from you, as well?" He was so close that Abby could feel his clove-scented breath on her lips. "For, I promise you, I find you infinitely more tempting than your niece."

Abby merely stared at him. There was no laughter in his eyes now. He appeared to be perfectly serious.

Of course. He was using her to get to Violetta. That was the explanation. How thoroughly unprincipled of him! Abby opened her mouth to tell him he needn't play his tricks on her, for she was wise to them, when he picked up a book of architectural drawings from the table.

"May I?" he asked with every appearance of keen interest.

"Of course," Abby said, surprised. "Are you interested in architecture?"

"Yes. These are magnificent."

"Such renderings are my one indulgence," Abby said, warming to him in spite of herself. "That one is my favorite." She pointed to a framed watercolor above the white marble fireplace. He sauntered over at once to have a look.

"It is the Royal Lodge at Kew," he said.

"You are correct," she said, surprised.

"Do you know it?" he asked without taking his eyes from the picture.

Abby gave a long sigh. "Every pane of glass and angle of roof," she said, "but only through books, alas. I have learned to my disappointment that it is not open to the public, more's the pity. I have been drawn to it ever since I saw a sketch of it in one of my father's books. Marvelous, is it not?"

"Marvelous," he repeated. His brow was furrowed, as if in thought.

"Imagine putting those high, arched stained-glass windows in a hunting lodge. I would give *anything* to see it."

He turned to face her at that. "Would you, indeed?" he asked gravely. "I wonder."

Before she could ask him what he meant by that strange remark, the maid arrived with the tea tray, and Violetta herself limped into the room, leaning heavily upon the doctor's arm. Emily followed with a light coverlet and the novel Violetta had been reading at breakfast.

"Doctor Simpson said I could come down to the parlor provided I keep my ankle up and spend the remainder of the day resting it," Violetta said. Her eyes had a bright, unfocused look. Apparently the doctor had dosed her with laudanum for the pain.

The girl stumbled, and Mr. Bourbonnais made a quick movement as if to go to her aid. Abby caught Violetta's arm instead and glared at him. He gave Abby a sheepish look and held his empty hands up in a humorous pantomime as if to show her he was harmless.

Abby didn't believe *that* for a moment! Lady Letitia was right. He was a rake and a scoundrel, and he had his eye on Violetta's money. Abby would bet her life on it. She could hardly say so now, however, with Violetta gazing at him as if he had personally set the sun in the sky.

"It is as you said, Mr. Bourbonnais," the doctor remarked. "Merely a bad sprain." He gave Violetta an apologetic look. "You are frowning at me, young lady, for that 'merely,' and you have a perfect right, for a sprain is more painful than a clean break."

"But the wedding . . ."

"You will be perfectly recovered by then, I assure you," he said. The doctor turned to Mr. Bourbonnais. "And where did you receive your medical training, sir?"

"I lived in Africa for some time," he said easily enough. Abby could see Emily's lips form the word *Africa*, and she knew by nightfall news of the fascinating Mr. Bourbonnais's sojourn in Africa would be all over the neighborhood.

"I did not receive any formal medical training, of course," Mr. Bourbonnais said stiffly.

"No, of course not," the doctor said sheepishly. It was hardly polite to accuse a gentleman of Mr. Bourbonnais's apparent breeding of condescending to learn something so useful to his fellow man as medicine. "I beg your pardon."

"Not at all," the gentleman said graciously. "I found

myself in a country, however, where medical aid is rare, so like many residents of that place, I learned enough to take care of myself and my dependents.''

"You have children?'' Emily squeaked. She looked crest-fallen.

Mr. Bourbonnais smiled at her. "I was referring to the servants.'' He turned to Abby. "Miss Pennington, I must take my leave,'' he said, rising. "My mother will be anxious for news of Miss Violetta.'' He took a last swallow from the teacup and set it on a table. When Abby rose, he took her hand and bowed over it. "*Au revoir*, my dear lady,'' he said.

He had remembered he was to have a foreign accent again, Abby thought sourly.

"Thank you for bringing me home,'' Violetta said.

"A pleasure,'' he replied, bowing.

Drat the man! Abby could hear Emily's and Violetta's sighs from where she stood. He had a little smile on his lips when he looked at Abby, for all the world as if he knew she was ready to intervene if he had the effrontery to kiss Violetta's hand or perform some other gallant nonsense.

Emily made a show of fanning her flushed face when he was out of sight, and Violetta gave an inebriated-sounding giggle.

"I had not the slightest hope that I would actually meet him,'' Violetta's so-called friend exclaimed. "What famous luck!''

"Yes. Famous luck that Violetta has been injured due to *your* lack of judgment,'' Abby said sternly.

"He is *so* strong,'' said Emily, unrepentant. She licked her little pink lips like a cat. "He carried Violetta all the way across the yard, into the house and up the stairs, and he wasn't even breathing hard.''

"He smells of bay rum,'' Violetta murmured dreamily.

And his breath smells of cloves. A thoroughly spicy *man*, Abby thought. Then she brought herself up short. She had no intention of joining in the litany of praise for her vexatious neighbor's gallant manner and large, graceful, fragrant male . . . person.

Before she could put an end to the young women's transports and—it must be admitted—her own, Mr. Whittaker, flushed and breathing hard, ran into the room.

"Violetta!" he cried upon seeing his betrothed seated with her swollen ankle elevated upon an embroidered footstool. He dropped to one knee beside her chair and took both her hands in his. "The servants tell me you have met with an accident."

Any other maiden would have been gratified by such a demonstration of concern, but Violetta only flinched, for in his zeal he bumped her injured ankle. "William! Must you be so clumsy?" she snapped.

"My poor darling, have I hurt you?" he asked anxiously.

"No. Not very much," Violetta admitted. "I'm sorry. It is very tender when it is jarred like that."

Abby remembered Mr. Bourbonnais's large, gentle hand on Violetta's injured limb. By comparison, she had to admit that poor Mr. Whittaker must seem the most bumptious clod.

"I am so sorry, my dear," he said, averting his eyes quite properly from the exposed limb. "How did this happen?"

"Mr. Whittaker," Abby interrupted before Violetta could answer, certain that telling the girl's concerned fiancé his beloved had tumbled off the garden wall while she was ogling Mr. Bourbonnais would serve no useful purpose. "Violetta is quite fatigued from her ordeal and must rest. The doctor has given her laudanum. Perhaps you should save your questions for another time."

"*I* will tell you," Emily said eagerly. "We climbed the garden wall to watch Mr. Bourbonnais and Violetta fell off. He just swept her up into his arms and carried her all the way up the stairs to her bedchamber."

"Thank you, Emily," Abby said with a sigh. "That was very helpful."

"It was the most *romantic* thing," the girl said with a dreamy expression. "I wish it had been me!"

"So do I, dear," Abby murmured. "So do I."

"I see," Mr. Whittaker said, straightening up and regarding his betrothed with rather less affection than his impetuous entrance would have suggested. "Well, I gather that my presence is superfluous, then."

"Of course not," Abby hastened to say. She gave Violetta

a speaking look and, to her credit, the girl looked instantly contrite.

"Do not go, William," Violetta said, catching his hand and wincing when the motion jarred her injured ankle again. "Maybe Emily wishes it had been she, but my ankle hurt so much that I hardly cared how I got upstairs."

Mr. Whittaker's face softened. "My poor darling," he said soothingly.

Abby sighed with relief.

"Mr. Bourbonnais has been to Africa!" Emily said as Mr. Whittaker gazed fondly at his bride-to-be. "He lived in a place where there were no doctors, so he was able to tell that Violetta's ankle was sprained rather than broken just by feeling it."

"*Thank* you, Emily," Abby said in resignation as William's head shot up. "Did you not say your mother expected you home by three o'clock? You had better go at once, or you will be late."

"Heavens! I forgot the time in all the excitement," the girl said. "Good day, Miss Pennington, Mr. Whittaker. I hope your ankle feels better soon, Violetta."

"Thank you, Emily," Violetta said, looking with some trepidation at her fiancé's thunderous expression. "Goodbye."

"I'll call on you tomorrow," Emily said gaily. "To cheer you up."

Abby took the girl's arm and ushered her from the room before she could say another word. When she returned to the doorway of the parlor, it was to see that Violetta had succeeded in soothing Mr. Whittaker's ruffled feathers. Neither had noticed Abby standing there, watching.

"I only climbed up on the wall because Emily would not come down unless I did," she was saying tearfully. "I lost my balance, and she would do nothing but shriek so loudly it made my head hurt. No wonder poor Mr. Bourbonnais came running. Everyone in the neighborhood must have heard. It was so embarrassing."

Mr. Whittaker tenderly stroked her cheek. "There, there, love. The last thing in the world I would want is to make you cry."

She smiled and looked up at him with her big, moist brown eyes. "I would never climb up on the wall to spy on our neighbors of my own volition," she said. "What an undignified figure I should cut!"

Abby had to smile to herself. The girl sounded just like *her*.

"In many ways," Violetta continued, "Emily is a very silly person. You would not credit the way she hangs on Mr. Bourbonnais's every word."

Suddenly Abby didn't feel so smug, for she heard the unmistakable note of jealousy in Violetta's words. Silly or no, her niece saw Emily as a rival for Mr. Bourbonnais's attentions, and Mr. Whittaker would realize it, too, if he were not completely besotted with Violetta. Thank heaven for small favors.

Abby sailed into the room. "There, now," she said briskly, causing Mr. Whittaker to straighten and move to a more decorous distance from Violetta. Eager as Abby was to have the lovebirds cooing at one another again, she had no intention of leaving them unchaperoned for too long. "Mr. Whittaker, I hope you will stay to dine."

"With pleasure, Miss Pennington," he said with a slight bow.

The man was quite restored to good humor. Such kind eyes he had. He was devoted to the girl, had Violetta the wit to see it. Never would he give her a moment's worry if she married him.

If? When *she married him*, Abby amended mentally. This marriage *must* go forward. Abby would fight with her last breath to ensure Violetta's happiness. And Mr. Bourbonnais, or whatever he chose to call himself, was *not* going to stand in the way.

The rest of the afternoon went well enough, and dinner was quite informal, for Mr. Whittaker was their only guest and it seemed ridiculous to have Violetta toil up the stairs to change into evening dress for the meal.

After they had dined, Abby settled on the sofa with her embroidery, and Mr. Whittaker entertained Violetta by reading from Lord Byron's *The Siege of Corinth*. Mr. Whittaker's fine tenor voice was well suited to stirring literature, and by the time he was finished, Violetta's eyes were aglow.

Abby cleared her throat, and both looked at her guiltily.

She suppressed a fond smile; they had completely forgotten her existence. "It is long past time for you to retire, Violetta," Abby said. "You will recover from your injury much more rapidly with adequate rest."

Violetta yawned and looked up at Mr. Whittaker with a sleepy smile. "I *am* tired," she admitted. "William, will you carry me up to my room?"

Mr. Whittaker glanced at Abby for permission, for although they were old friends, she had made it abundantly clear that he would take no liberties with *her* niece, even if he was betrothed to her.

She hesitated, uncomfortably aware that the stairs were steep, and even a slip of a girl such as Violetta was hardly the mere feather in a man's arms of poetical whimsy. For all that Violetta had been in excruciating pain that afternoon, the gallant and muscular Mr. Bourbonnais's masterful performance had to have impressed such a romantic girl despite her protestations to the contrary.

Abby knew Mr. Whittaker would cheerfully put his hand through fire for Violetta, but where the spirit was willing, Abby very much feared the flesh was weak. Mr. Whittaker's chosen pursuits, for all that he rode whenever circumstances warranted it, and he was an excellent dancer, were more scholarly than athletic. She was about to make some excuse to spare his pride, when Violetta raised her arms to her fiancé and the scenario Abby feared was placed into inexorable motion. The ardent Mr. Whittaker could no more refuse the appeal in his beloved's beautiful brown eyes than he could fly.

He lifted the girl carefully into his arms, and Abby began to have hope that all might be well. Mr. Whittaker held her high to his breast—in the best style of all romantic heroes—as he bore her out of the room and to the foot of the stairs. Abby followed with the coverlet and Violetta's book.

When Mr. Whittaker put his foot on the first step to the upper floor, Abby noted his breath was a trifle labored, but she told herself there was no real cause for pessimism—yet. Violetta seemed to see nothing amiss.

"William," Violetta said, "I was thinking about the doves."

Abby felt a thrill of alarm. She had every hope Mr. Whittaker could make it to the top of the stairs without mishap on sheer determination alone, but *not* if Violetta expected him to engage in conversation with her.

"The . . . doves?" he said.

Abby's heart sank. He was already wheezing a little.

"The doves I will be carrying with my wedding bouquet," she said, fluttering her eyelashes at him in a show of maidenly modesty.

Minx! Abby had found out that laudanum would most probably kill the birds, so she had put her foot down on the matter. No doves. Out of the question.

Because Violetta could not get around Abby on the matter, she was going to work on Mr. Whittaker while he was in a softened mood. "I thought if we put something to eat in the cage, some birdseed and maybe some water as well, the doves would be content until it is time to release them. What do you think?"

"What do I think," he repeated between gasps of air. "I think . . . Miss Pennington is right. . . . Live birds have no place in a wedding ceremony. If you have all that in the cage, it will have to be enormous. And you will be . . . spilling birdseed and dripping water all the way up the aisle."

"I was sure that *you* would understand," Violetta said, tearing up.

By now, poor Mr. Whittaker was puffing like a bellows and straining manfully to hide it. Abby's hands clutched the rail as she watched the disaster unfold.

First Mr. Whittaker staggered on the stair and tried to get a hand free to clutch the railing. Even the single-minded Violetta had to know what was wrong, so she let out a shriek of alarm, got a death grip on her cavalier's neck, and started kicking her feet, which no doubt made her injured ankle throb all the harder. Having a distressed female squeak in his ear so unnerved Mr. Whittaker that he lost his balance and started to fall backward. Abby quickly moved to one side of the stair to avoid being caught up in the inevitable accident.

Down Violetta and her cavalier tumbled, both screaming, until they landed in a jumble of limbs. Hearing the alarm, every servant in the house came running. Mr. Whittaker managed to protect his beloved by landing on the bottom, and his head had made a sickening crack as it struck the wood of the banister. His eyes rolled back in his head, and he lay still.

"Mr. Whittaker!" Abby cried as she ran to his side. The poor fellow opened his eyes and blinked.

"Violetta," he said faintly.

"William," gasped the girl as she painfully shifted position from where she had landed on top of Mr. Whittaker to turn his face to hers. "Darling, are you injured?"

In reply, his eyes watered, his nose ran, and he was violently sick. Violetta had the presence of mind to roll away from him to keep from having her face splattered, but he managed to desecrate her arm and her dress.

This caused Violetta, not surprisingly, to dissolve into hysterics. "My ankle!" she cried. "No! Don't touch it, Abby!"

Abby gave a silent signal to one of the footmen, who came forward at once to carry Violetta upstairs. Then she called for soap and water, and she cleaned Mr. Whittaker's face and clothing as well as she could. Another footman helped the embarrassed gentleman to his feet and half supported, half carried him to the sofa. Abby dispersed the rest of the servants and was concerned to see Mr. Whittaker was still extremely green about the gills.

"I will just catch my breath and be on my way," he said weakly.

"But you should not go home now," Abby exclaimed. "I will send for the doctor again."

"No," he croaked, an utterly broken man. He looked sadly up the stair, where his fiancée had been borne off in hysterics. "I do not think I should stay any longer."

Despite Abby's protests, Mr. Whittaker took his departure,

although he did agree to permit one of her footmen to accompany him and summon the doctor as soon as he got home.

When he was gone, Abby resisted the compulsion to give in to hysterics of her own. This was all Mr. Bourbonnais's fault, with his handsome face, gallant manner, and his bulging muscles. No wonder poor Mr. Whittaker had no choice but to try to compete with him for Violetta's admiration.

Knowing Violetta and her romantic nature, Abby was sure the girl was utterly disgusted with the man who adored her and lived only to make her happy.

"Violetta, dearest," Abby whispered later as she smoothed a damp ringlet from her niece's face. "Are you awake?"

The girl opened bloodshot and slightly unfocused eyes to Abby. Her maid had given her some more laudanum, obviously, for the pain. Violetta had been washed and dressed in a clean night rail. There was still a cloth dampened with vinegar water across her temples. She looked so very young like this, not much older than she had been at thirteen, when she'd come to live with Abby, bereft of both her parents and starving for the maternal love that Abby was starving to give her.

It wasn't easy to take responsibility for a half-grown child at the tender age of three-and-twenty, but Abby had managed. She couldn't love Violetta more if she had been her real mother.

"It hurts," the girl whispered.

"I know, darling," Abby said soothingly. "I am sorry for it. Shall I bring you a cup of tea and some toast? Or some soup?" It was a foolish question. Violetta hardly needed sustenance so soon after dinner, but Abby needed to do *something* for her.

"No, I thank you. Is William better?"

An excellent sign. Abby gave thanks to the heavens for it. "He sustained a nasty bump on the head, but he insisted upon going home. I made him promise to send for the doctor."

"William dropped me," Violetta said with the gusty sigh of a disappointed child. "And then he . . ." She swallowed and could not finish the description of the distasteful scene that had followed their fall. "I never thought William would drop me." A teardrop glistened in her eye and coursed down her flushed cheek.

"He did not mean to do it," Abby said gently. "He would not have hurt you for the world."

Violetta turned her face to the wall. Her voice was barely audible. "But he did," she whispered in a voice choked with sobs.

Abby spent the rest of the evening in her own room, letting her irritation grow and fester, for she could not concentrate sufficiently on her abandoned embroidery or her book.

If only that . . . distracting man had not moved into the house next door with his charm and careless gallantry to turn Violetta's head. Then, Violetta would not have been coaxed onto the wall by that silly little ninnyhammer, Emily. Violetta would not have fallen off the wall and twisted her ankle, giving Mr. Bourbonnais a perfect opportunity to sweep the girl into his arms and carry her into the house and all the way up the stairs as if she weighed no more than a sack of feathers. Mr. Whittaker would not have felt honor bound to carry Violetta up the stairs, nor, in fact, would the girl have expected it. And Mr. Whittaker—put on his manly mettle—would not have dropped Violetta, cracked his head, and subsequently disgraced himself all over the girl's favorite pink day gown.

It was all that wretched man's fault, Abby thought with rising indignation. He was going to ruin her precious girl's life. She just knew it!

Chapter Four

Abby began to think she'd been worried about nothing the next day when Violetta, holding court in a charming sprig muslin gown of primrose yellow with her hair tied up in ribbons and her injured foot propped on a footstool in the parlor, smiled warmly at Mr. Whittaker as he placed a nosegay of daisies in her hands.

"How pretty," the girl said, sounding pleased.

Mr. Whittaker had the good sense to call on his fiancée in what appeared to be his best clothes with his blond hair brushed until it shone. "How is your ankle, my dear?" he asked anxiously. "If I have made it worse, I will never forgive myself."

"It will be all right, William," Violetta said. She placed her delicate hand on his, and Abby knew she wasn't just talking about her ankle. She had forgiven him for not being a maiden's dream of all that was romantic. Thank heaven!

But Abby's gratitude to Providence was premature, for at that moment two maids carried in enormous bouquets of roses. "For you, miss," one smiling maid said as she handed a bouquet of pink roses to Abby. The other maid placed a bouquet of yellow rosebuds tied with white satin ribbons into Violetta's waiting arms. The fragrant blossoms covered her lap, and the little nosegay of daisies rolled onto the floor, forgotten.

"From Mr. Bourbonnais, miss," the maid said helpfully. She flinched when Abby glared at her. "There is a card."

"How beautiful they are," Violetta said, taking the card. "Will you read it to me, William?"

Mr. Whittaker cleared his throat and obeyed, poor man. To do otherwise would have seemed churlish.

"I hope these flowers will cheer you, Miss Violetta," Mr. Whittaker read. "Be assured that you and your aunt are welcome to view our garden at any time—preferably from *our* side of the garden wall. —Bourbonnais."

Violetta gave a delighted peal of laughter. "Does your bouquet have a card, Abby?" she asked innocently.

"No," Abby lied, crumpling the thick white linen paper in her hand. She had already read it: I imagine your cheeks are as pink as these roses at my effrontery in sending them. A thousand pities I am not there to see them. —B.

"How very, very kind of Mr. Bourbonnais," Violetta exclaimed. "Oh, look, Emily, at what Mr. Bourbonnais has sent me!"

"Miss Branshaw," intoned the butler as Emily rushed right past him.

Oh, good, thought Abby, thoroughly vexed. In her eagerness to poke her nose into the yellow roses, Emily carelessly trampled Mr. Whittaker's little bouquet of daisies underfoot. The look on poor Mr. Whittaker's face as he retrieved his abused offering made Abby want to weep.

"I'll have one of the maids put it in water," Abby said kindly as she removed the nosegay from his hand. She excused herself and gave the daisies with her instructions to the first maid she saw. The girl bobbed a curtsy and accepted them.

"Shall I put your roses in water, too, miss?" the maid asked.

Abby had forgotten them. They were still clutched in her other arm. "No," Abby said with gritted teeth as she carelessly tossed them onto a table. "Leave them to rot." Then she turned away from the startled maid to rush back into the parlor—as if she could stop matters from getting any worse! She found Mr. Whittaker in a sulk and Violetta ignoring him completely to listen to Emily's colorful tale about how one of their sillier friends had swooned—actually swooned!—merely because Mr. Bourbonnais smiled at her from atop his magnificent white horse when he drew abreast of her mama's carriage the previous afternoon at Hyde Park.

When the butler handed her Mr. Bourbonnais's visiting card, she rose at once, determined to make some excuse to get rid of the wretched man.

"*Now* what have I done to offend you?" Mr. Bourbonnais asked with one glance at Abby's face when she met him in the hall and blocked his access to the parlor with her hands on her hips. "I was certain the flowers would restore me to your good graces."

"You were never *in* my good graces," she said, and he laughed.

To her annoyance, she saw the maid had not taken her at her word when she told her to leave the man's roses to rot. No, indeed! She had put them in water and displayed them in a place of honor on a hall table where every visitor— including Mr. Bourbonnais—could see and admire them.

"To what do we owe the honor of your presence, Mr. Bourbonnais?" Abby asked with a sweet, insincere smile. "Were there so few silly little chits in Hyde Park for you to impress today that you must come here to find more?"

"Ah, you've heard about that, have you?" he said ruefully. "The girl had been riding in an open carriage in the sun. That, no doubt, accounts for it. Are you receiving? I was just passing by your house and thought it would be unforgivably rude of me not to call upon you to inquire about Miss Violetta's condition."

"*I* would have forgiven you," she said.

"No doubt," he said dryly. "What is it you think I am going to do to the girl? Seduce her under your very eyes? I shall be on my best behavior, I promise you."

"Oh, all right," she said ungraciously as she ushered him into the parlor.

The crushed daisies had been placed, as Abby instructed, in a small crystal vase at Violetta's elbow. The maid had done her best, but they still looked insignificant.

"Miss Violetta," Mr. Bourbonnais exclaimed with genial good nature, "I find you quite restored! It is a miracle!"

"Your roses have done it, sir," she said cheerfully. The bouquet was still in her lap. "And William's daisies, too, of course," she added with a kind afterthought to her fiancé. Instead of being gratified, the poor man looked ready to sink. For the next quarter of an hour, Mr. Whittaker endured the torture of watching Violetta sparkle and laugh appreciatively at Mr. Bourbonnais's amusing observations about town life. For all the attention the girl paid to her fiancé, he might as well have been invisible.

"Mr. Bourbonnais, my aunt is hosting a ball in honor of my betrothal on Friday next," Violetta said. "You and your mother *must* come. William and I insist, do we not, William?" she said. When Mr. Whittaker did not answer at once, she managed to tear her eyes away from Mr. Bourbonnais's face for the first time since he had entered the room. "Do we not, William?" she repeated a bit more forcefully.

"Of course," Mr. Whittaker said with an edge to his voice. What else *could* he say? "We insist."

"You are both very kind," Mr. Bourbonnais said, taking Mr. Whittaker's reluctant compliance at face value, "but it is for the hostess to extend such an invitation, is it not? Miss Pennington, will you permit us to attend your ball? It would be an act of kindness and generosity to a pair of lonely wanderers who have strayed far away from their home."

"And precisely where would *that* be, sir?" asked Mr. Whittaker in a voice too harsh for politeness' sake. "I do not believe you have mentioned it."

"Ah, my home," Mr. Bourbonnais said sadly. "It is a fair question, Mr. Whittaker, but one that I regret I am not at liberty to answer."

"Your mother speaks fondly of Vienna," Violetta prompted. "And you have said yourself that you lived for some time in Africa."

"Please, Miss Violetta," he said. "My history is a sad one in many ways, and it is painful for me to speak of such things."

"Why is this so, if you have nothing to hide?" demanded Mr. Whittaker.

"But I have not said I have nothing to hide," Mr. Bourbonnais replied with perfect equanimity. "Is there even one among us who truly has nothing to hide?"

"*I* have nothing to hide," Mr. Whittaker declared.

"You are a fortunate man, then," Mr. Bourbonnais said.

"One hears some outlandish speculation as to your paternity, Mr. Bourbonnais. It seems you claim to be of royal birth, if the gossips are to be believed. Perhaps you would care to enlighten us."

"William!" gasped Violetta.

"Let him answer the question," Mr. Whittaker said with a sneer. "If he can. Perhaps his mother herself does not know the answer."

Mr. Bourbonnais bore down on Mr. Whittaker with a menacing stride and drew the man out of his chair by his collar. "You may say anything you wish about me. I care nothing for it. But I do not permit *anyone*," he said through clenched teeth, "to cast aspersions upon my mother's honor."

"Then she was not the Prince Regent's lover?"

"My mother is a proud and virtuous lady who has suffered much," Mr. Bourbonnais said angrily, "and I will demand satisfaction of any person who seeks to damage her reputation." He shook Mr. Whittaker like a rat. "Do you comprehend, sir?"

"Y-yes," Mr. Whittaker said, completely cowed. "Beg your pardon."

"Very good," Mr. Bourbonnais said, releasing his adversary with a suddenness that forced Mr. Whittaker to do an undignified little dance to remain upright.

Mr. Bourbonnais bent to take Violetta's hand. "Good day, Miss Violetta. My mother will be delighted to hear you are sitting up, enjoying the company of your friends." Turning to Emily, he said, "Miss Branshaw, your servant." He gave a curt nod to Mr. Whittaker, who sneered at him. Abby noted with dismay that Violetta was staring at her fiancé as if she had never truly seen him before.

Abby rose to hasten Mr. Bourbonnais's progress to the door. The sooner she got him away from Mr. Whittaker, the better!

"Good day, Miss Pennington," he said without looking

her in the eye when they reached the door and a footman had handed him his hat and walking stick.

"And to think this was your *best* behavior," she murmured.

He gave her a wan smile. "I am sorry to have made such an unpleasant scene in your house," he said.

"It was not entirely your fault," she admitted. "Mr. Whittaker should not have spoken so."

"No. He should not."

Abby felt a pang of conscience. The treatment her neighbor received that day did not show either Mr. Whittaker or herself to advantage. "Mr. Bourbonnais?"

He looked at her, she realized, without the least expectation of a kind word. "Thank you for the flowers," she said softly. "It was most considerate of you to send them."

"A pleasure," he said solemnly, and left.

Abby returned to the parlor to find a heated argument in progress between Violetta and Mr. Whittaker. Emily was on the edge of her seat, adding a word here and there to stoke the fire.

"How dare you say such things about Mr. Bourbonnais!" Violetta said to her betrothed.

"What do you truly know about him, Violetta? All a man has to do is assume a false foreign accent and an oily manner, and all the totty-headed females are ready to fall in love with him."

"Who are you calling a totty-headed female, William?" Violetta demanded.

"I apologize," he said stiffly. "I only meant to imply that you are too trusting, perhaps."

"Gullible and stupid, you mean."

Abby stole a look at Emily, who was flushed quite as much with indignation as Violetta. She took a long, steadying breath and leaped into the fray. "Violetta, Mr. Whittaker. Please calm yourselves."

"He is the king's own son," Emily said hotly. "*Everybody* knows it!"

"Oh, for the Lord's sake," Mr. Whittaker said in disgust. He rose to his feet and stalked to the door. "I can tell I waste my time here."

"Mr. Whittaker, please," Abby said, desperate to put an end to this argument. "Violetta," she prompted in an urgent undervoice. "You must not let him leave like this!"

"William," Violetta said at once, sounding distressed. "I do not wish to quarrel with you."

Mr. Whittaker's heart was in his eyes when he looked back at his fiancée. "I must go now," he said with an air of obvious regret. "Your precious Mr. Bourbonnais was never in Africa, I'll wager, or Vienna. I would not be surprised if he has not a feather to fly with and his whole object in coming to London was to inveigle some naive heiress with more hair than wit into marriage with him."

"More hair than wit! Is that what you truly think of me, William?" Violetta demanded.

"I did not have any particular heiress in mind," he said deliberately. "But since you are so quick to take me up on it . . . you would not be the first young woman of fortune to have her head turned by a rogue intent upon making mischief."

"How can you speak so cruelly of a man you do not know?" Violetta objected. "You are merely jealous."

"I *am* jealous," he admitted readily enough. "But the man is a scoundrel and a thief, and I shall prove it to you." With that, he stomped from the room. Violetta stared after him with quivering lips.

"I must take my leave now as well," Emily said, now that the show was over. "I only came to cheer Violetta. Just think, Violetta! You have a prince living next door. How very exciting!"

"He wouldn't be a prince, Emily, even if the rumors are true," Abby pointed out, "given the status of his birth."

The situation was quite bad enough without Emily planting the idea in Violetta's head that marriage with Mr. Bourbonnais would somehow make his fortunate bride a princess. Was anything more needed to make her dissatisfied with poor Mr. Whittaker?

"Well, he *looks* like a prince!" Emily said. "Good day, Miss Pennington." The girl walked over to Violetta and bent down to sniff the yellow roses again. When she did, she somehow jarred Violetta's ankle and made her wince.

"Good day, Violetta," she said, impervious to this. When she turned, she knocked over the sad little nosegay of daisies and sent a puddle of water and broken flowers onto the Turkey carpet. "I will come tomorrow to see how you get on."

I wager you will, my girl, Abby thought cynically. *"Thank you, Emily,"* she said as she took the girl's arm firmly to usher her to the door.

Chapter Five

To Abby's dismay, she and Violetta saw nothing of Mr. Whittaker for the next two days. Fortunately, he was engaged to escort them to the opera on the third evening, along with his parents, who had a box at King's Theater for the season.

No matter how much his pride had been damaged by Violetta's admiration of Mr. Bourbonnais, Abby felt sure Mr. Whittaker would never be churlish enough to renege on a promise of this proportion.

By now, Violetta's ankle was much better and she hardly limped at all, although Abby was careful to see she rested for two hours in the afternoon on the day of the performance. She was determined her niece would look her most beautiful that night, and be in her best humor. This evening *must* bring about a reconciliation for Violetta and Mr. Whittaker. Everything depended upon it.

Abby had awakened twice in the night with her heart pounding after suffering nightmares that the wedding had been called off. After that, it was impossible to sleep.

The evening started out quite well. Abby began to think Mr. Whittaker had acted with rare good sense in staying away from Violetta for two days because the girl's face glowed with pleasure and relief when he appeared in the drawing room dressed in his best evening kit. His golden hair was brushed to a high gloss, and it was plain he was determined to be conciliating.

Violetta looked exquisite in her new ice-blue gown, with white lace ribbons entwined in her upswept hair. Her late mother's pearls gleamed softly at her throat. "Oh, William, I have missed you so much," the girl said softly when he gallantly raised her gloved hand to his lips.

"You look very well tonight, Miss Pennington," Mr. Whittaker said absently when he greeted Abby, which just proved he only had eyes for his fiancée.

After her sleepless night, Abby was well aware that she was not in her best looks. Her eyes had slight circles under them, and the light-green color of her second-best evening gown only increased the pallor of her skin. The color had never been flattering to her, but it had been all the crack a year ago when Violetta persuaded her to purchase it. Unfortunately, Abby's best gown was almost the same color blue as the one Violetta was wearing, and she hadn't wished to dilute the impact of her niece's appearance tonight. Abby's hair had been dressed simply and hurriedly because Violetta's maid had fallen ill and Abby sent her own maid to her niece first. This evening, Violetta's was by far the most important toilette. Abby was merely invited along for politeness' sake, so she felt sure no one would be looking at *her*.

Indeed, Mr. Whittaker and Lady Margaret barely gave her a glance as they warmly greeted their future daughter-in-law, and the happy prospective bridegroom solicitously installed Violetta in the best seat in his parents' box.

"A very pretty girl, your Violetta," Lady Margaret commented to Abby. "She will do William credit, I am certain."

After such an auspicious start to the evening, Abby was certain the lovebirds were in a fair way to being devoted to one another again, so all was right with her world.

Before the curtain opened, though, all her optimism fled, for their seats afforded them an excellent view of Mr. Bourbonnais enthroned in a box situated in the most desirable location in the theater. The houselights were still up, so Abby could clearly see Violetta's mouth water. Indeed, Abby's mouth was watering, too. Drat the man, he looked good enough to eat.

His tall, well-made figure was clothed simply and elegantly in black with blindingly white linen. His hair, normally in artistic chestnut disarray, was ruthlessly brushed back to display his high, noble brow. A crimson sash pinned over his chest contained several glittering orders and medals. He looked every inch the prince, as Lady Margaret tactlessly remarked to her husband in an undervoice that carried clearly to her son, judging from that gentleman's stiffened posture.

"I will admit," Lady Margaret observed, "he has a great look of the king in his youth. What a man *he* was before his physique was ruined by so much riotous living. He made the ladies' hearts flutter, I can tell you, Miss Pennington. Of course, *I* was a mere child at the time," she babbled. "I thought the rumors about Mr. Bourbonnais's parentage were nonsense the first time I heard them, but after seeing the fellow, I am not so sure. He certainly carries himself well, and breeding, my dears, is something that will always tell."

Mr. Bourbonnais and his mother apparently were guests this evening of the very rich, very powerful Earl of Stoneham, for it was his box they occupied. The great man himself sat next to Mrs. Bourbonnais, who was glittering with diamonds and egret feathers. The earl beamed at the smattering of audience members who applauded until Mrs. Bourbonnais curtsied, and her son, with some show of reluctance, made a solemn bow to the house.

Violetta applauded with rather more enthusiasm than was seemly. Abby tapped her niece's wrist lightly in warning, but the damage was done.

Abby had known Mr. Whittaker for several years before Violetta grew up so beautifully and he fell head over heels in love with her. In fact, Abby had hopes at one time that he meant to offer for *her*, but she never thought about that now. Or, at least, almost never.

Abby knew as surely as if she could look into Mr. Whittaker's mind that all his pleasure in the evening was spoiled, even though he made a valiant effort to hide it. No doubt he had been looking forward to impressing Violetta this evening with his family's wealth and prestige. His mother was the daughter of an earl, after all, and his father's country estate was one of the most valuable in Yorkshire.

Instead, poor Mr. Whittaker had merely afforded Violetta an excellent view of Mr. Bourbonnais being applauded by Society and looking so elegant in plain black that Mr. Whittaker must feel quite the jumped-up country squire in his elaborate waistcoat.

"If Lord Stoneham means to take him up," Lady Margaret said thoughtfully, "there must be some truth to the rumor. He would not bother with Mr. Bourbonnais unless his connections were the most impeccable or there was some political advantage to gain by befriending him."

"That fellow," her son sneered under his breath.

"I think it is the fellow's mother Lord Stoneham is bothering with," Mr. Whittaker said to his wife in what he probably thought was a confidential whisper. In recent years the gentleman had grown quite hard of hearing. "He has not yet replaced his last lady love, and from the look of it, a new candidate has joined the list."

"Nonsense. Lady Letitia is with them," his wife replied, considerately lowering her voice in consideration of Violetta's innocent ears. "Lord Stoneham has far too high a regard for his family's consequence than to expect his sister to share his box with his mistress."

Abby had forced her eyes to turn away from Lord Stoneham's box to avoid the appearance of gawking at Mr. Bourbonnais, but she now saw that Lady Letitia was there, sitting on the other side of Lord Stoneham, but a bit in the background as if she were reluctant to be seen in public with her brother's guests. Even from this distance, Abby could tell the lady had her nose out of joint. It was not surprising, considering Lady Letitia had been warning all her acquaintance that the Bourbonnaises' objective in coming to London was a sinister one.

"Good point, my dear Margaret," the elder Mr. Whittaker acknowledged. "The son is certainly impressive, I must say. His horseflesh will stand comparison with the best to be offered in England and Ireland."

"Father, Mother. Please," the younger Mr. Whittaker said, sounding testy. "Can you not leave off discussing that fellow even for two minutes? The curtain is about to go up."

Happily, by the time of the interval, Mr. Whittaker had relaxed enough to join the general applause that followed the first act. He smiled fondly at Violetta, who had been completely enthralled by the performance, when she squeezed his hand and smiled up into his face with glowing eyes. "Thank you for inviting us, William," she whispered. "I will remember this divine music for the rest of my life."

"It is a pleasure, my dear," he said suavely. At his signal, the servants brought tea and a tray of tiny cakes into the box. Each cake had a V and a W on it entwined with a heart in pink icing.

"Lemon cakes," Mr. Whittaker said proudly.

"William!" exclaimed his mother. "What a charming surprise."

Violetta had just lifted a lemon cake to her lips when a footman in dark blue livery entered the box.

"Your pardon, sir," he said to the elder Mr. Whittaker. "Lord Stoneham requests your presence and that of all your party in his box for refreshments."

Abby could see Mr. Whittaker's feathers fall.

"Excellent," said Lady Margaret, who apparently considered being recognized by one of the most powerful noblemen in the land her due. "Tell his lordship we shall be most pleased."

Violetta had set her cake down and looked to Abby for guidance.

"Was this not thoughtful of Mr. Whittaker, Violetta?" Abby said, trying to convey a message to her niece with her eyes. "Lemon cakes are your very favorite."

"Yes," the girl said at once. She lifted the cake to her lips again and took a bite. She swallowed so quickly that she choked on a crumb and Abby struck her on the back rather more smartly than the occasion required to dislodge it. The rest of the cake crumbled in Violetta's glove and dropped to the floor.

Her fiancé watched its progress sadly. "Are you all right, Violetta?" he asked anxiously.

"Yes," she said, eyes watering. She accepted a cup of tea from Mr. Whittaker's hand and took a restorative sip.

"That is better. The cake was a bit dry." Abby poked her. "But delicious," Violetta added quickly. "Quite delicious."

"If you are recovered, my dear," Lady Margaret said to Violetta, "we must not tarry." She preened a little as she took her husband's arm. "Lord Stoneham and his party will be expecting us."

"But, Mother," William said, gesturing toward the platter of cakes.

"There is no question of declining, William," she said firmly, and sailed from the box with her husband in tow.

Abby glanced across the theater at the Stoneham box and found Mr. Bourbonnais's eyes upon her. He made her a slight bow, and she looked away to prevent herself from scowling at him. Since Lady Margaret's defection left her no choice, Abby rose and followed, leaving young Mr. Whittaker to escort his betrothed. The look on his face when they entered the Earl of Stoneham's box made Abby want to weep.

Servants presided over chafing dishes in every corner, and the large cake covered in whipped cream and decorated with fresh, juicy, glazed strawberries made Edward's pretty little lemon cakes look completely insignificant. Lord Stoneham must have paid the management of the theater a fortune to arrange this. Mr. Whittaker and Lady Margaret were already seated in the box, addressing filled plates with enthusiasm.

When Mr. Bourbonnais bowed over Abby's hand and told her how lovely she looked, Abby gave him a look that caused him to recoil in mock trepidation.

Liar! she thought. She felt like a dowdy old crone among all these fashionable people.

"Lord Stoneham, you spoil me outrageously," Mrs. Bourbonnais said gaily. "Miss Pennington, you must have some of this divine smoked salmon. And the lobster patties. Gabriel, release the young lady's hand at once so she can have something to eat."

"I am pleased to see you in such good spirits, ma'am," Abby said, smiling at Mrs. Bourbonnais. There seemed to be nothing of the invalid about her tonight.

"Thank you, Miss Pennington. Gabriel insisted it would

do me good to accept Lord Stoneham's kind invitation, and he was right, as always." She smiled affectionately at her son.

"Welcome," said Lord Stoneham to Abby. "It is good to see you again, Miss Pennington. Miss Violetta! Such a pleasure! And this is your fortunate fiancé. Welcome, sir."

The earl was still remarkably handsome for a gentleman on the shady side of seventy, and Abby knew he was much sought after by marriage-minded ladies. She had gone to school with his daughter-in-law, Lady Blakely, so she knew the family slightly. Still, she had no idea why she and her niece were greeted with such effusion by a gentleman who had always been a high stickler. She looked to Lady Letitia for enlightenment, but that haughty lady merely favored Abby with a cool inclination of her head, although she did condescend to sit down with Lady Margaret, whose blood was, after all, quite as blue as any in the kingdom.

"Do be seated and have some refreshments," the earl said as he shook hands with young Mr. Whittaker.

"Yes, you must," said Mrs. Bourbonnais. "Lord Stoneham ordered all these wonderful dishes merely because I feared the night air might be injurious to my health if I accepted his kind invitation to dine after the performance. The four of us could not consume a quarter of it."

"Thank you," Abby said firmly, "but we are engaged to have supper at the Piazza at Mr. Whittaker's kind invitation."

Lady Letitia sipped on a cup of tea and barely responded to Lady Margaret's attempts at conversation, which seemed to consist of a series of whispered questions. It was obvious Lady Letitia was in a miff, but from the sour looks she directed toward her brother and Mrs. Bourbonnais, her grievance was not with the Penningtons or the Whittakers.

Abby had never seen the imposing Lord Stoneham so animated. It was clear he was charmed by Mrs. Bourbonnais.

"Miss Violetta, may I help you to some cake?" Mr. Bourbonnais asked.

"Violetta," Abby reminded her niece, "you will not wish to spoil your appetite for supper."

"No, of course not," Violetta said. She sounded like a disappointed child.

"Eat it," her fiancé grumbled. "Eat all of it." Then he stomped out of the box. The elder Mr. Whittaker exchanged a look with his wife before he shrugged and returned to his lobster patties. Violetta looked hurt and confused, so Mr. Bourbonnais smoothed over the awkward moment by motioning for a servant to cut a slice of cake, which he took to her. He procured another for Abby, and she could hardly refuse. When the mingled richness of the whipped cream and the sweetness of the strawberries burst gloriously upon her tongue, she felt like a traitor.

Lady Margaret, whose mouth was full of smoked salmon, had to swallow before she could speak. "I apologize for my son, Lady Letitia. I do not know what ails him this evening," she said.

Abby was amazed by the woman's insensitivity. How could Mr. Whittaker's mother fail to realize how disappointed he must be at having his grand evening upstaged by Lord Stoneham and the outrageously good-looking Mr. Bourbonnais?

With a sigh of resignation, Abby watched Violetta accept a lobster patty and a finger sandwich from a servant with every appearance of pleasure. When Abby looked over at the Whittakers' box to see Mr. Whittaker's hunched figure sitting dejectedly alone with his arms crossed over his chest, she regretfully put her half-eaten slice of cake on a table in front of one of the chafing dishes.

"Shall I return to your box to keep Mr. Whittaker company?" Abby suggested to Lady Margaret, since the elder lady clearly had not completed her inquisition of Lady Letitia. She could not leave the poor man sulking all alone while his mother, father, and fiancée stuffed themselves on Lord Stoneham's ostentatious feast.

"Why, Miss Pennington," Lady Margaret said, sounding scandalized. "It would be vastly improper for you to be alone in the box with my son."

"Surely not," Abby said with a tight smile. "I have been on the shelf for years and years. Your son and I are such old friends, and he *is* betrothed to my niece. I will engage to sit quite on the other side of the box, if you think it necessary to satisfy the scandalmongers.''

"Quite right, my dear," Mr. Whittaker said. "Miss Pennington stands in the guise of a parent to Miss Violetta, so she's practically Willie's mother-in-law."

"I suppose there is no harm ... now," Lady Margaret said coyly to Lady Letitia.

Most unfortunately, Abby was blessed with excellent hearing.

"Once I thought Miss Pennington was destined to be my daughter-in-law. But it came to nothing, after all." She said this with the air of one who had experienced a close brush with disaster. It always had been abundantly clear to Abby that she did not measure up to Lady Margaret's exacting standards for a daughter-in-law.

Mr. Bourbonnais's head shot up, and he regarded Abby closely.

Finding the situation intolerable, Abby turned and started to leave the box. Before the footman could open the door for her, Mr. Bourbonnais caught her arm.

"Miss Pennington, wait," he said. "I will be happy to escort you."

"Thank you. I would rather be alone," she replied. "Oh!" she added, genuinely dismayed. "I did not mean it quite that way."

"I am quite certain you did not," he said blandly.

"We should all go back," Lady Margaret said with a coquettish little wave at Lord Stoneham. "The next act is about to begin."

She waited in vain for Lord Stoneham or Lady Letitia to invite her to remain, but when an invitation was not forthcoming, she rose smiling. After all, she had been seen exchanging pleasantries with Lady Letitia, one of the queens of London Society, in full view of the entire house, so she was quite satisfied with the way the evening had gone so far. She took Violetta's arm and walked with her out of the box. Her husband, who was engaged in conversation with the earl, did not rise to accompany them.

"I can hardly permit three such lovely ladies to return to their box without male protection. Allow me," Mr. Bourbonnais said as he extended his arm to Abby. She could hardly object to his escort without giving offense, so she accepted it.

"I was not aware," Abby said as they made their way back to the Whittakers' box in Violetta and Lady Margaret's wake, "that you were on such intimate terms with Lord Stoneham."

"He has been all that is kind to my mother," he said, deliberately slowing his pace to increase their distance from the other two ladies. "And to me, of course."

"How nice," Abby said. They walked along in silence until they had almost reached their destination. "Thank you for your escort, sir," she said, turning to him when Lady Margaret and Violetta had entered the Whittakers' box ahead of them. She extended her hand in polite dismissal. "You must hurry back, sir, or you will miss the beginning of this act."

"Do you think your Mr. Whittaker is about to call me out for feeding cake to his fiancée?" he asked, apparently amused by her attempt to send him on his way.

"He is not *my* Mr. Whittaker, but Violetta's."

"Then he is a fool," he said quietly. "Will you be all right?"

The concerned expression in his blue-gray eyes embarrassed her. She had been barely civil to him since the day they met, and he invariably had returned her coolness with kindness and consideration.

He alone had not missed the significance of the dark circles under her eyes or the pallor of her skin from her sleepless night. He somehow knew how melancholy she was at the prospect of being alone once Violetta was married, and how elderly she felt at being treated as a nonentity by Mr. Whittaker and his parents this evening, for all that she tried to hide it.

It was unnerving to find every secret in her heart exposed to a man she could not trust.

"I do not know what you mean, sir," Abby lied as she forced a bright smile to her dry lips. "I could not be happier for Violetta and Mr. Whittaker."

"My mistake," he said gravely. "Good evening, Miss Pennington."

When he had bowed and gone, Abby entered the box, sank into her seat, and covered her eyes with trembling hands. Mercifully, the performance had just resumed, so she was spared having to account for her tardiness in joining her party.

"Do you have a headache, Abby?" Violetta whispered.

"No. Not at all," she whispered back.

After the performance, they went to the Piazza as the younger Mr. Whittaker's guests, even though it was late and their host was in a less than affable mood.

Lady Margaret could talk of nothing but the wonderful hospitality of Lord Stoneham and the elegance of the refreshments set before them.

"You mark my words," she said gleefully. "The earl is seriously playing court to Mrs. Bourbonnais. Did you notice how Lady Letitia's nose was out of joint? She usually pays her brother's flirts no mind, but she is worried by this one. It would not please her at all, I assure you, to be displaced from her very desirable situation as her brother's hostess to make way for a new sister-in-law. She might even find herself banished to one of the earl's lesser properties to live on her legacy from her father, which would not be pleasant for one who is accustomed to commanding every extravagance at her brother's expense."

"Do you think Lord Stoneham will offer for her?" asked Violetta. "I wonder if we will be invited to the wedding. After all, I intend to invite Mrs. Bourbonnais and her son to mine."

Mr. Whittaker stared at her in dismay. "See here, Violetta—" he began.

"Mr. Bourbonnais has been very kind to me," Violetta said. "And his mother has been all that is gracious. I want them to come to my wedding. We need not blush to count them among our friends if Lord Stoneham does not."

"Can we not speak of something else?" Mr. Whittaker asked wearily. "I am sick of hearing the fellow's name."

"Lord Stoneham?" his mother asked in surprise.

"Bourbonnais," he said in exasperation. "The fellow is a cad and a bounder. I'd stake my life on it."

"Nonsense, William," his father scoffed. "He moves in the very highest circles. Those lobster patties served in Lord Stoneham's box were first rate."

With that, they ordered their supper. The food was not as fine as that served in Lord Stoneham's box at the opera, but the ladies praised and ate with all the enthusiasm they could muster.

Mr. Whittaker was not fooled, however, and ate his supper in bleak silence.

Chapter Six

"My son, I *forbid* you to droop about like some dreary blanket of fog merely because Violetta Pennington's tiresome fiancé has decided to have us investigated," the duchess said in exasperation as she watched her son pace back and forth across the carpeting. "It will come to nothing if you will keep your wits about you."

Gabriel did not pause in his pacing. In his mind he pictured the tiger stalking its hunting ground in the jungle, and wondered if it, too, was this restless before the kill.

"What if the truth is discovered before the time is right?"

"It will not be," she said sternly, "if you will stop allowing your concentration to be diverted by that prim little spinster next door. You are so accustomed to women swooning into your arms that you are obsessed by one who does not. Have I taught you *nothing*? She is a tool, like all the others. Nothing more. And it is a poor craftsman who fails to use the proper tool when it presents itself."

"The risk of discovery is too great. You could go back to Vienna. It is beautiful in summer. You still have friends there."

"Coward! It is a good place to die, you mean."

"*Maman,*" he said reproachfully.

"I am going to die, my son. Would you deprive me of my last wish?"

No, he would not.

In return for a handsome settlement—long since spent—she had promised never to return once she had been expelled from England in her youth for committing the unpardonable sin of attracting the amorous attentions of a gentleman of royal birth. Soon afterward she bore a son, although who the father was, neither she nor Gabriel would ever say. The duchess, as she styled herself, dragged her child to all the principal cities of Europe, pretending to be one lost princess or another, and credulous souls were all too eager to shower riches upon her. When she suspected the ruse was about to be discovered, she would simply flee to a new base of operation.

She knew who Gabriel's father was, all right, although that gentleman was hardly in a position to acknowledge him before the eyes of the world.

Young Gabriel—who inherited his mother's histrionic talent—had received a colorful and varied education at his mother's knee until he came of age and went to breed horses at his father's plantation in South Africa, where he was passed off as a distant relative of the gentleman.

But six months ago, his mother had come to him, pale and languid, and told him she was dying.

It would take a harder man than Gabriel to say no to her last wish.

Her plan was audacious in its boldness. And her son, who had played the role of mysterious, long-lost rightful heir of one throne or another from the time he was a child, was the key.

He didn't mind, really. It was exciting. He thought every one of these complacent people deserved their fate at his mother's merciless hands, except for Miss Abigail Pennington.

Until now, Gabriel had not believed such a woman existed. There didn't appear to be a vain or avaricious bone in her body. All her energy and ambition was settled on her niece. But Gabriel knew a passionate and loyal heart beat beneath that prim exterior.

Oh, to be the man to capture it! Were all these phlegmatic Englishmen blind? How could even the unimaginative Mr.

Whittaker have spurned such a treasure to court the little heiress instead?

He would not have been so stupid.

Unfortunately, Miss Pennington had recognized Gabriel at once for a scoundrel. His charm didn't work on her. And he wanted it to, very badly.

What had he done wrong? The question plagued him. Yet, as essential as it was to his masquerade that he fool her, something inside him wanted one person to see him for what he truly was and accept him for it. Some days he was so tired of pretending. Perhaps, deep inside, his mother was, too.

Of course, the duchess could have a place with Gabriel in South Africa as long as she did not reveal the truth of her relationship with his father. The old gentleman had been most generous, although his mother would no doubt think the caliber of Society in that remote part of the world sadly inferior to what she had long enjoyed in the major capitals of Europe.

The duchess was through with compromising. She wanted to wreak havoc on the country that had wronged her, and she would succeed with her dying breath.

"That girl next door—the elder one," his mother said impatiently when he turned a blank face to her. "I trust I may depend upon you to put aside your gentlemanly scruples with regard to Miss Pennington. You *must* persuade her to set the next stage of our plan in motion by any means necessary."

"I will," he said, careful to hide the pleasurable anticipation he felt at the prospect of matching wits with the lady, even as he regretted the necessity of earning her trust only to betray it. After all, enacting the role of cad and deceiver was one of his primary skills.

The literary circle was meeting at Abby's house that day, just when she needed all her attention to deal with the increasingly complicated wedding arrangements. Add to that the anxiety of worrying that the lovebirds would decide, after all, to call off the wedding, and Abby could barely conceal her eagerness to be rid of guests whose company she normally anticipated with much pleasure.

It soon became apparent that these otherwise sensible bluestockings were no different from all the other unwanted guests who had flocked to her door since the Bourbonnaises moved into the neighborhood. They spent far less time discussing the fine arts than they did ogling Mr. Bourbonnais from her windows.

To Abby's consternation, the gentleman himself came to call before the meeting was over. She frowned when the butler presented his card. She could hardly pretend her caller was anyone else when the entranced ladies had watched his sauntering progress from his house to hers with eager eyes. Abby knew from their running commentary that he had a bouquet of flowers in his hand.

At this rate, the gentleman who rented his property to the Bourbonnaises would find it quite denuded of blooms by the time his tenants took their departure.

"The gentleman apologizes for the intrusion, miss, and begs the indulgence of a few moments of your time," the butler murmured to Abby in a tone that suggested he was repeating the gentleman's exact words.

"I am not receiving, Lumley, as you can see," she said in gentle rebuke. "Deny me to the gentleman, if you please."

"By no means!" exclaimed one of the ladies, whose intellect, until now, Abby had greatly admired. "That is to say," the lady added sheepishly, "it may be important."

At that moment the gentleman himself entered with a radiant Violetta on his arm. With a flourish, he presented the flowers to Abby, who dutifully sniffed them, murmured her thanks, and handed them over to a maid to put into water. She did not miss the knowing looks exchanged by the ladies of the circle.

"What was Lumley about, leaving poor Mr. Bourbonnais in the hall?" Violetta said with a sunny smile. She stopped short at the sight of six ladies gazing at Mr. Bourbonnais with all the longing of a pack of slavering wolves. "Oh! I forgot your literary circle was meeting here today," she added apologetically.

"Your pardon," Mr. Bourbonnais said at once. "I will call another time, if I may."

"No need," said the lady who was generally acknowledged to be the leader of the group. "We were just about to adjourn."

"Do join us," Abby said in resignation because, really, good manners left her no choice.

"We were discussing the Colossi at Memnon on the plain of Thebes, Mr. Bourbonnais," the leader of the discussion explained. "It is said that in ancient times the northern statue emitted a wailing sound at sunrise. I wonder if it is true."

"Perhaps not," Mr. Bourbonnais said with a smile, "but the legend is an interesting one. Memnon was the son of the goddess Aurora, and it is said that after he was slain by the hero Achilles at Troy, his effigy received the beneficial caresses of his mother every morning with a gentle moan. It is the northernmost statue that made the sound, which must have been quite disconcerting."

"It makes no sound now, apparently," said one of the more skeptical ladies. "I suspect it never did."

"The phenomenon was mentioned by the Greek geographer Strabo, and confirmed by Pausania and Juvenal in the second century," Mr. Bourbonnais said. "It was only after Septimus Severus restored the colossus and rebuilt the upper part that it ceased to make this sound."

"I did not know you were a scholar, Mr. Bourbonnais," the leader of the discussion said with a regal nod of approval. "I must say I am most impressed by your knowledge of ancient sites."

Abby, too, was impressed, even if she did suspect the shameless scoundrel made the whole story up.

Mr. Bourbonnais gave the lady a self-deprecating smile. "Do not be, I implore you," he said. "I merely became interested in learning the history of the colossi after I saw them in Egypt some years ago."

"You have seen them?" Abby said, awed. "You have *been* there?"

"Several times. They are most impressive at dawn, when Memnon's mother bathes them in her rays. The sight is romantic enough, I assure you, to convince even the most determined skeptic that the legend is true.''

"Oh, how wonderful it must have been,'' Abby cried. "I should dearly love to travel.''

"Why have you not, then?" he asked.

"By the time I was my own mistress, I had the care of Violetta, of course,'' she said, smiling at the girl. "Sadly, that will not be for much longer.''

She looked from Violetta to see Mr. Bourbonnais watching her carefully. He answered another woman's question seemingly at random.

The ladies soon took their departure and Violetta made her excuses to go for a drive in the park with Emily Branshaw and her mother, but Mr. Bourbonnais lingered on, which made Abby feel uncomfortable in a nervous, excited sort of way.

He favored her with a crooked smile. "Come, Miss Pennington,'' he said. "You do not find my company *that* disagreeable, do you?"

"Of course not. That is, it is not entirely proper for us to be alone together.''

"Did you not say yourself that you have been on the shelf for years and years?" he asked teasingly.

Abby's eyes widened when he approached her and cupped her cheek with his large, warm hand. His touch sent delicious little tingles of pleasure dancing across her skin.

"My apologies,'' he said. "Your complexion is so lovely. I could not resist this opportunity to discover for myself if your face is as soft as it looks.''

"Do I pass, sir?" she asked with one raised eyebrow. She was too old, she told herself, for maidenly shrinking.

"Magnificently,'' he assured her. "If you were indeed on the shelf, I would be tempted quite strongly to . . . handle you further.''

"Mr. Bourbonnais!'' she exclaimed. "What have I done or said to persuade you that I would welcome such attentions from you?"

"Nothing, my dear lady, but look at me with all the passion in your soul when I spoke of the Colossi of Memnon at sunrise. You must not deprive yourself of your heart's desire any longer."

"I . . . I do not know what you mean." He was standing too close. She couldn't *think* when he was standing too close. Her heart's desire. Did he somehow know she dreamed at night of being in his arms?

"Soon you will be free. Where will you go?"

"Go?" she asked, all at sea. His lips were close enough to touch hers.

"When Miss Violetta is safely married. Where will you go first? To Egypt?"

"To Egypt? I cannot go to Egypt! What are you thinking of?"

"The Sphinx, the Colossi of Memnon, the Pyramids all await you, Miss Pennington. How I shall envy you seeing them all for the first time."

"I cannot go to Egypt. What would people say?"

"That is the beauty of being alone. You need not care." He lowered his voice to an intimate rumble that made her skin quiver. "And if it is companionship you desire, I would gladly offer my services as guide if I did not think you would box my ears for my presumption."

"Mr. Bourbonnais," she said uncertainly. "Are you making an improper overture to me?"

"No, Miss Pennington," he said softly. "I am trying very hard not to."

At the look in his eyes, Abby found herself quite short of breath. "Unfortunately, I have not the means to go to Egypt, or any other of those exotic places I long to see," she admitted.

There. That should dampen his ardor. There was nothing so destructive to a man's interest in a lady, Abby had learned long ago, than his discovery that she is not as rich as he had supposed.

"How is this?" he asked with a frown as he looked about at the magnificent furnishings of the parlor.

"Oh, the house, you mean? It is true my brother left it to me, but when Violetta leaves my care, the generous allowance her trustees provided to me will stop. It is a shocking expense to keep an establishment of this size in repair. My brother expected me to marry and for the house to be used as my dowry, I suspect, but after all this time it is highly unlikely.''

"Then you are dependent upon your niece for your living?" he asked. She could not bear the look of pity in his eyes.

"It is not quite so bad as that. My brother also left me a small independence, and it will enable me to live in tolerable comfort if I am very frugal. But while I may be able to afford the occasional holiday by exercising certain economies, my means will hardly extend to Egypt.''

"If not Egypt, then, what do you say to the Royal Lodge at Kew?" He gestured toward the watercolor over the fireplace mantel. "It is not nearly so far.''

"I do not understand you, sir.''

"The Royal Lodge at Kew. What would you give to see it?"

"It does not matter," she said with a regretful sigh. "It is not open to the public.''

"It is open to me.''

"But how is that possible? It has been a Crown property for hundreds of years.''

"That is true. But it is open to me, just the same.''

"You are toying with me," she said, but she could hear the hopefulness in her own voice. She looked at the fading watercolor above the fireplace—the graceful gothic arches, the stained-glass windows, the ornamental gate with royal lions flanking the entrance. It fired her imagination now, just as it had when she was a child.

"No," he said. "You said you would give anything. What say you to one day? Just one day in your company. That is my price.''

"I . . . but—"

He gave Abby a look from those compelling eyes that made anything but surrender impossible. "One day," he said.

Bereft of speech, she could only nod her head.

At that he grasped Abby's shoulders and gave her a brief, exultant kiss on the lips. "Tomorrow, then," he said with a smile of triumph that made her heart hammer against her ribs. "The Royal Lodge is one of my mother's favorite retreats, and I am certain you will enjoy it. I shall call for you at seven o'clock, for we will wish to return to the city before nightfall. Do not bring your maid. The proprieties will be observed, I promise you."

Numbly, she nodded again.

He bowed and left her.

When he was gone, she sank into a chair and put one hand to her throat. What had she done?

Chapter Seven

All of Abby's stomach muscles quivered when she saw the carriage leave the Bourbonnaises' house next door. The coachman looked neither left nor right, as though he might have been made of wood. He drove very slowly, for it was known his mistress was in frail health and could not bear to be jostled on the road. The coach's progress was so slow that Mr. Bourbonnais, walking his horse beside it, could easily keep pace. By the time it arrived before her own house, Abby's blood was hammering in her ears.

She felt a pang of relief mingled with disappointment as she resigned herself to spending the entire journey in close confinement with Mrs. Bourbonnais, who would probably object to the least ray of sunlight being allowed to penetrate the gloom of the coach. It seemed a pity that all the curtains were drawn against what promised to be a perfect spring day. But Mr. Bourbonnais had promised her that the proprieties would be observed, and she must be glad that he kept his word.

His eyes were unusually solemn as he bowed and handed her into the coach. Abby ducked her head and called a cheerful "Good morning, ma'am," to the darkened interior, but no other lady returned her greeting. Not even a maid.

Abby turned at once and attempted to leave the coach so quickly that Mr. Bourbonnais had to reach out with both hands to steady her. She braced her forearms against his chest to keep from being crushed against him.

"Your mother is not within," Abby said breathlessly.

"No, she is not." His expression was inscrutable.

"But I cannot go off with you alone! Can I?"

"Only you know the answer to that question, Miss Pennington. I will abide by your decision."

Abby bit her lip. She should go at once into her own house. Instead she remained where she was, staring into his eyes.

"You did say, did you not, that you would give anything to see the Royal Lodge?"

She had, of course.

Mr. Bourbonnais watched her with an expression on his face that suggested anxiety. But surely she must be mistaken. He could have his choice from among the most beautiful women of the *ton*. Why would he choose her?

"It is for you to say," he prompted when she did not answer.

"What do you want from me?" she asked.

"It is as I have already said. One day. Can you not give it to me?"

One day. It was all he wanted. And, Lord help her, she wanted it, too.

Tears of emotion filled Abby's eyes when she first beheld the Royal Lodge from the carriage window. Sunlight gleamed against the stained glass of the high-arched gothic windows, and the gate stood open and welcoming, just as it did in her cherished watercolor.

When the coach stopped, she could hardly wait for Mr. Bourbonnais to lower the steps and assist her to the ground. He wiped a tear from her eye with a gentle forefinger, and Abby laughed giddily as she stepped forward to take it all in. "It is wonderful! As wonderful as I imagined it. Thank you for bringing me here!" Impulsively, she threw her arms around his neck. "Thank you."

His arms closed tightly around her, and he pressed his lips to her forehead. Then he smiled at her and touched her cheek. "Come inside," he said softly. "The caretaker is expecting us."

"Your Majesty," said the wizened little woman who opened the door to them. She started to sink into a curtsy, but Mr. Bourbonnais caught her forearms to prevent her from doing so.

"None of that, if you please, Mrs. Warren," he said pleasantly. "I am certain Miss Pennington will be glad for a cup of tea, if you will be so kind."

"Right away, Your Majesty," she said as she scurried away to do his bidding.

He turned to Abby with a rueful smile. "You must forgive Mrs. Warren," he said smoothly. "She has served the royal family for many years, and she mistakes any gentleman with reddish-brown hair and light eyes for His Majesty. I found it quite disconcerting at first, but one grows accustomed."

"Do you . . . come here often, Mr. Bourbonnais?" Abby asked.

"As often as time allows. This is a favorite retreat of my mother's, as I said. She came here often with my—ah, here is our tea." He took the tray from Mrs. Warren and gave her a nod of dismissal as Abby's mind absorbed the implications of the Bourbonnaises having the run of this personal possession of the royal family anytime they pleased.

Did he bring women here often? Mrs. Warren certainly didn't seem surprised to see her. She shook that unwelcome thought from her mind as Mr. Bourbonnais set the tray on a table and turned to her with an indulgent expression on his face.

"Well, Miss Pennington, what do you wish to do first? Have a nap to rest from the journey? Explore the house? Have a picnic on the lawn?"

"Everything except the nap," she said, turning in a circle to admire the small but charmingly furnished room. "I refuse to waste a single moment of my stay in this wonderful place by sleeping."

"Well said," he agreed, handing her a cup of tea. "I will just have a word with Mrs. Warren to arrange things. I shall return in a moment."

* * *

"A man in my position is not free to marry where he will," Gabriel said as he loomed above Abby on the impossibly green grounds of the Royal Lodge. There were bluebells growing between the tender shoots of green. A straw hamper filled with bread, cheese, wine, and little sweet cakes was at her elbow. There was even a bowl of strawberries and cream. And a bottle of champagne. His coat had been discarded hours ago, and his rolled-up shirtsleeves bared his powerful forearms. His loosened shirt collar revealed the strong, sculpted column of his throat. "Or, I swear to you, I would make you mine." His blue-gray eyes were darkened with intensity.

He meant, Abby supposed, that like any self-respecting fortune hunter he had no choice but to marry a wealthy woman, and he did not want to raise any expectations in Abby's breast that would prove embarrassing later. She had to admit he did it well.

"Do spare me your protestations of regret," she said. "Has no one told you that a woman is more likely to be persuaded to succumb to your wiles if you refrain from insulting her intelligence?"

He laughed out loud. "I marveled, at first, that a lady of your beauty would remain unclaimed at your age, but now I understand."

"Well, that's frank!"

He pushed her backward onto the carpet of bluebells.

"Mr. Bourbonnais!" she exclaimed.

"Gabriel," he corrected her as he removed the pins that had been holding her hair in a prim chignon at the nape of her neck. "Such lovely hair. I have longed to see it like this." He seemed genuinely moved.

Then he kissed her.

She had to admit he did *that* well, too.

When she felt his fingers expertly undo the top buttons at the back of her gown, she gasped for air. Until now she could pretend she was living in some dream. But he was obviously so adept at removing a lady's clothing that she could no longer deny to herself it most probably was an everyday occurrence for him.

"I must compliment you on the dexterity of your fingers," she said dryly. "Do you knit to keep them in readiness for this purpose?"

He hesitated for a moment in the process of kissing a sensitive spot at the junction of her jaw and ear. "You have discovered my secret," he admitted. "Relax, my dear. You've gone all stiff. I promise you, I will not hurt you."

"Mr. Bourbonnais—Gabriel!" She gasped with sudden panic as she felt his fingers delicately caress the bare skin of her back. "I have made a dreadful mistake! I cannot do this!"

"What? This?" He kissed her with a thoroughness that left her panting.

"I am sorry," she said, tearing herself away from him. "I cannot." Then, to complete her humiliation, she burst into tears.

He pulled her into his arms. "There, there," he whispered. "It is all right."

"I let you bring me here under false pretenses. At least, I meant to—but now I find I cannot— it would be contrary to everything in which I believe and make me a stranger to myself."

"I am sorry for it, but it is no great catastrophe," he said as he turned her around and did up her buttons for her again. "There," he said, patting her shoulder. "All safely locked away, to my everlasting regret."

"But . . . I promised you the day."

"Yes. And I shall still have it. Just not the way I had dared hope." He gave her a smile full of warmth and laughter. Then he stood and reached for her hand. "Come, my dear. Let us explore."

It was dusk when Gabriel reluctantly handed Abby back into the coach for London. As compensation he had the infinite pleasure of sitting across from her to watch the dying sun play across her features.

He would give his soul to possess this woman, but whatever the outcome of his deception, the lovely and often surprising Miss Pennington was lost to him. Too bad it was not as easy to gain entry to her heart as it was to gain entry to an unoccupied royal property merely by presenting oneself on the doorstep and encouraging the senile caretaker's delusion that he was the king as he had appeared at an earlier age.

When Miss Pennington started to doze, he crossed to the other side of the coach so he could guide her nodding head to his shoulder. She smelled of wildflowers, but whether it was a scent she purchased in one of the shops in London or the lingering perfume of flowers from the Royal Lodge's grounds, he could not tell. Her golden hair was still undone, and a strand of it clung to his coat. Her eyes were closed, and her eyelashes were fair, feathery half moons against her slightly flushed cheeks. Gabriel did not doubt that he was holding her for the last time. It was time to spring the trap.

He stared at her face until she opened her eyes and smiled at him.

"Thank you, Gabriel," she said.

"For what?"

"For the day. For honoring my wishes. For serving as my pillow. For everything."

"It is I who should thank you," he said, and kissed her.

She made a small sound, like a sleepy kitten, and kissed him back.

His hands wandered. He could not stop them, and wouldn't have, if he could. She was so soft. So delicious. He wanted more, and he could tell she did, too.

He had to say it now. It was either that or draw her into the soft cushions and ravish her. "Abigail—Miss Pennington," he said as he straightened and leaned away from her. "I have a confession to make."

Abby blinked at him for a moment, and then she straightened, too.

"Very well. What is it?" Abby said, bracing herself for the worst. He had a wife and a brood of children. Or a lover. Or perhaps he would admit that he was merely toying with her, and he intended to have a hearty laugh at her expense at White's with the so-called gentlemen who had wagered a monkey that he couldn't persuade the prudish Miss Pennington to surrender her virtue to him.

"I am not the king's son," he said all in a rush.

He looked dumbfounded when Abby burst into laughter. "Is *that* all?" she demanded. Relief made her giddy. "Forgive me for laughing, Gabriel, but I never, for a moment, believed that you were the rightful Prince of Wales."

"No," he said, looking rueful. "I am the bloody King of England."

She stared at him in disbelief for a moment, then she rolled her eyes. "Credulous fool that I am, I thought you were going to tell me the truth," she said in disgust. "I should have known better."

"My grandmother was Hannah Lightfoot, a Quakeress who married George III secretly when he was still the Prince of Wales. The Royal Lodge was one of several places where he kept her during the years of their secret marriage. It belongs to me through a legacy handed down to my father."

"Of all the Banbury Stories," Abby scoffed. "You should be ashamed of yourself."

"The marriage with Hannah Lightfoot—my grandmother—took place before his state marriage to Charlotte of Mecklenburg-Strelitz, whom he would acknowledge as queen," he continued in that same earnest voice. "My father was born before the gentleman who is to be crowned king, which makes me—"

"The rightful King of England," she said skeptically. "I see."

"Abby," he said, taking her shoulders and looking deeply into her eyes. "When I said we could have only one day, I meant it. And I regret it more than I could ever express. There can be no future for us."

She drew away. "You need not invent pretty lies for me," she said in words that grated against her suddenly swollen throat.

"It is no lie to say I would marry you tomorrow if it were possible. But I must make a marriage of state. My blood and the blood of my ancestors demands it."

"I suppose the fortunate woman has already been chosen for you."

He gave a long sigh.

"There is talk of an Austrian princess. She is related to my mother."

"Yes. You Hanovers are mad for European princesses," Abby said archly. "How fortunate that there seems to be an endless supply."

"Abby, my darling, please do not be like this," he whispered.

"Be like *what?* Do you honestly expect me to believe this ridiculous tale?"

He gave a long sigh. "I can only tell the truth. It is not my fault if you do not believe."

"Very affecting," she scoffed. "If you are the rightful King of England, why have you not come forward before now?"

"For fear of my life," he said quietly, "which I have put into your hands by telling you this, but I owe you the truth."

"The truth!" she said skeptically.

"There are political factions in government that would not hesitate to have me murdered to keep the present administration in power. If my secret becomes known before the time is right, my death and possibly that of my mother will be on your head."

"But the whole tale is so preposterous."

"The nursemaid who took an assassin's bullet meant for me when I was an infant would have disagreed with you," he said grimly.

"A woman was killed?" Abby said in disbelief.

"In Paris. Before my mother fled with me to Vienna. The authorities never apprehended the assassin. Nor did they try very hard. My mother was of noble birth, but she had committed the crime of marrying George Rex, the firstborn son of the Prince of Wales. Even her birth could not protect her. Or me."

Abby hesitated. His words rang of absolute conviction. Then an amazing thought occurred to her. "You are here to stop the Coronation," she breathed. "That is why you and your mother have come to London now after keeping your silence for so long."

He nodded once in confirmation.

"I do not know what to believe," she said. "You ask too much of me."

"Too much? Are you speaking of your trust, or of this?" he asked, and then he took her into his arms and kissed her.

"No," she protested, but he ignored her. She had to put a stop to this. Now. She pushed against his chest with so much force that she knocked him off the seat and onto the floor of the coach. "Just in case you mistook my protest for a false one," she said when he gave a loud groan.

"Unnecessary. I believed you," he said dryly. "I think you have broken my nose."

"Don't be a baby," she scoffed. "I barely tapped you."

"I have been prone to nosebleeds since I was a child." He had both hands over his face. "Damnation! My mother will insist I have her precious coach reupholstered if I stain the cushions."

Abby sank to her knees beside him in an instant with her handkerchief in hand. Violetta, too, was prone to nosebleeds as a child, and Abby was an expert at dealing with them. "Hold still," she said as she pried his hands from his face, "and let me see. If I put pressure right *there*—"

Suddenly he sprang, and she found herself on her back on the floor of the coach as Gabriel kissed her with a passion that robbed her of breath. "Never . . . trust . . . a scoundrel," he gasped when they had to break apart to breathe.

"Mr. Bourbonnais! What are you about?" she demanded.

"Call me Gabriel," he said softly. She could hear the smile in his voice. "And I think you know very well what I am about."

She tried to rise, but he gently restrained her. "Please, Abby," he coaxed. "You did promise me the day, and there is some sunlight left. Do not let us waste it."

"But it is very uncomfortable here on the floor," she lied. "And cold."

"Let me warm you," he said as he lowered his lips to hers.

Gabriel stole into the quiet house and found his mother waiting for him.

"Well, my son," she asked. "Did you bait the hook well?" There was nothing of the duchess about her now, but she was no less imperious than that delicate figment of her imagination. Her eyes blazed like live coals in their sockets. She must have a touch of the fever again.

"I did," he replied with a sigh. "I have set the stage for her to betray my trust."

His mother gave a delighted cackle. The duchess, had she truly existed, would have been shocked by its coarseness. "Excellent," she said.

"Perhaps she will tell no one. I told her that to betray my confidence could be worth my very life."

She laughed again. "An amusing touch," she said appreciatively. She gave him a playful bat on the shoulder. "Sleep well, Your Majesty." She swept him a grand curtsy and left him.

In the library, Gabriel took out a decanter of brandy and seated himself at the desk. He and his mother had chosen their dupe carefully, for Abigail Pennington was considered by Society to be a sensible lady with an aversion to repeating idle gossip. From her lips, the tale of the rightful king being denied his throne by a cruel fate would gain credence.

How she would hate him when she learned the truth.

Chapter Eight

Abigail could not sleep. She gazed out the window at the single candle burning in Gabriel Bourbonnais's house.

The King of England.

How could he expect her to believe such a preposterous tale? Yet he seemed absolutely sincere.

Something inside her needed to believe he was an honorable man. However, she was a devoted daughter of Great Britain, and if he was an impostor, his objective must be to defraud the government.

She must investigate his story. If she did so discreetly, there would be no danger to him. That decided, at the crack of dawn Miss Pennington sent for her solicitor to give him her instructions to investigate the existence of a George Rex with the stipulation that he was to keep all findings confidential and report only to her.

"My, your inamorata has been busy," the duchess said coyly to Gabriel when the butler presented the Earl of Stoneham's visiting card four hours before the appropriate time of making polite social calls. "I must say I underestimated her. I thought it would take at least a week for word to come to the ears of the government."

They were still at breakfast, and Gabriel wished his mother

would just be still and drink her tea. His head hurt like the very devil, and it appeared he would have no choice but to drag his sorry self out of the wings and onto the stage at this reasonable hour.

"The news will be all over London before the cat can lick her ear," the duchess positively cackled with glee. "King Gabriel the First will be paid a great deal of money to leave the government intact, and for the good of Mother England, we will fade into obscurity. The men in power are nervous now. I promise you they will make us an offer soon."

"Either that, or one of them simply will put a bullet through my head as soon as I show my face in public," her son said dryly.

"Nonsense! These English pride themselves on their civilized behavior. It will be bribery, my son. Mark my words. Besides, who among them would want to be responsible for murdering the grandson of King George III?"

Despite her eagerness to move in for the kill, Mrs. Bourbonnais kept Lord Stoneham waiting in the parlor for quite a quarter of an hour before she made her entrance. "Good morning, my lord," she said with a faint but cordial smile as Gabriel solicitously helped her into her chair and arranged the cushions at her back.

Lord Stoneham had, of course, risen to his feet when they appeared, but he did not accept the hand the lady extended to him. "You promised me, madam, that you and your son would be discreet until your claims could be properly investigated," he said sternly.

"I do not understand you, my lord," she said, sounding bewildered and a little hurt. Her voice and manner betrayed not a twinge of guilt as she looked Lord Stoneham straight in the eye. It was not the triumph of acting that one would suppose, for, truly, Gabriel knew she felt no guilt. She never did.

"A London solicitor has received instructions on behalf of his client, Miss Pennington, to investigate your claim to be the legitimate son of one George Rex. How would she know the name of a gentleman exiled to South Africa years ago unless one of you told her?"

"I am afraid I am the culprit," Gabriel admitted. "I took

Miss Pennington into my confidence. I can only assure you my reasons were good ones. I trusted her to tell no one."

Lord Stoneham gave him a look of stern disapproval. "It seems your trust was misplaced," he said dryly. "The solicitor traced your movements from Cape Town and uncovered all the old speculation about the exiled Mr. Rex being the firstborn legitimate son of George III, and having agreed to renounce his own claim to the throne. Fortunately, Miss Pennington's solicitor came in confidence to my son, Lord Blakely, at Whitehall, with his revelations. Between the two of us, we persuaded the man that his investigation must not continue."

"Then you have proof my son's claim is true."

"Not quite yet, Mrs. Bourbonnais," Lord Stoneham said. "It must be established without a shade of doubt that George Rex, the man you claim was your legally wed husband and the father of your son, was, indeed, the legitimate son of our late king."

"Surely *you* do not doubt my word," Mrs. Bourbonnais said, the very picture of wronged innocence.

Lord Stoneham gave a long sigh, but his voice was soft when he replied to Gabriel's mother. Gabriel realized the man had a sincere kindness for her. He wasn't sure how he felt about that.

"It is not quite so simple a matter, Mrs. Bourbonnais," the earl said. "We are speaking of the potential collapse of the government."

"So my son, your rightful sovereign, should slink back into obscurity for the sake of your *convenience*," Mrs. Bourbonnais said bitterly. "You disappoint me, Lord Stoneham. I thought you a man of honor."

"If our investigation could have proceeded in secrecy at its own pace, the situation would not be so dire," the earl said. "But we have learned that Mr. Whittaker, your neighbor's fiancé, has been making inquiries as well. Of course, he has been quite vocal in his dislike of Mr. Bourbonnais's attentions to his fiancée, so I rather doubt anything he says to your detriment will be paid the least heed. As a precaution, I have called upon him, and impressed upon him that he will incur the severest displeasure of His Majesty's government if he does not desist immediately. He, of course, does not know of your son's alleged relationship to Mr. Rex, or his claim to the throne.''

''Then there is no harm done,'' Gabriel said. He expressed a confidence he did not feel. Miss Pennington's solicitor obviously discovered the trail that he was meant to find, but if Gabriel knew Mr. Whittaker—and he felt sure he did— he would not rest until he found some unpalatable truths to hang him with. Lord knew there were plenty of them to find if the fellow looked in the right places.

''I think it would be best if you disappear from town for a short while,'' Lord Stoneham said. ''My country house is at your disposal. We will leave tomorrow. I fear I cannot guarantee your son's safety if you refuse. I will post guards there, as well.''

Mrs. Bourbonnais brought one pale, trembling hand to her throat. ''Do you think my son is in danger?''

''There are those who would not hesitate to assassinate a claimant to the throne who threatened their own positions in government.''

''It shall be as you command,'' she said in defeat. ''I care not for myself, for I am a dying woman. But I pray you to protect my son—'' She then dissolved into a fit of coughing, and Gabriel bent over her solicitously. She had the cheek to give him an audacious wink, knowing that Gabriel's position hid her face from the earl's scrutiny.

''Madam calm yourself,'' Lord Stoneham said in consternation. ''I would not distress you for the world.''

''My lord, I think it best that you leave now,'' Gabriel said gravely.

The earl stretched out an impetuous hand toward Mrs. Bourbonnais. But when she refused to look at him, he bowed and left.

When Lord Stoneham was gone from the house, Mrs. Bourbonnais gave a whoop of triumph and threw her cashmere lap robe into the air. ''Success, my son,'' she crowed. ''Suddenly I feel like dancing.''

''Success, is it?'' Gabriel said dryly.

The duchess laughed at him. ''I refuse to listen to your pessimistic old grumbling, my son,'' she said gaily. ''Did

I not tell you all would be well if you would but keep your head? The threat of Mr. Whittaker's investigation is neutralized by the full authority of the goverment. Your Miss Pennington is now convinced of the truth of your claim and so is her solicitor. I do not care if they promised to remain silent until they were blue in the face; no one can keep such a good story secret for long. And the best part—the *very* best part—is that the goverment can no longer afford the luxury of a thorough investigation into your claim. They will be forced to pay us off, and without delay."

Gabriel gave a sigh of exasperation and ran a weary hand through his hair. "Tomorrow we will be completely in Lord Stoneham's power," he pointed out. "What if he decides it will be more convenient, after all, to assassinate me than to pay us to disappear?"

"That is tomorrow, my son. Tonight," she said with a smirk, "we are invited to a ball in honor of the king's approaching coronation. And I promise you, it shall be memorable!"

The ball was in full swing when Gabriel and his mother arrived. Sourly, he noted that she was clinging to his arm with more than customary frailty. She was every inch the martyred aristocrat determined to make any sacrifice to see her son and liege restored to his rightful place.

"Mrs. Bourbonnais," said Lord Stoneham, frowning, when they appeared before him in the reception line. He lowered his voice. "You should not be here."

"Nonsense," she said, smiling at the curious bystanders glittering in all their finery. "Did you not send us an invitation?"

"Yes, I did, but that was before—"

"Precisely," she said, moving on to greet Lady Letitia. "Such a lovely party."

Gabriel bowed over Lady Letitia's hand when it was his turn to greet her. She fairly snatched it away from him. Apparently she still considered his mother a threat to her position as the earl's hostess.

He looked quickly around the room and found Miss Pennington talking with Lady Blakely, the wife of Lord Stoneham's son, at one end. He recalled the earl saying that the two women had been at school together as girls.

Lady Blakely," he said, bowing.

"I am glad you could come," the beautiful brunette said with a cordial smile. She reached out to take Mrs. Bourbonnais's arm. "I must steal your mother from you for a little while, Mr. Bourbonnais. There is someone here who is most anxious to renew her acquaintance with you, ma'am," she said to the elder lady as she indicated a beautifully dressed, red-haired woman sitting on the sidelines.

"Ah, it is Lady Madelyn!" Mrs. Bourbonnais exclaimed. "What a delightful surprise! We met in Vienna some time ago."

"Miss Pennington, I hope this waltz is not bespoke," Gabriel said when his mother had gone off with Lady Blakely.

"No," she said, looking at him with her heart in her eyes.

Never had he seen her look so lovely. She was dressed in an extremely flattering pink-and-white gown he had not seen before, and her beautiful hair was pinned up and crowned with small white, star-shaped flowers. Her cheeks matched the gown.

"Pink becomes you," he murmured.

He knew instinctively that the new gown, the elaborate upswept arrangement of her golden hair, the little star-shaped flowers were all for him, and he could not help devouring her with his eyes. She blushed delicately when she stepped into his arms.

"What is this?" he asked teasingly when she avoided his gaze. He waited for the beat of the music and guided her into the rhythm. "My collar seems to be exerting a fascination for you that I am quite at a loss to comprehend."

"Please do not mock me, Your Majesty," she said softly.

"Abby, no," he said, appalled.

"I wonder that the sight of me does not disgust you after my appalling behavior yesterday," she said. "I do not know what came over me. I completely lost my self-control. Like a . . . a cat in heat."

"Not completely," he said with a rueful sigh. "Unfortunately."

"How can you joke about it?" she said in disbelief as she averted her gaze.

"Abby, look at me," he said compellingly.

She obeyed.

"Your honor is intact," he said. "I assure you that I will continue to regard you with the utmost respect, and I do apologize for distressing you with my attentions."

"Thank you, Your Majesty," she whispered.

"My name is Gabriel," he corrected her.

For now, at least.

"I do not deserve your kindness," she blurted out. "I did not believe you, and I had my solicitor investigate your . . . father. Lord Stoneham paid me a confidential visit and told me I must never tell a living soul what my solicitor found out—and I will not, I swear. Can you forgive me for doubting you?"

"Of course," he said, knowing that too soon she would know the truth about his so-called claim to the throne and his treachery in using her to extort money from her government.

"You must excuse me," she said when the waltz was at an end. "I must . . . I must go."

Gabriel frowned as she walked away. Wonderful. The woman he adored was so cowed by his false pretensions to the throne that she could hardly bear to look at him.

Suddenly a hush fell over the room. The guest of honor had arrived.

When His Majesty George IV came into the room flanked by Lord Stoneham and Lady Letitia, every lady and gentleman bent the knee in a waving sea of plumes and diamonds. With an affable smile, the First Gentleman in England bowed to the assembled guests. Applause broke out.

"Your Majesty," said Lord Stoneham, "will you have some refreshment? Or will you join the gentlemen in the card room?"

"Some wine, perhaps," the king said graciously.

Lord Stoneham signaled a servant, but took the wine to present it to the king personally.

"Your health, Stoneham," the king said as he sipped delicately from his glass. His smile faded when he spotted Gabriel's mother sitting by the side of the ballroom with Lady Blakely, Lord Stoneham's daughter-in-law, and Lady Madelyn Langtry, a grand lady in international diplomatic circles.

Mrs. Bourbonnais's face paled.

Gabriel had no idea how she managed it. He'd never missed a cue in his life, so he rushed to her at once and stood behind her chair with both hands on her shoulders as if to lend her support.

The king had heard the rumors that Gabriel was his illegitimate son, of course. No wonder he looked at Mrs. Bourbonnais as if he were trying to place her in his memory.

The duchess, with a great show of gathering her strength, stood with head held high and sank into a low curtsy.

Gravely, the king bowed to her. He favored Gabriel with a regal inclination of his head, and Gabriel bowed in return. Gabriel could feel the other guests' eyes travel from one to the other, noting their resemblance in coloring.

Gabriel knew they would see him as every inch a Hanover if they were looking for a reason to do so.

Lord Stoneham's eyes narrowed and he stepped forward quickly when the king started to approach Gabriel and his mother.

"I will escort you to the card room, Your Majesty."

The king shook himself from his reverie and smiled at the earl. "Thank you, Stoneham," he said. As he left the ballroom, he looked back once at Gabriel's mother, who was still staring at him. Never had Gabriel seen her so imperious.

The clever adventuress had callously banked on His Majesty's celebrated gallantry toward the fair sex not to denounce her as an impostor in the middle of a *ton* party.

When the king was out of sight, the whispers and significant glances started. He helped his mother, who gave a show of sudden weariness, into her chair and left Lady Blakely and Lady Madelyn to fuss over her with their vinaigrettes.

Gabriel badly needed some air, and made for the open French windows of the balcony.

Unfortunately, his steps led him right past Miss Violetta and her jealous swain, who appeared to be having some sort of argument. Her cheeks were hot spots of high color. Her companion was glaring at her with hostility in his eyes. Finally he stomped off and left her alone.

Gabriel tried hard to ignore the heartrending spectacle of

Miss Violetta allowing tears to course down her cheeks without making the least effort to check them. Her nose was turning red. In a moment people would leave off their stupefaction at the extraordinary scene that had just unfolded between his mother and the king, and then they would titter at her. He sighed. He really could not leave the chit to make a spectacle of herself. "Come along, my girl," he said in a brisk undervoice as he took her arm. "You may tell me all about it, but not here."

She looked at him with watery worship in her eyes.

Oh, good Lord, he thought impatiently.

"All I said," she told him tearfully when he had ushered her into the unoccupied library, "is he is not the man I thought him when I agreed to marry him. I do not want to make a mistake I will regret for the rest of my life, so I told him I wanted to postpone the wedding."

"And you decided to tell him this in the middle of a party attended by the most influential people in London? Whatever possessed you?"

Her tears sprang forth anew and, with some impatience, he handed her his handkerchief.

"I thought he would not make a scene if there were people about."

"I suppose it did not occur to you that your behavior was unfair as well as cowardly?"

Her mouth dropped open, as well it might. He certainly was behaving out of character for the courtly Mr. Bourbonnais.

Well, he was in no mood to let the incorrigible little chit weep prettily all over his chest. "For pity's sake, girl," he said, not caring that Gabriel Bourbonnais's cultured continental accent had degenerated into a testy growl. "You should be on your knees thanking Providence for the fellow instead of holding him up to ridicule in public. It would have served you right if he had boxed your ears."

"How *dare* you, sir!" she cried in disbelief.

"The man would lay down his life for you. Does that not count for *something*?"

"William is right," she said coldly. "You are a scoundrel, and probably a thief as well."

He could not help himself. He burst into laughter.

Miss Pennington rushed into the room and put her arm around Violetta when she dissolved into angry tears. "What is going on here?" Abby asked, looking to Gabriel for enlightenment. He merely shrugged. "There, there, darling," she added to the girl as she patted her on the back.

"He is cruel, and hateful," the girl sniffed.

"Mr. Bourbonnais?" she asked in surprise.

"William! He said that I can cry off with his goodwill!"

"He doesn't mean it, love. Sit down and compose yourself. I will be right back," Miss Pennington said. She gave her niece's shaking shoulder a last pat. "Come with me, if you please, Mr. Bourbonnais." She took his arm and towed him from the room.

"Have I told you how beautiful you look tonight?" he said.

"Yes, thank you," she said in clipped tones as she stalked through the hall. He had to step lively to keep up with her. "I heard you shouting at my niece from the next room."

"Well, she deserved it. Where are we going?"

"To find Mr. Whittaker." When she saw her prey lounging against the fireplace with a glass of wine in his hand, she grabbed his arm and towed him all the way back to the library with a bemused Gabriel following. He had to step back to keep from being splashed by the startled Mr. Whittaker's libation.

"Miss Pennington! What do you think you are doing?" Mr. Whittaker demanded.

"I have had enough of this nonsense," she said. "I have planned a wedding for you, Violetta, and three hundred guests." She shoved him into the room, and Violetta looked up with a tear-stained face. "I expect the two of you to either make up right now, or call it off. I do not care which. Understand, though, if I have to cancel all the arrangements and you decide to marry after all, you can find some other poor fool to plan your next extravaganza!" With that, she stalked from the room with Gabriel in her wake and slammed the door so hard behind them that the hinges shuddered.

Gabriel leaned against the wall and dissolved into laughter.

"Stop it," Miss Pennington hissed, but her lips began to

quiver and she started laughing too. "Whatever possessed me to do that?"

"Crude but effective," he said, making a pantomime to indicate applause. "I must say, my dear, I admire your methods." Then his smile faded and he gave a wistful sigh. "Lord, I shall miss you," he said.

"Miss me?" she echoed.

"Your solicitor did his work well," he said.

She blushed to the roots of her hair. "I stressed that the investigation must be done with the utmost secrecy."

"I am sure you did. He confided in Lord Blakely, who is in the diplomatic service at Whitehall, and he told his father, Lord Stoneham, who already knew about my claim to the throne. It is why he has been in my mother's pocket since we arrived in England."

"What have I done?" she whispered.

"Nothing that wouldn't have been done eventually, anyway," he said. "But there is no hope now that the news won't leak out. My mother and I are being sent away tomorrow. Lord Stoneham will not guarantee our safety otherwise."

"It is all my fault," she said.

"It is not," he insisted. "It would have happened, sooner or later. The government was doing its own investigation. You have only accelerated events."

He cupped her face in his hands and forced her to look at him. "Abby, after tonight I may never see you again," he said earnestly. "Try to remember me with ... some kindness."

"I will. Always," she said. Her whole heart was in her beautiful eyes.

"Farewell," he said softly, and left her.

Abby was sitting dejectedly in a chair in the hall outside the library when Violetta and Mr. Whittaker emerged from it. Seeing Abby, he made her a brief, ironic bow and walked quickly away.

"All is at an end," said Violetta, and burst into tears all over Abby's new pink gown.

Chapter Nine

Gabriel had made his farewell speech to Miss Pennington, and it was well past time to get off the bloody stage.

It wouldn't be a moment too soon. He was sick to death of the whole business.

A glance around the room revealed his mother, flanked by Lady Blakely and Lady Madelyn, two of the most influential hostesses in the *ton*, as one guest after another clamored for her attention. Now that she had been acknowledged by her former paramour, the king, her status as an important personage who would one day be in a position to grant favors was confirmed.

His mother hadn't the least difficulty juggling the roles of royal mistress and wronged queen mother at the same time.

Gabriel's affectionate smile was quite wiped from his face when he saw a familiar tall, slender gentleman with pomaded golden hair and a handsome face. "Mother," he said quickly, extending his arm. "I have had one of Lord Stoneham's footmen fetch the carriage. Let us go now."

"Gabriel, what is wrong with you?" she said with a frown. "We have only just arrived."

"Do stay," said Lady Blakely. "We are so enjoying your mother's reminiscences about Vienna."

"You know how injurious the night air is, Mother," he said desperately.

To his dismay, Lady Madelyn gave a little cry of pleased surprise and waved to the newcomer, whose face was suddenly illuminated with honest pleasure as he increased his speed. Gabriel turned away and tugged on his mother's sleeve. She slapped his hand away.

"Stop it," she hissed at him.

"Vanessa, you remember Mr. Wyndham, do you not?" Lady Madelyn said.

"Of course," Lady Blakely said with a tinkling laugh. "He became betrothed at our Christmas house party two years ago." She turned to the gentleman with a sweet, expectant smile on her face.

"Jack! Jack Sunderland, is that you?" Gabriel's nemesis cried out. Mr. Wyndham seized his hand and wrung it with enthusiasm. "What are you doing so far from Cape Town, you old rascal!" Mr. Wyndham turned to his companion. "Jack and his cousins breed the best racehorses in South Africa. Beauties, every one! I would have died of boredom if it hadn't been for old Jack when I was posted to South Africa years ago."

"Come along, Cedric," Gabriel murmured. "Let me get you a glass of wine."

"Had enough, thank you, old fellow. Wife doesn't like it if I come home foxed. Do you still act in amateur theatricals in Cape Town? Lord, you could have made a fine living on the stage in London. Jack used to keep us all in stitches with wild tales about how he toured Europe as a child, masquerading as the lost heir of some kingdom or another with his mother," Mr. Wyndham announced to the company at large.

A muttering went up all around them, and Lord Stoneham looked thunderstruck. At his side was Mr. Whittaker, who looked as if the heavens had opened up and granted him his dearest wish.

But Gabriel only had eyes for Abby, who stood with her niece at the edge of the circle of shocked guests.

Mrs. Bourbonnais might be in many ways an unsatisfactory parent, but she knew her duty. She gave a great gasp

and rolled her eyes upward. Then she sank gracefully into
Lord Stoneham's arms. While the guests' attention was
diverted, Gabriel ran for the doors.

Abby was there waiting for him. "Come with me," she
said, grabbing his hand. "There is no time to lose."

"Halt!" cried Mr. Whittaker. "Stop that man!" But he
was too late. Abby and Gabriel were already running down
the street.

"I had already called for my carriage because Violetta
was so upset," Abby said. She was holding up the front of
her skirt so she could run faster. "There it is."

They leaped inside, and the coachman whipped up the
horses. "Home, James," Abby called out.

"It was all a lie after all," Abby said to him in the
darkness of her carriage.

"Which part do you mean?" he asked with a shrug. "The
part about me being the king of England? Yes. Sadly, that
was a lie." The cultured foreign accent had dropped away
and left this stranger. It was as if the man who had captured
her heart no longer existed.

"I knew it all along," she said.

"But if you mean the part about my marrying you if I
were free to do so, that part was the absolute truth."

"Please do not insult my intelligence any more than you
already have!" she demanded. "How will you get away?"

"It is better if you do not know," he said.

Before she knew what he was about, he grasped her shoulders and gave her a brief, hard kiss. "Farewell, Abby," he
said. "Try not to hate me too much."

Then to her horror, he opened the door and leaped from
the moving carriage.

Violetta cried herself to sleep that night, and cried some
more when she opened her eyes to the rainy morning.

"Come downstairs, love," Abby coaxed. "You cannot
spend all day in your room."

Violetta turned her face away. "Yes, I can," she said.

How could Abby take it so calmly? Mr. Bourbonnais was a fraud, a thief, a scoundrel. There weren't enough bad words for what he had tried to do.

"You have a visitor," Abby said. "Mr. Whittaker desires a word with you, and I think you owe him that much."

"I do not think I can face him," Violetta said. Her pretty face crumpled.

"Courage, my girl," Abby said.

In a half hour, Violetta went into the parlor to find William waiting for her. He stood and took both her hands in his. "Are you all right?" he asked. His expression was anxious.

She couldn't help it. She burst into tears.

"Please don't cry, Violetta," he said, patting her on the shoulder. "I just wanted to apologize for my behavior last night. Of course we must not marry unless you are convinced we will suit. Take all the time you need. I hope you will decide to marry me because I love you so very much."

Violetta gave a great sniff and touched her handkerchief to her eyes. "Oh, William. How could I have been such a fool," she sobbed.

"Well, you weren't the only one," he conceded. "That fellow had almost everyone in London convinced he was the son of a king."

"I don't mean him," Violetta said disdainfully. "I meant fool enough to tell you we would not suit."

"Violetta, my darling!" he cried. "Does this mean—"

"Oh, William, I love you so much," she said.

He opened his arms and she rushed into them with a sigh of relief. "There, there, my love," he said as he rained ardent little kisses on her lips, her cheeks, and her closed eyelids. "I love you, too."

"Does that mean you will marry me after all?" she asked hopefully.

"Yes," he said.

Violetta's smile faded.

"What is wrong?" he asked.

"Abby has washed her hands of us. She said so last night. She said if we change our minds, we must make our own wedding arrangements."

"We don't need Abby, Violetta. We only need each

other." He reached behind a chair and emerged with a big box. "I have a gift for you."

Intrigued, Violetta untied the silver ribbons.

"I had it made for you," he said all in a rush. "I hope you like it."

Violetta's heart melted. "Oh, William! It's beautiful! It's perfect!"

The birdcage was made of thin, graceful strips of brass. A big white satin ribbon was tied at the top. "I have the doves, too," he said. "But I didn't think they'd like being in the box until you opened it."

"You're right, William," Violetta said softly. "We only need each other."

"Have you come to arrest me?" the duchess asked when Lord Stoneham was shown into the parlor. Her trunks were waiting by the door. She was sitting in her usual chair, but today the draperies were open to let the sunlight shine into the room.

When he did not answer, she stood and faced him proudly. "Do your worst," she said with a tight smile. "I care not what happens to me. I can only rejoice that my son has escaped."

Several of the Bourbonnaises' London benefactors from among the opposition party who had hoped the ascension of Gabriel I would bring them political favor, had been vociferous in wanting their money back. Many had filed lawsuits, but they couldn't get blood from a turnip. Mrs. Bourbonnais had spent every cent and run up a mountain of debt besides.

"Where will you go?" Lord Stoneham asked softly.

"To prison, I assume," she said. "Is that not why you are here?"

"No. Your creditors have all been satisfied." He moved forward to take her hand, and she burst into near-hysterical laughter.

"Do not tell me you have settled my debts out of pity for the gallant dying widow," she said when she had recovered her voice. "The more fool you."

When he said nothing, she gave him a wry smile. "What a gallant adversary you are, my dear friend," she said softly.

"I didn't exactly do it for pity," he said.

She raised one eyebrow. "My lord," she said in a chilly tone. "I do hope you don't expect me to be your mistress in exchange for settling my affairs. If so, you will be making a very poor bargain."

"No, actually. I was hoping you would agree to be my wife."

"Your wife!" She turned pale and put a hand to her throat as she sank back into her chair. "Your wife," she repeated faintly.

"My dear Mrs. Bourbonnais, shall I call your maid?"

"Don't you dare," she said with a tremulous smile. "I am perfectly all right. It's just—" She closed her lips and clutched his hand convulsively.

"It's just—" he prompted.

"I have never received a proposal of marriage before," she said, and burst into the first genuine tears she had cried in years.

"Please say yes," he said as he laid his hand against her damp, rouged cheek. "It will be my honor to make your last days happy ones."

"Oh, dear," she said in dismay. "I suppose you will find out sooner or later."

"I beg your pardon?" he asked.

"About this dying business," she admitted with a sheepish look. "I'm afraid I lied about that, too."

The wedding of Miss Violetta Pennington to Mr. William Whittaker was attended by all the leading members of London Society, most notably Lord Stoneham and his bride, whose surname had been a bit murky, but no matter—she was Claudia Logan, Countess of Stoneham now.

Violetta was radiant in a gown of white taffeta trimmed in silver ribbons, and after the party emerged from St. Paul's into the sunlight she opened the ornamental cage she carried with a flourish to release a pair of snow-white doves.

With a coo of pleasure, the birds flew out of the cage as

the guests applauded. Then the applause died when the birds circled once and dove for Lady Letitia's elaborate hat.

"Get them off! Get them off!" the lady shrieked when one of the creatures grasped one of her dyed blonde curls in its beak and tugged.

Her brother flapped his hat at them and they finally winged their way heavenward.

Lady Letitia turned an accusing look at her loathsome sister-in-law. "She did it," she snarled. "I *know* she had something to do with it."

"Nonsense, Letitia," Lord Stoneham said, looking displeased as he took his bride's arm. The countess gave her sister by marriage a smug smile and kept her own counsel.

"Abby!" wailed Violetta in distress. But she wailed in vain, because Abby's work was done. She had already walked across the street and accepted her coachman's hand into her waiting carriage. She didn't look back once.

The carters had already taken her trunks to the ship, and the new owners would take possession of her house in a week. The watercolor of the Royal Lodge at Kew was the only thing she intended to keep.

Miss Pennington had finally earned her freedom, and she didn't intend to waste a single moment in pining over a certain handsome rogue who hadn't even possessed the courtesy to find a way to let her know whether he was safe.

Chapter Ten

September 1821
Egypt

Her guide and porters complained bitterly about traveling out onto the Plain of Thebes in the darkness, but Miss Pennington was adamant. She had journeyed many miles to see the Colossi of Memnon at sunrise, and she was determined that no one would deprive her of it.

Miss Pennington alighted from her donkey like the seasoned traveler she had become in the past several months. She adjusted her sun hat and shook out the sturdy riding skirt she wore with her practical linen shirtwaist.

As she lifted her face to the rising sun to see the first rays of morning caress the forms of the huge statues, she felt tears of emotion well in her eyes.

Then she heard it—a long wail of sorrow echoing on the wind. It was enough to make the hair at the back of her neck stand on end. She whirled around in alarm, only to confront an exotically robed man astride a white Arabian stallion as he threw back his head and laughed.

"My apologies for startling you. I could not resist," he called out in perfectly accented English.

He dismounted with athletic grace and approached with a panther's stalking gait as he removed his flowing headgear to reveal picturesquely windswept chestnut hair. He held the horse's reins in one hand, and the animal minced daintily across the sand. His blue-gray eyes were laughing, and his big, mischievous grin shone white against his sun-burnished face.

She blinked in astonishment. It could not be! Her eyes were playing tricks on her!

"Do not be alarmed, Miss Pennington. It is only I," he said, just as if he could see into her mind. He took her hands in his. "Are you not glad to see me?"

"Gabriel," she croaked when she found her voice. No, that wasn't right. "Jack?"

He gave an approving inclination of his head and turned her around so they could watch the sun climb in the morning sky together. The only sound was of the wind and the birds greeting the sun.

"But . . . how?" Abby asked as she savored the sensation of his strong hands at her waist.

"Mother, of course," he said wryly. "She writes to me faithfully to record all of her social triumphs now that I live quite out of the world in Cape Town."

"And she told you what I've done."

"Of course. Sold that monstrosity of a house for a good price and gone off despite the shocked protests of your solicitor, your niece, and your friends to see the world. Well done, Abby! All of London thinks you've run mad. The only thing that has caused a greater sensation is Mother's marriage to the earl and her pitiless torment of Lady Letitia for daring to oppose the match. I have been here every morning for a month, waiting for you."

"And is your latest imposture that of a desert sheik?" she said with an edge to her voice.

"Certainly not. I merely wanted to impress you. I have it on good authority that I look rather dashing in this guise, do you not agree?"

She could hear the cocky grin in his voice.

"My days of pretending to be someone else are at an end," he said. His voice was perfectly serious now. "The only role I want to assume now is that of husband. To you."

"And you expect me to accept you, just like that," she said with a catch in her voice.

"Certainly not. I have far too much respect for your intellegence to expect any such thing," he said as the blessed rays of the sun bathed them in rosy light. He seized her around the waist and lifted her to the saddle of his horse. He looked up at her with adoring eyes. "I intend to propose to you at the foot of the Pyramids, under the eyes of the Sphinx at sunset, before the ruins of the Ramesseum—in short, at every blessed monument in Egypt until you give in."

He mounted the horse behind her, and she leaned back against his broad chest with a sigh of contentment.

She could hardly wait.

Afterword

One expects an author to make up outlandish tales, but the most surprising element of my story is the real-life controversy surrounding George Rex, who is believed by many to be the legitimate heir to George III by his secret—but legal—first marriage to one Hannah Lightfoot, a Quakeress whom the king is said to have kept at a series of retreats in England until her death.

Soon after King George III's own death in 1820, various articles purporting to report the truth of this prior legal marriage appeared in the newspapers, and it is said at that time several imposters came forward to masquerade as George Rex or his heir. I see no reason why one of them couldn't have been my hero.

George Rex, himself, made no such claim. He first appeared in Cape Town in 1797, and he died in 1839 at his luxurious estate in Knysna on an extensive land grant deeded to him by the English Crown.

For a fascinating account of the family legend of George Rex, read *George Rex of Knysna,* which was written by Sanni Metelerkamp, George Rex's great-granddaughter, and published in 1963 by Baily Bros. & Swinfen, London.

Oh, one more thing—don't bother looking for the Royal Lodge at Kew on your next tour of England. I made that bit up.

Kate Huntington
February 7, 2002

A ROGUE'S RESCUE
Donna Simpson

Chapter One

Ingram stalked the crowded ballroom, his presence at the edge making the others nervous, like prey at a waterhole will raise their heads and sniff the air to catch the scent of the black panther rustling through the underbrush. Some, sighting him, moved away, pulling their impressionable daughters away from him as if the merest touch of his shadow would taint.

But the Viscount Lovell Melcher, Lord Ingram, did not appear to notice. He scanned the throng for a particular face, weak-chinned, bespectacled, but vicious rather than foolish in its vacuous emptiness. And there was his despised quarry. His gaze sharpened; his dark eyes narrowed. *There* was the man who had escaped without paying his rightful debt and would now suffer the consequences. He started forward but was blocked in place by a sudden movement of the crowd.

"That, my dear," a voice near him hissed, "seated so forlornly at the edge of the ballroom floor, is Miss Ariadne Lambert. Poor, *poor* woman. Looked after her elderly aunt for fifteen years; devoted herself *wholly* to the old woman's care. Wasted all her youth. Too bad, really. She was only just passable as a girl, but of course, the sickroom, and all that ... She has dwindled into the fright you see before you."

Ingram, unwillingly caught in one spot by the press of

the crowd, became the reluctant confidant of a woman he hadn't even seen yet, her shrill voice cutting through the murmur like a knife through curd. The elegant blue-and-silver ballroom was stifling, and there was a general movement just then toward the supper room; even he could not worm through.

And the voice droned on.

"She should be in caps, of course. But look at her! For all the world as if she thinks a beau is going to stride out of the crowd and *sweep* her off her feet." The woman tittered. "She must be . . . oh, all of three-and-thirty? Now she lives for tea, gossip, and to read the most dreadful of novels, you know, only gothics and romances. Too bad. She was rather good *ton* at one time; never top notch, of course, but acceptable. 'Course, she is rich now. Oh, yes, positively *oozing* money. The old aunt left her pots and pots of filthy lucre, if I must be vulgar, and that makes up for a multitude of faults. Gains her access to these events."

Ingram, impatient and restless, leaned against the stout back barring his progress—his quarry was sure to move on and be lost in the crowd if he did not accost him soon— but the big fellow in front of him was wedged securely and could not move. And he would not retreat, as there was supper yet to be had. Hostage to his spot near the curtained entrance to the refreshment room, Ingram sourly observed the pair who were gossiping. The gossip purveyor was a thirtyish matron, well-dressed, well-moneyed, and she spoke to—

He frowned. Where *had* he seen the other woman before?

The matron sighed. "I just hope poor Ariadne does not fall for the first gamester or adventurer who says a pretty word to her, for she is terribly, *terribly* gullible, poor dear. She would give her last *sou* to be married, or at least courted."

At that moment the stout fellow moved and Ingram could see the woman being indicated by the tilt of the gossipy matron's plumed headdress.

She sat alone at the edge of the ballroom, her slippered toe tapping in time to the country dance that was the last number before supper. She *was* plain, gaunt of face and angular, with spectacles firmly planted on her nose and a hideous dress in pea-green highlighting her sallow complexion. Even alone, though, she seemed cheerful, smiling and nodding as a couple passed by her.

Ingram turned away, intent, once more, on finding the man who owed him money, for the fellow was going to be beaten badly within the hour, though he did not yet know it. Ingram let no man cheat him without the severest of reprisals. In that moment, as he passed by the two gossiping women, he remembered who the one listening so intently was. She was sister to Dapper Dorsey, an ineffectual cardsharp and villainous roué who skirted the edge of respectability so successfully that he managed never to be paid back for his incursions on feminine purse strings. The viscount cast one look back at the gaunt spinster, and then at the two gossiping women. Damn, but he should warn that foolish, gossiping idiot whose ear she was dropping such precious information in.

But no. Not his business. He turned and spotted his prey. *There* was his business. In ten minutes he would be breaking a nose in the back alley. That would satisfy the debt between them.

Ingram nursed his knuckles. Who would have thought the cheating dolt would have such a hard chin? And give as good as he got? Limping, Ingram was heading to the supper room to have a bite to eat before leaving the stifling affair, when his progress was arrested by the one sight he had hoped not to see.

The spinster—what *was* her name?—was still sitting in the same chair on the edge of the ballroom floor. But at her side was Dorsey, gazing at her with a kind of stunned adoration. Nobody was better at that look than he, and women found it irresistible, without exception believing in his fervent declarations of devotion. To Ingram's eye the man was too good-looking, almost pretty, with curling fair hair and smooth skin. But perhaps that was just the opinion of a man who had had his nose broken on three separate occasions and whose jaw did not quite run straight, the way nature intended.

Ingram plunked down in a nearby chair. Dorsey was leaning toward the woman, whose foolish face was lit with a brilliant smile, displaying strong, even white teeth in a most unladylike display of joy. Dorsey's sister must have whispered in his ear about the woman's fortune, and now he was going in for the kill. He was a skilled seducer, and would have the idiotic woman parted from her money in a trice, especially if she insisted on bestowing those radiant, surprisingly beautiful smiles on him.

Damnation.

Fighting with his conscience, Ingram stayed planted on the blue brocade chair as the party swirled around him, frolicsome young women dancing the waltz with dark-clad gentlemen, nobody sparing a glance for the foolish rich spinster and her amorous swain.

Where was her friend? She should be warned. Ingram glanced around, but the woman who had gossiped so effusively about her acquaintance's money was now nowhere to be found.

Damnation.

Dorsey was kissing her palm, and she was coloring an unattractive flame red.

Hellfire and damnation.

Ingram looked away. He should leave. He had done what he came for, and that was to plant a facer on a lying, cheating knave. He could leave and forget he had ever seen . . . what was her name? Miss Ariadne something. No one had talked to him and he would ask no young lady to dance. Ingram was skirting the fine edge of being considered bad *ton*; another scandal and he would be dropped from the invitation lists of all the better hostesses. He knew it, and he didn't give a damn. Or so he told himself often. Right now, because he was a viscount and well-moneyed, he was invited everywhere. When people stopped inviting him, he would concentrate on his business enterprises and consort with those who valued him for who he was.

The irony was that Dorsey, with no money and of doubtful *ton*, was invited everywhere because people genuinely liked him and thought him a fine fellow. His occasional "lapses," as they were called in polite circles, had been successfully hushed up to preserve the women in question's reputation. In fact, most of his thievery had gone undetected. But Ingram cruised in many circles, and Dorsey was known in the moneylending spheres, his name bandied about as a card-sharp and cheating varlet.

Miss Ariadne Whatever-her-name-was, eyes wide in an absurd parody of the most innocent of green girls, was listening intently to Dorsey's honeyed words.

Ingram, unwilling hostage to his own conscience, rose from his seat and moved closer, concealed by a couple at the edge of the ballroom who were having a whispered conversation of their own.

". . . knocked flat on my back," Dorsey was saying, his emotion-filled voice quavering. "Never have I met a lady who has done that, who has made my heart beat faster just at the sight of her brilliant eyes and . . . and handsome . . . handsome teeth."

Ingram rolled his eyes. This was Dorsey's idea of flattery? Surely the woman would tell him to take flight.

"Mr. Dorsey," she said, in a breathy, high-pitched voice. "You . . . you overwhelm me with your kindness."

"No, my heart, my *life*, you overwhelm *me*! I am stricken, flattened. Please, tell me there is no one else. Tell me I do not need to feel the agonizing pangs of jealousy."

"I . . . I have no other beaux." Here, she giggled.

Ingram was set to walk away. There were hundreds of foolish spinsters and it was not his business—

"Then say you will meet me at . . . oh, anywhere. I long to see you in private, to touch your hand. I would suggest my little house at Richmond . . ."

"Mr. *Dorsey!*"

Good. She was going to tell him he was an impudent donkey for suggesting such a thing. He strained to hear her next words, to make them out through the hissing altercation that consumed the standing couple.

"Mr. Dorsey," she said. "I could never meet you out of town like that. But perhaps we could have a moment alone somewhere closer. . . . Vauxhall, mayhap?"

Oh, for—Ingram circled the quarreling couple that had concealed him till now and presented himself before Dorsey and his quarry.

"May I have this dance, Miss . . ." The name finally came back. "Miss Lambert?"

Chapter Two

Ariadne glared up at the strange man who had just asked her to dance in such an abrupt and ill-tempered manner. He had a bruised chin and his bare knuckles were grazed and bloody. "No," she blurted out.

Dorsey's beautiful blue eyes were wide. "Ingram!"

"Do you know this man, Mr. Dorsey?" Events had taken a peculiar turn. Ariadne had not expected to have her hand solicited for a dance, and certainly not in such a manner. The man who stood over her appeared angry, as though he had been forced into making the request.

And it had happened at such an interesting juncture, just as she and the terribly handsome Mr. Dorsey were coming to an understanding.

"No?" the angry man said, folding his arms across his broad chest.

"No," Ariadne replied, folding her square hands together. "I do not know you, sir."

The angry man turned to the still-seated gentleman. "Introduce me, Dorsey!" he barked.

"This is Ingram," Dorsey said, forcing the words out, his voice quavering.

"Viscount Ingram, at your service, miss," the fellow grunted.

She expected that Dorsey would find some way to get rid of the viscount—she really could not believe such a swarthy, brutish-looking fellow *was* a viscount—but instead her beau melted away, with just a whispered, "Your servant, Miss Lambert."

Ariadne gazed up at the man in front of her. He now wore a self-satisfied smirk. So his intent was to get rid of Dorsey, for some unknown and likely personal reason. She knew just the way to eradicate that complacent smile. She stood, her height about the same as his. "I have changed my mind. I *will* dance with you."

"What?"

"I said, sir, that I have changed my mind. A lady's prerogative, you know. I would be *delighted* to dance with you."

A sprightly minuet began that moment. She eyed his stocky, broad-shouldered figure. Let them see who would have the most satisfaction. She did not dance well, and he was certainly not built for the elegant minuet. They joined the dance.

As they came together and parted in the figures, saying nothing, she examined him. Her first impression of brooding, glowering anger was not diminished, but she felt an unwilling stirring within her. He was not handsome, certainly not like Mr. Dorsey, who had the fair good looks of a seraphim.

But he was compelling. His nose was crooked, his chin pugnacious, his shoulders broad, and his eyes dark and piercing. His whole personality simmered as though he were a cauldron. One could not guess at his true nature except in glimpses as it broke the surface.

And now she was being just fanciful.

But when he took her hand and put his other to her waist as they turned and stepped down the line of dancers, she felt a little flushed. He knew the dance, she had to admit. And he did not look as foolish on the floor as she had assumed he would. She regretted her earlier mean-spirited assumptions, and admonished herself that a book would not always be known by its cover, something she should understand better than anyone.

The dance over at last, he walked her back to her chair. She expected him to depart, but he glanced around and then sat beside her. And did not talk. Was his sole purpose of seating himself with her to guard her, like a dog does a bone it does not particularly want but will share with no one?

The thought made her smile; when she looked again at the man next to her it was to gaze directly into his eyes. She swallowed. No, he was not good-looking, but many a woman would swoon at the expression of glinting steel behind the dark eyes. He was brooding, but not in any pretty, Byronic way. She was not a foolish enough woman to find menace fascinating, and yet—

"At whom are you smiling?" he asked, his dark eyes narrowing.

Ariadne rolled her eyes. "I was just thinking how funny it was to have a guardian at this late stage in my life."

"What?"

"Nothing. Are you really a viscount, sir?"

"I am," he said, shifting in his seat as if admitting it made him uneasy. "Lovell Melcher, Viscount Ingram at your service, ma'am," he said, and put out one hand.

"Miss Ariadne Lambert, spinster, at yours, my lord," she said, shaking his hand.

He flashed a smile, and she felt her heart thud. How odd that just the briefest of smiles, there and gone in a heartbeat, should have that effect. Mr. Dorsey was much more free with his, and they did not have near that impact. Perhaps that was the secret.

Spotting Mr. Dorsey lingering in the distance, there one moment and then concealed again by the crowd, Ariadne swallowed. She turned to Ingram and desperately scrabbled for conversation. "I have three cats, my lord, whom I have named Prinny, Maria, and Caroline. Prinny, as you may have guessed, is the tom, and he spends his time mostly with Maria; oddly enough, he despises Caroline and they hiss at each other whenever forced to share the same bowl of milk. Do you think I forced that relationship on the three when I named them?"

Ingram gazed at her with a furrowed brow. "Really, uh, I do not know," he said. He glanced around and rose. "I have business to attend to. Your servant, Miss Lambert."

Ariadne sighed. "Good evening, my lord." Now that she had chased him away, she felt bereft. How silly. But now she could go on with her evening's plans. She rose, patted down her ugly skirts, and began to circle the ballroom.

* * *

"He got away, Olivia. I could just strangle that man with my own bare hands." Ariadne Lambert was walking with her friend in the front garden of her Chelsea home the morning after the ball.

Olivia Beckwith, whom Ingram would have recognized as the gossipy matron, frowned. "Strangling Dorsey would not serve, Ari. It would . . ."

"No, my dim friend. Dorsey got away; I was not able to tempt him back to my side at all. And I could strangle Lord Ingram for causing it. He frightened my quarry away with his dark looks. I would almost think there was something between them. Is it possible they are confederates and the viscount was warning Dorsey?"

Olivia considered it as she plucked a full-blown rose and twirled it under her nose. "I do not think so. Ingram is a different sort than Dorsey. Just as dangerous, but in another way entirely."

"How so?" Ariadne took a seat on a carved wooden bench overlooking the river and patted the spot beside her. She would never admit to her friend that she found the brooding viscount intriguing, attractive even. She was *not* some gothic heroine, to be drawn to danger. She was just evaluating a man who could be allied with the enemy.

"Mmm, he is a dangerous man to cross, I have heard. And he has a despicable reputation."

"Despicable?"

Olivia leaned toward her friend, the signal that truly delicious gossip was about to be imparted. "Despicable. At the age of just three-and-twenty, it is rumored that he . . . er . . . forcibly seduced a married woman."

"Forcibly seduced?" Ariadne frowned and cocked her head sideways. "Olivia, what *does* that mean?"

The woman colored. "Best not to ask, Ariadne. Especially someone like you."

Someone like her? Ariadne shook her head. "The man is well into his thirties. Has that scandal lasted all this time?"

"Oh, no, there is more. He went into business with a number of men, but when they lost everything—a ship sank, or some such thing—he was said to have cheated the investors of their money.''

''Olivia! 'It is rumored,' 'He is said to have done this.' None of it is fact.''

''You have seen his face. The man has a reputation as a fighter and he does not fight by any recognized rules. Last night he was seen beating poor Sir Jeremy May in an alley behind the house.''

Ariadne turned away and stared down at the sparkling river as her friend chattered on. A barge on its way to London took advantage of the current to make time on its run. She watched, absently, counting automatically the vessels making their voyages, noting the different ways lowly scow and stately sail craft slipped through the flow.

She didn't want to admit it. Pushing back stray tendrils of stubborn hair loosened by the stiffening breeze, she put her head back, easing the tension knotted in her neck muscles, as Olivia still rambled on. No, for some reason she didn't want to concede that Lord Ingram was a nasty lot, a brute and a villain. An unrepentant rogue.

And yet, she must acknowledge the likelihood. It was not the first she had heard of the viscount. He was reckoned a bad enemy to make, drifting on the outside of Society, barely admitted to ballrooms. She had never seen him before last night, and it appeared that she was as foolish as any other woman she had ever castigated for an idiot. She did not want to believe the gossip, did not want to admit that it was possibly true, and all because of a moment's powerful attraction to his undeniably masculine presence.

Ultimately it did not matter what she believed him to be, because it certainly did not make sense that he was in with Dorsey on his swindles. Dorsey had appeared afraid of the other man. And so Ingram did not figure at all in her plans. Which, thinking of that, they must just alter, as the night before had not worked out quite as they had planned. She would forget Ingram and concentrate on the task at hand.

And until then she would go back to work.

She stood. ''Olivia, you must excuse me. If you hear where Dorsey is to be next, let me know; I will need an invitation. Until then I must get back to work.''

Chapter Three

Ingram handed the wizened fellow a half crown, and peered at him through the thick cloud of smoke that was an ineffable part of the infamous Battersea tavern, the Jolly Roger. It was a place where if you were wise, you watched your back, and yet Ingram felt completely at home, the misspent years of his youth preparing him far better to be a denizen of one of these taverns than to grace a ballroom floor. "So, what have you heard?"

"Feller in livery stable of th' rooms Dorsey an' that doxy whut 'e calls 'is sister lives in, 'e says Dorsey were boastin' o' the juicy nest 'e were goin' ta land in come a week or two from now."

"Is that it?" Ingram asked, ready to snatch back the half crown.

"No yer don't!" The fellow clutched it in his grimy fist and stuck it down his even grimier pants. "Better'n better. 'E says 'e's a goin' ta . . ." The old man glanced around and leaned closer to Ingram, and then whispered a string of words containing several very nasty words for copulation.

Ingram felt his stomach turn. So, Dorsey intended to seduce and compromise Miss Lambert, and then threaten to ruin her reputation if she did not hand over a large amount of money. It was the most despicable act yet in a long line of contemptible actions. If revealed, it would send him fleeing out of London and even the country, and would destroy Miss Lambert in the process.

Why did he even care? Miss Lambert was certainly old enough that if she wanted to make a fool of herself, no one could stop her. But this went beyond merely making a fool of herself. The woman appeared to have little social stock but her good name, and Dorsey intended to ruin that. Or seduce her first, and then *threaten* to ruin her. It would be a devastating blow. Ingram had seen how innocent were the woman's eyes; she would be no match for the practiced wiles of a man of Dorsey's stamp, especially as idiotic as she seemed to be. A cat named Prinny! Good God!

Ingram hammered his fist on the table. How did Dorsey get away with it repeatedly? He supposed it was still a sorry old world where a fair face was deemed a reflection of the soul, where good looks were assumed to presage a good heart. It was rarely true. The two had little or nothing to do with each other.

The old man had drifted away, secure with his half crown and now treating his cronies to a round of bitter. Ingram quaffed his own stout, relishing the bitter taste and wiping the foam from his mouth with the back of one hand. He had come looking for information; now, what would he do with it?

Ariadne laid down her quill and cupped her cheek in her hand. Spring sunlight streamed into her study, the room chosen carefully by her as the only ground-floor room that had a view of the river. When she had first seen this Chelsea house, it was the situation overlooking the river that had first attracted her, and then she had entered.

It was a light and airy dwelling, with large square rooms and painted walls, white paneling and marble floors. Modern, clean, filled with light, she had fallen in love with it immediately, but concealing her admiration, she had dickered with the land agent until the price was more to her liking. Frugal by nature, a windfall could not change her now.

And what an unexpected stroke of luck her inheritance had been. Dutiful to the end, Ariadne still had never believed that her vinegary, ancient aunt would leave her fortune any-where but to the charities she had, in her lifetime, supported. So when Ariadne found herself in possession of a fortune beyond what she could have imagined, her first thought had been *what now?* It hadn't taken long to decide. What else would she do but devote herself to the dream of a lifetime, to write and publish a history of the River Thames? And where else to do it but this wonderful study?

And yet this morning the memory of a pair of coal-dark eyes intruded on her work. *Foolish spinster*, she castigated herself, even as she sighed and stared, unseeing, out the window. If even half the rumors about Lord Ingram were true, then his heart was as black as his eyes. And what did she have to remember? The feel of a square hand at her waist, the gleaming depths of his gaze, the gruff tone of his voice. So little. She was not eighteen, that a man's physical attributes or lack thereof should have such weight with her.

And yet she had liked his voice, the burr in it, the honesty. It appealed to her so much more than the soft, caressing tones of Dorsey's expert inflections. It was gruff, deep . . . she caught herself and straightened. "Ariadne Sophia Lam-bert" she said out loud. "You are not going to become that most foolish of things, a lovesick spinster, and over a man whose reputation is so very black! Most idiotic of women, behave and do something constructive."

And so she went out to the garden to pull weeds.

The card room was full to capacity. There was no place to sit, and no card game to join. Ingram drifted to the door and stood, smoking a cigar while he watched the ballroom, noting with amusement the nervous looks cast his way. If he had taken the trouble he probably could have cleansed his reputation long ago. His errors were mostly callow youthful ones, though he still enjoyed a good fight and had a punishing left hook; that much was true.

His gaze drifted, but then sharpened. He straightened, his muscles tensing. Damn and damn again. There she was, and there was that weasel, Dorsey, paying court to her as if she were the Season's diamond.

He butted out his cigar, and straightened his jacket. Fatuous spinster or not, Miss Ariadne Lambert did not deserve to be taken advantage of, and he would take it upon himself to stop him.

Ariadne simpered coyly. "La, Mr. Dorsey, but you do talk such foolishness. A girl might be forgiven for thinking you were a practiced flirt."

Dorsey pressed her hand warmly. "Miss Lambert," he whispered, his tones caressing. "I would never merely flirt with a lady of your caliber. You deserve so much more. My intentions . . . but there. I get ahead of myself."

Sighing inwardly at the role she must play, Ariadne tried again. She swallowed her distaste at the dampness of his palm in the overheated ballroom and turned her hand so it was clasped within his. She widened her eyes and assumed her most beatific, asinine expression. "You may get ahead of yourself as much as you wish, Mr. Dorsey, for who is there to stop you?" She sighed dramatically and glanced away, eyes downcast. "I have no guardian or relative to protect me. I am so *alone* in the great, terrifying world!"

Dorsey moved closer. "No one?"

"Not a single person."

"But who takes care of you?"

"That is left to me," she said with a piteous smile.

"No lady of such tender sensibilities should be left alone to deal with finances. How deplorable! But then, if you do not have much money to worry about . . ."

"But I do! My aunt left me . . . oh, but it is vulgar to speak of sums." Ariadne glanced away to conceal her smile. She was enjoying this far too much. She should be moving on to the resolution of this little game as quickly as possible but she could not help dangling the treat in front of Dorsey's nose, only to snatch it away.

"You could never be vulgar," he murmured.

"You flatter me again, Mr. Dorsey."

"I only speak the truth. How I wish I could be the one to shield you from life's harshness," he said. "But I have no right . . ."

''You have as much right as anyone,'' Ariadne said.

''If only that were true. If only I could prove to you . . . would you meet me somewhere private, Miss Lambert, somewhere where we could discuss . . .''

''I have often longed to go to Vauxhall . . .''

''Highly overrated,'' a deep voice said from above.

Ingram. Ariadne looked up into the dark eyes she had dreamed of the night before. She seemed to have lost her voice and knew her mouth hung foolishly open, her expression as vacuous as any dimwitted gudgeon of more breeding than brains.

Dorsey bolted to his feet. ''Ingram, old man. Thought you never went near ballrooms, and yet here you are . . . *again*.''

''I have come to ask Miss Lambert to stand up with me,'' he said grimly.

Ariadne pressed her lips together and pushed her glasses up on her nose with a swift, impatient gesture. *Infuriating* man. He was asking her to dance yet again, but with a tone of voice that told her it would be more chore than pleasure. Was he merely in competition with Dorsey? Was that the beginning and end of his seeming preference for her company?

''I have no wish to dance,'' she said.

''Are you refusing me?'' Ingram asked, dark brows furrowed.

Ariadne clenched her fists. Dorsey would surely wonder if she did. It would look peculiar, and perhaps there was a way after all to use this odd turn of events. She cast a fluttering glance at Dorsey, eyes wide, as much idiocy as she could feign forced into her smile. ''Why, no! But I must beg leave of Mr. Dorsey, who has been so kind as to sit with me this half hour.''

''You do not need to beg leave of anyone,'' Ingram growled, and took her hand, leading her to the dance floor.

A waltz was just starting, but Ariadne was too busy watching Dorsey, and stepped on the viscount's toes. ''I beg your pardon, sir,'' she said. They bumped into each other and her glasses skewed to one side. She righted them.

''Miss Lambert,'' he said through gritted teeth, facing her and taking her hand in his. ''Mr. Dorsey will not go away, not while he thinks there is a chance of your favor.''

That was enough to gain her attention, and she gazed into his dark eyes. She took a deep breath as he swept her onto the ballroom floor. This was a most unaccustomed feeling. As he had proved in their minuet, he was a rather good dancer, with an athletic grace she would not have thought such a stocky, muscular gentleman would possess. Where Dorsey was lithe and slim, Ingram was heavy-set. Dorsey's cherubic fairness was the opposite of Ingram's swarthy darkness.

She stuttered back into speech, saying, "D-do you think he seeks my favor?"

Ingram's generous mouth turned down in a scowl. "I think he seeks to loosen your purse strings. I must most strenuously warn you, Miss Lambert, not to entertain that scoundrel alone. I have it on good authority that he means to rob you of your money in a most disagreeable way."

Ariadne gasped. This turn of events stunned her. What was Ingram doing, seeking out such information? Was he still playing his own game, as she had conjectured from the beginning? Or was he trying to do her a good turn? She had never heard him spoken of as quixotic, and yet, how else could one interpret this behavior?

He took her speechlessness as horror. "I am sorry if I have shocked you," he said, his voice more gentle but still easily heard through the music. "But Dorsey does not have a good reputation."

"He is invited everywhere, sir." She lost her footing for a moment, but Ingram expertly righted her, and they moved on effortlessly.

"So am I, but that does not mean I am good company." His tone was bitter.

"Are you warning me away from yourself, as well, sir?"

His gaze caught hers and held. There was a searching look in his eyes. The music drifted over them, and in that moment they both seemed to become aware of what they were doing. He was holding her close—closer than before—and they were swaying together, his broad hand at her waist. Her cheeks flushed and she was mortified, worried that he would misinterpret—or would it be only too correct to judge her affected by his nearness?—her pinkness.

"I would ask you to be careful, Miss Lambert. I would not see you hurt."

She swallowed. This was not good. He sounded far too much like the gallant Ingram of her dreams, and she had determined that *that* Ingram was a phantasm raised by her own rich imagination. Everything she had heard of Lord Ingram had served to make her cautious. He was regarded as a blackguard, a dangerous man to cross.

She looked away.

There was Dorsey at the edge of the ballroom, speaking to his sister, if sister she was. Ariadne was not convinced of that. He was glancing their way, and whispering again with the young woman.

And so she must be cruel, must be rude to the viscount, to give him a disgust of her. If Dorsey felt too threatened by Lord Ingram, he might slip off the hook. He did not appear to be the kind who would stand up to a man of Ingram's dangerous stamp.

"I will take your warning under advisement," she said frostily. "Though most assuredly, is that not a case of the pot blackening the reputation of the kettle?"

Unexpectedly, Ingram grinned. The effect was to twist his pugnacious visage and light his dark eyes. "Between the two of us, ma'am, Dorsey and I, there is enough black to spread, trust me."

Feeling her lips twitch, so badly did she want to smile with him, Ariadne assumed instead the faintly idiotic expression she was growing weary of. How awful to make herself appear so in front of a man whom she had reluctantly begun to like. And that after he had already crept into her maidenly dreams. People would be shocked if they knew what kind of dreams Miss Ariadne Lambert experienced, but then, they would be shocked by much of her thinking, if she was so incautious as to reveal her deepest musings.

The music ended, and Ingram returned her to her place. "May I call on you, miss? What day are you at home?"

This unexpected twist left Ariadne genuinely flabbergasted. "I entertain Thursday afternoons."

"Good. I expect I can find out where you live," he said. "I shall get to meet Prinny."

"P-prinny?"

"Your cat." Ingram bowed and pushed through the crowd, toward the card room.

Olivia Beckwith approached Ariadne. "My dear, what are you doing dancing with Ingram? How did that come about?"

"He asked me."

"How strange." Olivia's bright gaze followed Ingram's progress, people parting before him like the sea before Moses. "He never asks ladies to dance."

Ariadne shook herself. "Stranger still, my dear. He asked me to dance to warn me away from Dorsey. Can you credit it?"

Olivia gave a hoot of disbelieving laughter. "Is that not the most . . . oh, dear. I must slither away, Ari. That despicable Dorsey is coming this way and I do not want to be seen talking to you too long. We are supposed to be merest acquaintances." She drew herself up and assumed her haughtiest look, difficult in so plump and pleasant a woman. "My dear Miss Lambert," she said in a stagy voice as Dorsey approached. "You would do well to stay away from men of Lord Ingram's stamp. He can only be trouble for an unwed lady." She serenely cruised away.

Thanking the quick wit that her friend so seldom exhibited, Ariadne put one gloved hand to her forehead.

"Miss Lambert," Dorsey said in melting tones. "Are you unwell? May I be of assistance?"

"Oh, that was a most unpleasant experience. Dancing with Lord Ingram, I mean, not speaking to Mrs. Beckwith."

"Did he upset you? I should challenge the beast!" Dorsey made a feint, as if to go after Ingram. When Ariadne did not catch his arm, as she was expected to, he turned back to her. "But perhaps I can be of more service by staying at your side?"

"I would appreciate your arm, Mr. Dorsey. I feel quite . . . overcome."

"Let me take you to the terrace, Miss Lambert, where you could get a breath of fresh air," Dorsey said.

Ariadne nodded with satisfaction. "I would like that."

"I live to serve you, my dear Miss Lambert."

Chapter Four

Ariadne sniffed the air appreciatively. There was a lingering scent of blooming hawthorn from a tree overhanging the terrace, and something else, something indescribable. Whatever it was made her buoyant, lighthearted, even. She was enjoying this far too much, considering the seriousness of her quest and the importance of success.

Dorsey had her arm and guided her to a dark corner of the terrace. There was a low stone wall, and he seated her there and knelt at her feet. Chafing her hand, he then peeled back the edge of her glove and gently kissed her bare wrist.

His lips were wet.

Resisting the urge to hit him, Ariadne said, with a fatuous giggle, "Mr. Dorsey, you forget yourself!"

"A million pardons," he murmured. "I am overcome."

"You presume upon our acquaintance." She withdrew her hand from his grasp, grateful that her "maidenly confusion" act would cover the fact that she found his touch repulsive.

"I am so sorry," he said, taking a seat beside her on the cool stone.

Ariadne stayed silent. Still puzzling out the other scent on the air, the one she could not identify, she listened to all the night sounds of the city, the clop of horse's hooves, the cry of the night watchman. They were in Mayfair, miles from her Chelsea home, and she longed to be there this minute, in the solitude and shadowed peace of her terraced garden. The dance with Ingram still drifted through her mind, teasing her with unidentified longings that she would not linger over. Her great dread in life was to be ridiculous, and yet she feared she was on the verge of becoming so over a man whose character she worried was not all it should be.

"What did you and Ingram talk about out on the dance floor, Miss Lambert?"

His tone was casual. Too casual. Even if she did not know what he was, her suspicion would be aroused.

"To be honest, Mr. Dorsey," she said, adjusting her spectacles and smoothing down her puce skirts. "We spoke of you."

"Me? What could a creature such as Ingram have to say about me?" His tone was haughty, but there was a tremor concealed by the forceful delivery.

"I take it you do not like each other?"

"I barely know the man. But I have heard . . ."

"Yes?"

"Things no lady should learn of, nor ever will from my lips. Enough to say he is not to be trusted in a situation, say, like this one." He sidled closer to her and pressed his damp palm over her folded hands, the moisture permeating her gloves.

"But how am I to judge? He says things about you; you say things about him. Who should I believe?" She had said it all with a plaintive whine in her voice. This was good. It was actually playing into her hands. She needed to express just enough doubt to not pique his suspicions. Too easy a pigeon, and he would not expose himself so thoroughly as she intended he should.

"I have proof. Did he offer you any proof of *his* nasty lies?"

"Nooo," she said. Her heart thudded. Proof? What would he say? She hated gossip in the ordinary course of life, but some demon tweaked her to ask, "What proof do you have, sir? And of what?"

Another couple drifted out onto the terrace and descended

the stone steps into the garden, disappearing down a path sheltered by a hedge. Dorsey was silent until they disappeared, flirtatious laughter floating behind them, and then he said, "I know the parties in this incident. I would not sully your ears with such a tale, but if you really want to know . . . all right. Ingram, to my certain knowledge, forced himself upon the wife of a very well-known gentleman. If that gentleman had not interrupted, Ingram would have . . . well, ravished her."

"But that is just old gossip, is it not, Mr. Dorsey?" It was what she had heard from Olivia, Ariadne thought. The same accusation seemed to be the only thing ever leveled against Ingram. "Did the lady not have him arrested?"

"Of course not! It would have ruined her to have it known that she had been so close to ravishment."

"Oh."

"Let us not talk of others, Miss Lambert . . . Ariadne. May I call you that?"

"You may," she said, her voice breathy. She tried to get back into character as the dim, fatuous spinster flattered by the good-looking young man's attention. "But only when we are . . . alone."

"I like the way you say that. Alone. I would like to be alone with you. Very alone."

"Would you?" Ariadne wanted to scream with impatience. Dorsey was getting closer, edging toward her. Twice now she had suggested the place they could meet to be private. What more did he need as encouragement? The man was far too cautious for the scoundrel he was. But perhaps that very caution was what had kept him from being found out on numerous occasions.

He was silent, merely pressing her hand with a heartfelt look of adoration.

Women described him as charming, but Ariadne had seen little evidence of that. Perhaps she just did not inspire him as other women had. She was a plain aging spinster, and yet that was just the type of woman men of Dorsey's stamp preyed upon.

Urging him back into speech, she repeated, "Would you *indeed* like to be alone with me . . . Edward?"

"Of course he would." A stocky figure, cigar in hand, stepped out of the shadows. "Then he could convince you to give him all your money or seduce you and threaten to ruin your reputation!"

"Ingram!" Dorsey cried and stood.

Ariadne wanted to scream with frustration. Just when . . . but had he been there the whole time? To hear his own reputation shredded?

As he emerged from the shadows, it was with a detached smile, not at all charming as his grin earlier had been. There was something sinister in his expression, and Ariadne wondered what the truth was. Was he the dastard people called him? And why did he concern himself with her money and the disposal of it?

This situation would take some work if she was to save it. What to do?

"Lord Ingram, I think it is very ill-mannered of you to eavesdrop like that. Not at all what one would expect of a gentleman." She snipped her words off like errant threads, made her tone as prim and foolish as possible. Let Dorsey think she despised Ingram's "low" behavior.

"I am not a gentleman. And neither is Dorsey, here." His drawl was lazy, but his dark eyes snapped. He strolled toward them, flicking ash away and circling the quivering Dorsey like a cat around a mouse.

Worse and worse. Ariadne tore her gaze away from Ingram's powerful form. He was too easy to watch, to admire, and her mind was storing up images that would likely haunt her dreams for many nights. She snapped, "I do not think it is incumbent upon you to decide what Mr. Dorsey is." Oh, dear. That had been incautious, for it was said in her normal tone, not that of the foolish, gullible spinster she was supposed to be.

Ingram's gaze fastened on her. "You puzzle me, Miss Lambert. I had pegged you as a silly woman. I *should* leave you to your own devices. And yet, I sense an intelligence beneath it all."

Oh, very much worse. The one thing she did not want Dorsey to think was that she was intelligent.

She made a moue of distaste. "Oh, my lord, how *cruel*

you are. Of all things, a lady must not be intelligent. I had much rather be thought"—she gagged, but then surged ahead—"pretty."

That had done it, given him the necessary disgust of her. Ingram nodded. "I have told you what I think, Miss Lambert. Just say the word now, and I will leave you with your . . . beau."

Backbone ramrod straight, she lifted her head haughtily. "I would like you to leave us, Lord Ingram."

He bowed, and then fastened his gaze upon Dorsey. "Be warned; I am watching."

Ariadne abandoned her quill and paced the floor. She had not been able to settle to anything all morning. The debacle of the previous night still haunted her, and she could not make up her mind what to do about it. She had hoped to be much farther along now, and yet it did not appear as if she was going to accomplish her goal, and all because of the mysterious Lord Ingram.

Dorsey had skittered off like a frightened beetle after the confrontation, and had said nothing about seeing her again. Frustrated, Ariadne had spent the remainder of the evening delicately sounding out the few she knew at the ball about Lord Ingram.

All agreed that he was a nasty customer to cross. One said that Ingram was a cheat and a thief, while another said that he was, at the very least, honest. Several hauled out the tired old rumor, the one about being caught on the point of ravishing a married woman. Ariadne was sick to death of that one, for no one could name the lady, nor could any ascribe a date to this supposed transgression; if it happened at all, it could have been a year ago or ten years. And yet all agreed it had taken place.

She paced to the window. He was at the very least perspicacious. He had picked out her intelligence, and she could not think of a thing she had done that had revealed that, except for a vague *something* in her tone. But a scoundrel could still be smart. And compelling.

As she pondered she realized that she had smelled his

cigar; that was the indefinable scent on the terrace she had liked so much. It had been *his* scent, memorized from their dance together, a blend of smoke and male musk.

All right, so she was attracted to him. She gave in to the knowledge, still not sure why it was so. He was not good-looking in any classic way. He was dark and solid and hard-featured.

But he made her feel . . . womanly. They were of a height, and yet she did not feel ungainly with him. She was intelligent, but she did not feel superior to him, sensing a mental acuity at least the equal of her own. Her besetting sin was a tendency to look down on those with less in the brainbox than herself. His masculinity was thrilling and enticing, calling out to something within her she had never suspected was there, a longing to walk closer to danger, to reach out and touch fire.

And yet there was no fear—or hope—that it would go past what it now was, an acquaintance formed by him for the purpose of warning her about Dorsey. He was certainly the kind of man who would look for at least beauty in a woman, if not sophistication and elegance. She could boast none of those attributes. Her strength lay in her intelligence and a ruthless honesty. But he *had* bothered about her. Worried about her.

Why did he care?

"Miss, someone at th' door," Dolly, her maid, said, poking her head into the room.

"Dolly, how many times have I told you that while I am working, I will not be disturbed?"

"Oh, Ari, it is just me!" Olivia burst in and bustled over to the window where Ariadne had stopped her pacing. "I have the most delicious news. And a triumph, of sorts."

"Dolly, tea please," Ariadne said, with a warning glance for her exuberant friend.

The maid closed the door behind her, and Olivia laughed. "My dear, you are too cautious! She is just a maid."

"There speaks a woman who never ventures below stairs in her own house," Ariadne said dryly. "You would be horrified not only by how much your servants know about you, but also how much they see fit to gossip about, and to whom they divulge their information. Anyone with a ha'penny would know the secrets of your boudoir.''

"It doesn't matter," Olivia said, waving her hands, a letter clasped in one of them. "We are almost successful. A few days only and we will see our plan complete.''

"What do you mean? I told you what happened on the terrace last night. Dorsey will never come near me now.''

"Oh, yes he will. I spoke to his ... ahem, 'sister' just this morning. She approached me at Gunter's, and gave me a message for you. From Dorsey!''

Ariadne's eyes widened and she drew her friend down to sit in a couple of hard chairs that were drawn up to a table by the window. "Tell me all!''

"No, first things first! I will tell you what I heard after you left last night.''

Dolly brought the tea tray and set it down with a *plunk* and a slosh. *I really ought to discharge that girl,* Ariadne thought, and then abruptly dismissed it from her mind as the maid left the room. "What have you heard? If it is just gossip, you know I do not care for it.''

"Ah, but you will when you hear who it concerns.''

Ariadne poured, waiting patiently as Olivia drew off her gloves.

"I was waiting for my carriage in the anteroom,'' she finally said, "when I overheard two men quarreling. This is not gossip, my dear, but direct hearsay!''

Ariadne did not correct her friend's word usage, but listened.

"One of the men was Lord Duncannon. He is that Scottish laird, you know. And he was speaking to ... *Lord Ingram!* I would know that ill-tempered growl anywhere. Sounds exactly like my husband when he first awakens.''

"And so?''

"So, it is what they were saying! My dear, Duncannon told Ingram that he had better get the money to him soon, or it would be '*too late.*' ''

"What?''

"Ariadne ... it would be '*too late*'. That is a threat! Ingram must owe Duncannon money and is unable to pay him back. Or perhaps blackmail for some indiscretion of

Ingram's! In either case, it clearly indicates he is out of funds! Perhaps he has spied you out for himself, and is trying to cut Dorsey out. Is that not interesting?''

Ariadne felt a pang. Unfortunately, it all made too good sense. She had just been wondering why Ingram was bothering about her, but if he needed money, and she had been pointed out as wealthy . . . he was no better than Dorsey after all.

She took a sip of tea and composed herself. She could not trust her voice just yet, and so she motioned to the letter on the table as she sipped.

"Ah, yes," the other woman said. "The letter. It is a note to you from Dorsey. Open it!"

"You already know its contents, I do not doubt."

Shamefaced, Olivia nodded. "I could not resist."

Opening the letter and holding it up to the light, Ariadne adjusted her glasses. It was a brief note, poorly spelled. *My deer Miss Lambert*, it read. *I kno there are Thos who would miss represent me, but I wish to Tell You All. Meet me at Voxall Friday nite and we can bee privat. Your dev'ted servent, etc., Dorsey.*

"The idiot does not say when or where to meet him!" Ariadne exclaimed.

"His 'sister' said about seven, at the gate."

They discussed their plans, bickering over them, now that it appeared they were coming to fruition. Ariadne was in a contrary state of mind, and she did not want to think too deeply why that was so. By the time Olivia left she had a headache, something that generally only happened when she had been working too hard.

But she should be glad Dorsey had not been frightened off, after all. He must be truly desperate. And so must Ingram.

She sourly decided that no more work would get done that day, and was just ready to climb the stairs for a nap when a knock came at the door. "Dolly! *Dolly*! Oh, heavens." She went to answer it herself and pulled it open with an angry jerk.

There, standing on her pristine doorstep, was Lord Ingram himself.

Chapter Five

He was no better-looking in the light of day than by candlelight, but unfortunately he still appealed to her just as much. She was speechless.

"Miss Lambert," he said. "May I come in? You did say you entertain on Thursdays?"

She silently stood back and then bustled past him, leading the way into her drawing room. He followed and glanced appreciatively around, and then frowned. "Somehow I expected Prinny and Maria and Caroline to have pride of place in your drawing room, Miss Lambert. Silk cushions, bowls of cream." He paused. "Diamond collars."

"I beg your pardon?"

"Your cats," he said, gazing at her thoughtfully as he strolled the perimeter of the room, touching a Rouen jardiniere that held a jade plant, and then stopping to admire a wood piece on a gilt stand. "What is this?" he asked, reaching out and tracing the carving.

"It is a carved finial from a pew in a Norman church that was torn down many years ago in my home village. I rescued it. They were going to use it for firewood."

He touched it lightly. "Lovely carving. How many would think of making it such an interesting object of statuary?" He straightened and gazed at her again.

She shrugged.

"So where are they?"

"What?"

"Where are Prinny *et al.*?"

"Oh. Dead."

"All of them?"

Ariadne snapped back to her senses. "Non-existent, merely. I was having fun with you the other night, my lord. My own little joke. I have no cats. I dislike them."

"Really? I rather like cats. They generally have impeccable taste in humans, and they are smart and calculating. I like intelligent beasts. And intelligent humans."

She was *not* going to ask him to sit down, nor would she give him tea. She crossed her arms over her chest, and stared at him as he stalked the room. It was no wonder he liked cats; he was very much like them, prowling and stopping to evaluate objects, touching her favorite brass bowl and a Waterford crystal decanter. What was he doing there? What was his purpose?

He walked toward her desk by the window and she tensed; had she left the note from Dorsey out? She could not remember and could not see from her viewpoint by the door. But he merely glanced at the desk and then strolled to the window.

"You have a lovely view here," he said, staring out the window. "I own some property in Chelsea, but I have not yet developed it. Your house gives me the impetus I have been needing."

"What do you mean, my lord?" Reluctantly, she moved from the door and joined him at the window.

"I like your house very much. It is modern. Airy. I live in a convoluted medieval horror in the heart of the old city; this is much more to my liking."

"I am overjoyed that you approve," she said.

His gaze swung to meet hers, and she was caught once again by the intelligence gleaming in his dark eyes.

"Sarcasm. I like that in a woman."

"Do you indeed?"

"Yes. Don't suppose you would care to sell me your house?"

"No," she snapped. "Lord Ingram, what do you want?"

She was sorry the moment the words came out of her mouth. People seldom rattled her equilibrium, but Ingram was successful whenever he tried. It was irritating. She bit her lip. How could she descend back into the idiocy she had been trying to feign without Ingram becoming suspicious?

The gleam died and his eyes became flat, unreadable. "I want to know why you are encouraging Dorsey."

She wanted to tell him that was none of his business. She wanted to ask him why he cared. But neither of those responses would further her aims. She simpered and widened her eyes in a counterfeit of coquetry. "Mr. Dorsey is a very handsome man, do you not think so?"

"Oh, he is that. Is that the beginning and end of your attraction to him?"

She gritted her teeth. "Need there be more?"

His expression inscrutable, he said, "I suppose not. I should take my leave, Miss Lambert. I was curious about your house. Now that I have seen it, I am curious about you. But common courtesy dictates I take my leave."

"I am surprised you are bound by the laws of courtesy, even the *common* variety," she snapped.

He grinned, that unexpectedly attractive expression she had surprised him into before. "I cannot help but think that there is more to you than I have yet discovered, Miss Lambert."

"I think you will find I am exactly what I appear to be, Lord Ingram."

"If I knew what that was, I would know how to think of you," he answered. He bowed. "I will leave you to ... whatever you were about to do."

Friday was dull and rainy, but by afternoon the weather had cleared and Ariadne stood staring into her wardrobe, nervously fretting over her clothing. It was a problem, dressing to appear like a fatuous fool. Her taste in garb was simple. She liked good fabrics, now that she had the money to indulge that taste, and clean lines. She had no illusions about her figure; she was thin and angular, and would not stoop to cotton wadding to amplify what nature had seen fit to deny. Nor would any amount of lace compensate.

But for this evening she must appear to be a fool convinced that she was about to embark on a romantic adventure. How had she been drawn into this ridiculous undertaking? When Olivia had first approached her with the tale of Dorsey's predation on a dear friend, her fertile mind had unfortunately been tickled by the idea of setting a trap; but she had not at first thought the bait would be herself, until her friend had pointed out how perfect she was to play the part. Ariadne had admitted that she was relatively unknown to those of the *ton*, so her intelligence or lack thereof would be unascertained, and she had enough truth in her tale to make the story ring true.

She had, indeed, tended an ailing aunt for many years, and been left her fortune. That she had done it out of love and gratitude, not need, was not an issue that needed to be canvassed. The simple fact was, she was now what she called wealthy, in that she had been able to purchase this house and devote herself to her work. Never again would she need to find employment or scrape to get by.

And so it made a perfect story. Olivia had pointed out that when they were both girls at school, Ariadne had been inordinately fond of amateur theatrics. What she did not say but they both knew, was that she was also of a "certain age" and unmarried, and, most people would assume, desperate; added to all that, she was plain. The only thing left to ask was, could she play the part of a wealthy idiot?

She had made up her mind to try. She was not, however, willing to invest the kind of money it would take to buy an entire wardrobe of ugly clothing befitting that character. And so she must make do with what she had and find a way to dress it up.

She reached into her wardrobe and pulled out her least favorite dress. As the fool she wanted to appear, she must alter the gown somewhat, and she needed the help of someone with abominable taste. "Dolly!" she shouted, leaning out the door and staring down the hall. "I need your help."

*   *   *

Ingram strolled past the entrance to Vauxhall, wondering if he had misread the note on the desk in Miss Lambert's elegant drawing room. He had only a second or two to peruse it, scanning it and committing it to memory in a way he did not truly understand but had employed on previous occasions. It was almost as if his eyes recorded a visual record of the note for him to read at his convenience. But it was not a perfect skill. It could have been a future Friday to which the note referred.

But logic told him it would be soon, for men of Dorsey's stamp did not pursue their objects in a leisurely fashion. He would not put it off to a future Friday, and so it must be this day.

He scanned the crowd and his senses sharpened as the familiar silhouette of Miss Ariadne Lambert emerged from the crowd. Familiar, and yet different somehow. He watched her for a moment, taking in the hideous confection of mint green overdressed with blond lace that she wore. Why would she choose that gown, of all possible colors? Green made her look sallow, washing out her coloring.

And there was indeed something different in her silhouette ... something ... Lord, she had padded her bosom! He rolled his eyes. She must be an idiot if she thought Dorsey or any man would not notice the difference immediately and attribute it to cotton wadding. She was alone, and he was about to join her to make sure Dorsey did not achieve his object that night, when a better idea occurred to him. Miss Lambert would never be satisfied until she learned the truth of Dorsey's character. So let her find out the truth. And he would be there to soften the blow, and make sure she did not lose her reputation. Then he would work out the puzzle of Miss Ariadne Lambert, who appeared at times so sharp and intelligent, and then descended so rapidly into idiocy.

He slipped behind a taller, broader figure and entered Vauxhall with a group of ladies and gentlemen.

Chapter Six

Ingram strolled along the infamous Lover's Walk of Vaux-hall smoking a cigar, letting the smoke curl up past his nostrils and eddy into the dark. He could hear the lilt of a waltz from the orchestra and the sounds of lovers cooing in the dim, leafy recesses of the walk. He had left Dorsey and Miss Lambert behind in their private booth, having dinner. He had heard quite enough of the rascal's flattery, and the lady's simpering giggles. Why he gave a damn he did not know, but Dorsey deserved a comeuppance. He had preyed upon innocent women—women whose only fault was stu-pidity—for too long.

He did not want Miss Lambert to suffer their fate—penury, and abandonment. Was it just the lady's contradic-tory nature, and the curiosity she engendered within him? He could not reason away the two disparate halves of the lady in question's personality. When with Dorsey she appeared the complete fool. Apart from him, she seemed a rational human being, even an unusually intelligent one at times.

But she would not be the first intelligent woman to become a fool for love. He pondered the subject while he strolled, waiting the requisite length of time it would likely take for them to consume their dinner and for the gentleman to propose a stroll down the caliginous avenues of the Lover's Walk.

He had known another woman who had allowed love to blind her. His youth had been spent on the streets of London as the forgotten branch of the title which he now held. There was a young woman there—a girl, really—who had been kind to him, but whose lover had been surpassing cruel. He had tried, but been unable to save her from her own poor judgment. She had died, pregnant and abandoned, in a sponging house.

A few short years later the serpentine twists of fate saw him elevated to the title of viscount. The lessons of his youth had never been forgotten; he would share his good fortune. Money as money did not appeal to him. It was only good for the use to which it could be put.

And he did use it, though few in Society knew that.

What it could not do was repair his reputation, earned when his title was new and he was naive. Too proud, or just too stubborn to make an effort, he did not have the knack of making friends among the *ton*. It took something he was not in possession of, an insouciance, a devil-may-care attitude that he just could not cultivate.

And that was the very heart of the problem.

As much as he denied it, he cared. He cared too damn much. No matter what people thought—and he knew what they thought, for far too many were willing to tell him— he *did* care about his dismal reputation. But pride, which he possessed in abundance, made him unwilling to do the social mending, the small talk, the making up to the right people, that it would require to encourage a forgetful mindset. If he would have publicized the many good deeds he did . . . but there. That was impossible, for his motives for what he did were buried deep within him and to have them canvassed by the general public would make him uneasy.

And so he existed in uneasy limbo, not a part of Society, and yet by virtue of his title, not to be disregarded.

In most cases he did not regret the few invitations denied him, but there were people he would like to meet on friendly terms, but whose poor opinion had been ensured by gossip. In an odd twist, he was invited almost everywhere and yet welcome nowhere. He went to spite those who would snub him. And he lurked on the sidelines making everyone uncomfortable.

He glanced at his pocket watch in the dim light shed by a fairy lantern, and then made his way back to the entrance of the walk. By his estimate he should have several minutes to wait before they made their way toward the walk—surely maidenly modesty on her part would make her pull back, hesitate—but no, there they were! Thank God he had not strolled longer or he would have missed them. He slipped into a gap in the grove of trees and extinguished his cigar.

Tedious. The man was tedious beyond belief. So hideously tiresome was his company that Ariadne was tempted to botch the whole episode and leave any woman who was idiotic enough to enjoy Dorsey's company to be taken advantage of as she surely deserved.

But no. This was for Olivia and her friend, Henrietta Godersham. The woman, a widow of good and solid reputation and of an even more solid figure, had been seduced by Dorsey and then had written some desperately improper letters to him—Olivia had seen one and assured Ariadne that they were intensely improper in their sexual detail—reminding him of what they had been to each other, and asking him to take her back into his arms and his bed. He had taken large sums of money from her already, but had fled her bed, presumably upon sighting a more tempting purse. Dorsey had apparently degenerated to practicing blackmail. He told Mrs. Godersham that without substantial and regular payments he would divulge all, publish the letters, and let her be incarcerated in Bedlam for "nymphomania," a lunacy that afflicted the female half of creation only. There was no corresponding name for a similar male affliction, Ariadne wryly reflected.

Ariadne glanced over at Dorsey. How this pallid, doltish, unctuous, fawning fellow could have inspired such febrile fantasies, she would never understand. Mrs. Godersham must indeed be a desperate woman to entertain flights of sexual fantasy about such an anemic and bloodless young man.

Now if it was Ingram—

She wisely left behind that line of thought for the time when she would be alone to enjoy it.

Dorsey guided her toward the entrance to the Lover's Walk.

She drew back. "Oh, sir, I do not think it right for us to walk thither!" she said, despising the sound of her own voice, lifted in breathless, girlish accents ill-suited to both her intelligence and her mature appearance. But the hideously transformed dress helped her attain the correct attitude, and Dorsey seemed wholly convinced.

"Miss Lambert," he said, in wounded tones. "Do you not think that your gentle, unassuming manners are first in my mind? I would never guide you to any place or occupation that I thought would shock or dismay you."

In faltering tones, she said, "But I have heard that gentlemen . . ."

When she did not go on, Dorsey bent his head toward her and said, "Yes?" in a caressing tone.

Now was the moment. With all the latent skill in acting she hoped she possessed, Ariadne looked at him with wide eyes, and injected a trembling note of quivering, breathless excitement into her words. "I have heard," she whispered, "that gentlemen, on occasion, will try to . . . kiss a girl on the walk!" She covered her mouth with her hand and giggled.

She could see the ill-concealed derision in his expression as he replied, "Ladies only get kissed on the Lover's Walk if they really want to, so mind you are not so naughty as to ask for it!"

She screamed in shock and playfully hit his arm.

He winced and rubbed it, then took her hand in his and pulled her down the dark walkway.

Ariadne felt a qualm, for Dorsey's hand was much stronger than she thought it would be, and held hers in an iron grip. But there were people all around, and she was safe, she reminded herself. This was just the next stage of the game, where the trap would be baited and the hook set.

Then, when the correct moment came, Dorsey would be revealed for the scoundrel he was. And made to pay.

Ingram slipped through the darkness, his eyesight and senses sharpening. Whisperings and murmurs came to him, voices and hushed pleas. Ladies giggled, their swains pleaded, mouths met, and hands slid and rustled over silk and cashmere. And then he heard the tone he was listening for. He slid past a branch and felt for the pathway that was close.

"Sir, it is so very dark!"

That was Miss Lambert's voice. Or one of her voices, for the fatuous tone was not the one she used when speaking to him. But then, she was not attracted to him as she was to Dorsey. The thought irritated him.

"Ariadne," came Dorsey's fawning tone. "Oh, Ariadne, if I could but tell you . . ."

"Sir! You forget yourself!"

"Oh, my dear lady, my deepest apologies, but I am a mere man, after all, and weak."

"I forgive you," she whispered.

"Would you forgive me if I did this?"

A scream and a giggle answered whatever incursions on her modesty Dorsey made. Ingram was about to turn to leave—if she truly wanted the pestilential idiot, then let her have him—but he could not abandon a lady of such good repute to the machinations of a practiced swindler like Dorsey. She did not know his true nature, after all, even though he had tried to warn her.

Ingram frowned into the dark. Why had she not listened to him? One would think she would at least ask for details. When he again paid attention to the pair, he could hear nothing but a muffled snuffling and a grunt.

Then—

"Mr. Dorsey . . . Edward . . . you make me forget my proper upbringing! My Aunt Constance would be shocked if she saw me now!"

"Your aunt?"

"Yes. I looked after her for the last years of her life. She told me a lady's reputation is like brass. She must polish it and care for it or it will become sullied.''

"You were truly blessed to have such a sterling character as your . . . aunt, you say? Did she pass away?''

"Yes, poor *dear* Aunt Constance. I was ever so surprised at the will reading, you know, to hear that she had left me all her vast estate! I never thought such a thing. I really do not know what to do with it all but leave it with my banker, for I do not understand the first thing about money, you know, and it is such a vast amount. Ladies do not, I fear, have very practical minds. I have made a will, but all I can think to do is leave it to the care of my cats, Prinny, Maria, and Caroline, and to a foundling hospital. I have no husband . . . or . . . or children of my own.''

"Would you like to marry?''

Ingram gritted his teeth. How foolish could she be to maunder on about her money to a virtual stranger! It was an invitation to thievery! And why was she speaking about her nonexistent cats again? Was she attics to let?

"I would like it above all things,'' she said in a breathless, girlish voice. "To have a gentleman to take care of all my finances, and . . . me.''

"Oh, Ariadne, the man would be blessed indeed to have you, such a . . . such a handsome woman . . .''

There was a rustling for a moment, and then a shriek of dismay. Ingram tensed. It was getting late; the walk was deserted now.

"Mr. Dorsey!''

Miss Lambert's voice was muffled; when she shrieked again and the sound of a branch breaking reached Ingram, he made his move.

Chapter Seven

Ariadne felt Dorsey's hand crawl up to her cotton-wadding bosom and she shrieked with what she hoped was convincing fervor. Now she would swoon and Olivia would—

As she began to close her eyes on the dim pathway, she heard a hoarse, angry shout, and felt a thud beside her as a handful of the cotton wadding was ripped from the low neckline of her hideous dress. It was certainly not the cotton wadding that had made such a noise. She screamed again and opened her eyes on a struggle; two figures—one of them certainly Dorsey—lashed about on the pathway, then with a shriek, her supposed swain struggled to his feet, shoved his assailant toward Ariadne, and fled along the path.

The stocky villain, off balance from Dorsey's quick movement, stumbled and landed on her. Not one to suffer the indignity of being robbed, she did what came naturally.

"Ow! For God's sake, Miss Lambert, let go of my ear!"

Ariadne released from her teeth the fleshy, and now bleeding, part of her "assailant" and stared up at him in the dimness. At that moment Olivia Beckwith, out of breath, erupted from the bushes.

"Aha, Dorsey! You are caught now. You will marry this young lady . . . or . . . suffer . . . the . . ." Eyes wide, Olivia said, "Ari, what on earth are you doing lying on the ground under Lord Ingram?"

"I am wondering the same thing." Heart thudding like
an infantry drum, Ariadne felt the unaccustomed weight of
the man on top of her, and then met his eyes. In the dim
light shed by a fairy lantern, she saw the utter confusion on
his face as he held his poor ear. And she burst into inappropriate laughter.

After a second's pause he did the same, rolling off her
and putting out his free hand, while he still gustily guffawed.
He helped her to her feet and wiped his eyes, wet from tears
of laughter. They both noticed her newly unbalanced figure
at the same time—she was lopsided from the lack of wadding—and fresh gales of laughter rippled over them as Ariadne held one hand to her bosom.

But inevitably the laughter died. And then they stood
staring at each other, with Olivia's bemused glance going
from one to the other.

"I think, Miss Lambert, that it is time you told me what
the devil is going on, because I cannot believe for a second
that a woman of your character and intelligence would actually harbor feelings for that scoundrel."

Ariadne gazed at him steadily for a moment; then, not
letting her eyes wander, she said, "Olivia, I think he is right.
I am not going to have a moment's peace until I tell him
what we are up to and why. It is likely all ruined now
anyway. Dorsey has run from my impetuous rescuer—I
assume that is what you thought you were doing, sir?—like
a rabbit from a wolf."

"But Ari . . ."

"My house in Chelsea. Tomorrow morning at ten, my
lord," she said to Ingram. "And not a moment sooner, if
you please. And have your valet see to your ear."

Ariadne bustled around her drawing room, making sure
the crystal was polished, pulling back the gauzy curtains to
show the view of the sun sparkling off the water of the
Thames. She couldn't imagine why she was nervous. After
the debacle of the previous evening—Dorsey had been
nowhere in sight when the threesome had emerged from
the Lover's Walk and departed—there was no point in the

charade anymore, and so telling Ingram the whole story was a wasted effort. But she wanted to. She wanted to talk to him without having to pretend to be an idiot.

Not that she had remembered to most of the time. He had a way of keeping her off-kilter, never knowing what to expect next.

He must have seen the note from Dorsey on the desk and read it in the very brief time he had, as he strolled past her desk during his Thursday visit. But why did he come to her rescue, a foolish spinster in his eyes?

Olivia was supposed to arrive first, but when Dolly showed in the first visitor, of course it was Ingram. Her friend had never been on time for anything in her life, even her own wedding.

He sauntered into the room, and Ariadne felt foolishly exposed. For seeing him again brought back all the forbidden feelings she had experienced when she first realized who it was lying on top of her in the dim recess of the Lover's Walk. Luckily, laughter had come next, along with the discovery of her depleted anatomy, and it had considerably eased the tension between them.

But now she felt it all again, the untenable pounding of her heart, the unexpected rush of something unnameable. She felt hot, but would not allow herself to look away from his dark eyes. His very *fine* dark eyes. He was still not a handsome man, but his parts, taken separately, were attractive: the dark piercing eyes under heavy eyebrows, the handsome mouth, the corner of which lifted in a quirky, attractive grin on very rare occasion, the powerful broad shoulders and muscular legs.

The bandaged ear.

He had greeted her, and she was staring inanely at him like an automaton doll. She jerkily moved forward and offered her hand.

"Lord Ingram, welcome once again to my home."

"Thank you. For a moment I thought you had forgotten inviting me."

"Of course not. I may have had to appear foolish on occasion, but I assure you, I am not wandering. My faculties are all quite sharp."

"As are your teeth." He ruefully touched his ear. "Yes, I had come to the conclusion that you are an extraordinarily intelligent woman. So why the charade for Dorsey? Do you really care for him? Is it to soothe his fragile self-image? You would not be the first lady to pretend to be less than she is to catch a beau."

"I had rather we wait for Olivia," Ariadne said, indicating a chair by the window. "Will you have a seat, sir? I will have Dolly bring in coffee. Unless you would prefer something stronger?"

"Coffee is fine. But I do not see the need to wait for Mrs. Beckwith when she so clearly already knows the whole story, and in fact is playing some part."

Ariadne admitted the truth of his statement. When Dolly arrived with the coffee tray and had been dismissed, she crossed and closed the door firmly behind her maid, and, coming back to the table by the window, poured heavy mugs of coffee for both of them.

"First, sir, I must apologize for biting you last night. I thought you were an unknown attacker."

"Apology accepted, Miss Lambert. And I apologize for landing on you with all my considerable weight. Dorsey caught me off guard. I expected him to fight, not attempt to flee immediately."

"Apology accepted." She handed him a cup and offered him cream, which he took. She left her own black and sugarless. She remembered in that moment the conversation Olivia had overheard between Ingram and Lord Duncannon. Was she making a mistake in trusting him? Did it really matter now?

It did not. "About Olivia, I suppose we must now say that she *was* playing a part. We should speak of it all in the past tense now, for Dorsey is surely lost to us."

"I take it I have befouled a plan to trap Dapper Dorsey?" He stirred his coffee, then crossed his legs and sipped the strong brew, sighing with satisfaction.

She nodded, studiously keeping her eyes away from his powerful legs.

"Why did you not tell me I was interfering early on,

when I was clearly complicating things by insistently saving you from him?''

She stayed silent. What could she say? She stared into her cup and chewed her lip.

"Of course," he said, nodding with sudden understanding. "You didn't *know* you could trust me to leave you be. Didn't know you could trust me at all."

"You have an . . . uneven reputation."

He grinned and she found herself smiling over at him.

"Miss Lambert, there is no need to mince words. My reputation is murky at best, black as night at worst."

And not justified. Somehow she felt that, though she would never be able to put that feeling into words. She edged toward verbalizing her feelings. "I didn't quite believe it. People kept telling me the same stale story over and over as proof of your perfidy, but there was no lady's name attached, nor time frame; it just did not hold together."

"Oh, but it is quite true, as far as it goes."

"What?"

"I assume you speak of the old scandal, my being accused of near rape?" His voice was hard and his eyes glittered.

Her cheeks burned and she nodded.

"You didn't believe it?"

She shook her head and his dark eyes lost some of their hard gleam.

"I . . ." She hesitated. She had been called honest to a fault. If she said something, it had to be the truth. "I still do not believe it."

His dark gaze softened, and the touch of it was almost physical as he stared deep into her eyes. "You are the first person ever to say that," he said, and cleared his throat. "It is true that I was accused of trying to rape a woman." He gazed out the window and furrowed his brow. "I was twenty-three, and I fell in love . . ."

"You do not have to explain," she said, her fist closing over the soft material of her elegant skirt.

"I know I don't have to." He gave her a crooked smile. "But I will anyway. You have honored me with your belief; I will justify it, if I can." Taking a moment to compose himself, he again stared out the window. "I do love your view, Miss Lambert. You have impeccable taste."

"Thank you. It is the reason I bought this house."

"Anyway, I fell in love. With a married woman much older than I." The words came out in jerky half sentences. "It was just after I attained my title. She was angry at her husband—he had taken a mistress of whom the wife did not approve—but I did not know that then. She arranged for him to catch us, to . . ." He frowned. "To catch us in the . . . the act. She wanted him to be jealous, to feel as she felt. Someone else was with him, though, and so the story spread. To save his wife's reputation—or perhaps the poor fool believed it—he told everyone that I was trying to ravish her, and that he rescued her from me."

"But it wasn't true," Ariadne said.

"Rather hard to ravish a woman when she is on top of one," he said with a wry grin.

Ariadne looked away in embarrassment.

"I'm sorry, Miss Lambert. That was an inappropriate story and a wholly unsuitable remark to make to a lady."

She let him think that was the genesis of her blush. How could she say it was still the memory of his powerful form on top of her, and how his words made her think of that again? She had dreamed of it the night before, for it was the closest she had ever come to being seduced, strangely enough, and it had left her feeling oddly breathless. But he would never know that.

Ever.

"Let me tell you about my dealings with Dorsey, such as they are," she said, pouring more coffee in his empty cup.

Olivia Beckwith had a widowed friend, Ariadne told him, without mentioning the lady's name. The woman was lonely, and wealthy. Dorsey was full of flattery and handsome. The outcome was inevitable; the widow was indiscreet and wrote letters, and now she was being forced to pay to keep those letters a secret. He was blackmailing her.

Ingram gulped his coffee and slammed the mug down on the mahogany table, making the vase in the middle jump. Ariadne pushed it back to the exact center.

"Filthy bloodsucker. How he gets away with such behavior, I do not understand," he grunted. He folded his arms across his chest. "He continually does such despicable things, but because no woman is willing to accuse him outright, he skirts the edge of respectability. A smoother rascal I have never encountered. When I saw him setting you up to take advantage of . . . well, it was more than I could bear."

"Why?" The question was out and hung in the air. Ariadne waited breathlessly.

He shrugged. "I just thought it was time to end his incursions on the feminine half of creation. I hate his type—smug, oily, oozing through life on charm. I could never see what ladies like about him."

Disappointed in his answer, Ariadne murmured, "Neither can I. I have been trying the whole time to understand women like Olivia's friend and what they see in Dorsey, but I am at a loss."

"You . . . were not attracted at all?"

"No. He made me ill. I found him revolting."

Cheerily, Ingram pushed his mug over for another refill. "So, what were you going to do about it? You clearly had some trap set. What was it and how can I help?"

Ariadne drained the pot into his cup. "Oh, all hope of that is over now. He will not come near me now."

"Why not? He never saw my face, I can guarantee that. I was just some anonymous assailant, as far as he knows."

"True. But after his behavior! How can he expect to get back into my good graces after abandoning me like that?"

"He did run like a frightened schoolgirl, didn't he?" Ingram chuckled.

"Worse. I have known some stalwart schoolgirls in my day. He squealed like a trussed pig."

Laughing, the viscount slapped his knee, and said, "But, like I said, he does not know it was me. If he thinks there is a chance you thought, oh, that he was running for help, he will be after you again. The temptation of your money will be too great. I assume that was the bait."

"Yes. The intent was to be foolish and yet canny, to let him know how much money could be his, but to hold out for a marriage proposal. Then, once he was hooked, he would find out that there was really not much money, and that it was tied up in such a way that I could not touch the principal—that is not true, by the way, but it is the story he would be fed. I would begin to speak of how if we married we would have to live very quietly in a village somewhere and raise sheep. Or something equally as ghastly.''

"Not bad," Ingram reluctantly said.

"Then, when he abandoned me after a very public engagement, we would ruin his reputation.''

Nodding, he said, "I see." He got up and paced to the window.

Ariadne, admiring his muscular grace, lost his next statement. She blushed as he stared at her with a questioning look. "I'm sorry, I was woolgathering. What did you say?''

"I said, that was not a bad plan to begin with, but it does nothing to get Mrs. Beckwith's friend's letters back." He paced some more, his dark brows furrowed. Finally he turned and leaned over the table, looking directly into Ariadne's eyes in a way that made her heart hammer again. "What would you say to a better plan? One that would tie him up for life?''

"I would welcome it, sir. Speak on.''

Chapter Eight

Ingram, standing in an alcove of the Conyngtons' ballroom, watched Ariadne, seated in the chaperon's area, and thought about their conversation of the previous day. She was not only clever, but witty and with an unexpectedly whimsical turn of mind. And her assertion that she believed in him had touched him more deeply than he liked to admit. He had learned to be casual about the "slings and arrows of outrageous fortune," but they still found their mark, and with every piercing volley had hardened his vulnerable heart. Lately, he had begun to feel frozen, finding more pleasure in the hearty and hardy company of the villains that thrived in the sour underbelly of London life than in company that could be called good.

Ariadne Lambert had thawed a little corner.

After working out their plan, they had gone on to talk of other things, and she had invited him to lunch. She had, she said, an excellent French cook, a talented gardener, a lazy footman, and a miserable maid. It showed that her priorities were first, her stomach, then her garden, with only a passing interest in social appearances and personal appearance. After lunch they had gone for a long walk on the Embankment from Battersea Bridge to Chelsea Bridge. Olivia Beckwith had never arrived, sending a note of apology with some scrawled reference to a familial emergency involving her youngest child.

He glanced again at her, sitting at her ease on the edge of the ballroom floor, her toe tapping to the music as she nodded to the occasional acquaintance. She wore again the hideous gown from the Vauxhall incident, having found, she told him, some measure of comfort that a sartorial mistake could have been put to some use.

As they had walked the riverbank, she had somehow winkled out of him his familial history, such as it was. How he and his mother had been abandoned by his aristocratic father, even though the man had legally married the woman he never openly acknowledged as his wife. He spoke of his childhood on the streets of London among the lowest of the low, pickpockets, rag and bone men, mud larks. And then the surprise when he found himself, as a young man, accosted by a solicitor and told that he was the legal heir, after some search and doubt, of the Viscount Ingram's estate.

Somehow during that afternoon, as they stood gazing out at the Thames winking and twinkling in the sun, he had found that he had her hand firmly clasped in his. When he had taken it he did not know, but the lady did not object. Every time he glanced over at her, he found new parts of her to admire, how straight her nose was, how full her generous mouth, how sculpted and perfect her high cheekbones, and how intelligent and beautiful her luminous gray eyes. By the end of the afternoon he would have leveled a facer on any man who dared call her homely.

Finally they spoke of lighter topics, the theater—both of them were aficionados—and the opera, which neither of them liked very much. But when the topic between them got around to books, and Ariadne had admitted her work, which was writing a history of the Thames, he offered to read the manuscript. She had said, "No, thank you very much."

At first he had been perturbed—he wasn't used to such flat denial—but after a few moments he was cheered considerably by the notion that she was merely shy about her work. Of course, she had denied that, too, when it came up in conversation. Then she had looked at him for a long, hard moment and said, "You are not one of those men, are you, who need an explanation every time you are told 'no'?"

Strangely, her direct behavior toward him was freeing. She treated him as an equal, not one to be deferred to. He was used to a strange sort of sneering deference, as Viscount Ingram, and it had always bothered him. He would prefer outright rudeness to forced obsequiousness. With Ariadne Lambert he would only ever get honesty.

Usually honesty had painful connotations. His last mistress had told him, when given her congee—only after she was safely in possession of a ruby necklace, of course— that he was so painfully ugly she could not help being glad to leave him, for bedding him had been an unpleasant chore. That was honesty of a sort.

He could not imagine Ariadne Lambert saying those words. Nor could he imagine offering her *carte blanche*. He watched her from his alcove, noting the shrewd gaze masqueraded by her vague smile.

His painfully honest mistress had been beautiful, lush and voluptuous, with glossy chestnut hair and milky skin, pouty lips and green eyes. And the morals of an alley cat, though to be ruthlessly honest, that hadn't bothered him while he was bedding her.

What would bedding a morally upright woman be like? Would it be stiff and awkward? Refreshingly different? Boringly clumsy?

Could that imaginary morally upright woman—a lady like, say, Miss Ariadne Lambert—be passionate in the bedroom?

He shifted, uncomfortable with his wandering thoughts. Miss Lambert was not now, nor would she ever be, anyone's mistress. The very thought was ludicrous. She deserved much more than a slip on the shoulder. What would she gain, after all? She was in funds, with no need of male support of any kind, financial or otherwise.

Nor—if one were inclined that way, which he was not— would she be anyone's idea of a conformable, demure wife. She had argued with him about the form of the plan they were about to enact, every idea of hers coming down on the side of boldness over caution.

Despite it all, she was interesting. And her laugh was delightful. And when she smiled, it changed her face completely.

As he studied her, her expression altered subtly.

Ingram glanced around the room and saw Dorsey. The fair-faced young man was paying court to a heavy-set girl who glowed with happiness at his attention. Ingram exchanged a glance with Ariadne, and pushed away from his lounging position by the wall to thread his way through the chattering crowd. Without a word he had let his confederate know he would find out who the young woman was, and whether she was rich enough to be in danger from Dorsey.

The terrace was dark. Ingram watched the glow of the tip of his cigar and waited, senses alert, the hairs on the back of his neck bristling. When she hesitantly stepped out onto the terrace, he absurdly wished their assignation was for another purpose than just the exchange of information.

"Ingram?"

Her husky voice was softer than usual, and a chill raced down his back. "Here," he said, stepping out of the shadows.

She moved toward him, joining him in the darkness near the potted shrubberies that lined the terrace. "What have you learned?"

"She could be in danger from our quarry. Her name is Miss Smith, and she is a coal merchant's daughter who has recently inherited an estate. The money and property is vast, and will all come to her husband should she marry. She is foolish enough to believe whatever Dorsey says to her, from all reports, and her chaperon is a fool."

"If she is so naive, she will not believe a word against him once he has his hooks into her." She frowned into the dark. "Do you think he will go so far as to marry her to gain her fortune?"

"Why not? He has done it before."

"What? He is married?"

"I have been doing some research on our friend since we parted yesterday. He has no siblings."

"So, his sister is not his sister but his mistress. How do they get away with it?"

"They are discreet. Very discreet. And though it seems like Dorsey has been in Society forever, he has only been in London a year. Before that it was Brighton. And before that Bath."

"And he is married?"

"Was. She died."

Ariadne drew in a long hissing breath. "Was he culpable?"

"No, I do not think anything so gothic as that occurred." He chuckled in the darkness and reached out to touch her shoulder. "You read too many romances, my dear. He is a villain, but not, I think, a murderer. But he went through his wife's rather modest fortune, it is said, and is looking for a considerably larger one now. He will not marry, I think, until he finds the right fortune on the right terms."

"Terms?"

"A fatuous young woman who will place all of her trust, and all of her money, in his hands."

"Why does he need so much money?" Ariadne felt Ingram's hand on her shoulder. He caressed her shoulder blade with absentminded strength and she felt a desire to move closer to him. So she did.

Sliding his hand over her shoulders and putting his arm around her, Ingram said, "He likes to gamble, and he likes to live well. He has no money of his own and he is neither a good nor a lucky gambler. Ergo, he needs funds to spend and has no desire to earn them. He needs, in short, a rich wife."

"Why did he not marry Olivia's friend, I wonder?" Her voice was a little breathless, she found, but steady.

"Her fortune was probably not large enough to tempt him." Ingram had dropped and extinguished his cigar and with his free hand caressed her hair.

Ariadne felt oddly detached from their conversation. It was quite odd, really, for two different things were going on. They were speaking of Dorsey and his machinations, but at the same time Ingram was, by degrees, taking her in his arms. Why?

"So we must find a way to tempt him away from Miss Smith before he entices her to do something rash."

"Yes. Something rash."

Ariadne felt the last of her reserve dissipate as Ingram's arms surrounded her. The moon peeked out from behind the plane tree in the garden, and she gazed up into the viscount's black eyes. He searched hers for a moment, and then lowered his mouth to cover hers.

She watched until the last possible moment, and then closed her eyes and waited.

Descriptions flashed through her brain, all the words of romance fiction. Dark swirling tunnels. Breathless moments.

But his kiss left her oddly unmoved.

Unmoved? She had dreamed of this moment, so why was she not melting into a puddle of feminine emotion? She opened her eyes. He smiled that quirky grin.

"Stop thinking, Ariadne, and relax. Close your eyes. I shall likely get coshed for asking this impertinent question, but was that your first kiss?"

Numbly, she nodded.

"And it did not meet your expectations. That is because you are thinking your way through it. Do not do that. This is one of those moments when you need to shut off that formidable intellect and just *feel*. Close your eyes."

She obeyed.

"Part your lips slightly."

Like an obedient infantry soldier, she did exactly as ordered.

"Now, more."

And as she moved her mouth, his closed over hers and his arms encircled her, pulling her close, holding her tight. Her heart, pounding, beat against his chest like the wings of an imprisoned bird, but she lost all sense of the thrum of her pulse as the moist velvet of his lips clung to her, and his tongue touched hers.

She was trembling, she knew, her whole body quaking with sensation now as she arched against him. Involuntarily, her hands moved up his broad back . . . and then she lost all memory.

A second or an hour or a lifetime later, she opened her eyes as he let go of her. "That was . . ."

"Stop, Ari," he said, his voice deep, his breathing raspy. "Do not try to categorize it, understand it, digest it. Just let it be."

She nodded and took in a deep, shaky breath.

"Now," he said. "We must go back inside and try to part that despicable whelp from the impressionable young lady he will beggar in a month, if we give him the opportunity."

Chapter Nine

"Where were you?" Olivia hissed, grabbing at Ariadne's
arm.

"Talking to Lord Ingram. Why?"

"You were gone for a half an hour! What on earth were
you talking about that could possibly take half an hour? And
why are you flushed? Are you quite well, Ari? And where
is Ingram? Why is he not here, too, if you two were talking
together?"

"He said it wouldn't do for us to reappear together, and
so he was just going to stay on the terrace and think for a
few moments longer. He wanted to have a cigar, he said."
She paused and frowned. "I don't think he was feeling quite
well. Perhaps he is coming down with something."

Olivia gazed at her steadily, her expert glance flicking
over Ariadne's flushed cheeks and glittering eyes, and the
loosened tendrils of hair that floated down over her shoulders. "What were you two doing out on that terrace? Ari,
do not be taken in by a man who is an even bigger scoundrel
than Dorsey! Remember what I overheard between him and
Duncannon." She frowned, her eyes narrow. "He was not
making love to you, was he?"

"Do not be ridiculous," Ariadne said briskly, pushing
her friend's hand away. She would not talk to Olivia about
Ingram anymore. When Ariadne told her that morning that

the viscount was going to help them, Olivia had expressed herself at length about the "gentleman" in question's suitability as a confederate, calling him a base-born scoundrel so many times, Ariadne had been forced to put an end to the conversation. She would listen to no more abuse of Ingram.

Ignoring the other woman's disapproval, Ariadne told her everything that Ingram had found out about Miss Smith. Olivia promised to discover more, but in the meantime, she sailed across the dance floor to meet Miss Smith and introduce her to more suitable young men than Dorsey. The girl was presentable enough, if plump and shy, and given exposure to other gentlemen, she might find that Dorsey's oily charm faded.

Dorsey, expertly finessed by Olivia Beckwith, moodily surveyed the room, and Ariadne abruptly glanced away. If he approached her, she did not quite know how to help him over the awkwardness of their last parting. She didn't want to, really. He deserved to be embarrassed for deserting a lady in his care when faced with what they both thought was an assailant.

But she needed him to come to her; it was vital to their plan that he be lured back in with the bait of Ariadne's money, and so she reluctantly turned her gaze back toward him and gave him a startled smile. She even beckoned to him. Very unladylike.

His look was even more surprised, but he advanced across the floor willingly enough, threading between the couples, evading a line of dancers. He bowed before her finally and said, hesitantly, "I do not deserve such magnanimous notice, Miss Lambert, after that unfortunate incident at Vauxhall. I must explain; you see, I ran to get help—our assailants were clearly so much larger than even I—but when I . . . when I returned, it was to find you gone. I searched, and even confronted the master of ceremonies, but he swore he saw no villains of any description, nor any lady of yours."

Ariadne was silent for a moment, admiring the brazen nature of his apology, if that was what it could be called. But then, what did he have to lose? His social cache was, ironically enough, higher than hers; if she accused him in public, he would just deny it and perhaps cast into question her own character for having "lured" him down the Lover's Walk.

However, she still must not appear too eager. There was a new plan brewing. "I must admit, Mr. Dorsey, I was surprised when you did not come back immediately. I was lucky, in that the villain—there was only one, sir—was frightened off the next minute by a group of people coming down the walk in answer to my cries."

"You should have stayed there longer, Miss Lambert," he said in tones of gentle reproof. He sat down beside her and took her gloved hand in his own. "I was so very worried when I came back and you were gone; I searched for you long and eagerly. I have worried myself to death!"

Ariadne drooped and sagged against him. "Oh, Mr. Dorsey, were you really so overwrought? That touches me deeply. I am so sorry for your worry!"

"There, there, Miss Lambert," he said, nervously glancing around the room. "Would you like to walk outside? The air will benefit you."

"I would like that," she said, giving him a simpering smile. The hook was reset, but the plan was slightly different. When Ingram had first told her of his idea, she had demurred. It had an element she could not be comfortable with, even now. It seemed to her that they were sinking to Dorsey's level. But Ingram was persuasive, and she willing to be persuaded. Her own plan was more vigorous, but Ingram's was devious. At length, she agreed to try his way.

Once out on the terrace, she maneuvered close to Dorsey, leaning against his chest, and said, "Oh, Mr. Dorsey, that awful experience at Vauxhall has made me even more aware of how much I really do need a gentleman to take care of me!"

It sounded ludicrous. Even if true, why would he think that she could possibly mean *him* when he had abandoned her with such alacrity?

"Do you really? Of course you do," he said.

He sounded distracted.

She put her hand on his chest and laid her head against him, noting that she felt none of the heart-pounding sensations Ingram engendered. "Sir, you make me feel so very safe. I am in unfamiliar waters, you see, for with all of this money that my poor auntie left me—a fortune such as I never expected to be mistress of—and not knowing what to do with it . . . Oh, I wish someone would just help me!"

"You mean, give you advice?" His voice was alert, now, his attention unwavering.

"No, I do not want advice. I do not want to take care of it at all."

"I could take over the handling of it for you," he suggested.

Ariadne demurred. "My poor, dead papa always said that the chore of taking care of a lady was to be handed over to a husband only. Her money was safe only then. Very adamant about that, was my poor papa. I honor his memory."

Was it going too fast? She raised her face in the dark and felt his breath on her mouth. "Mr. Dorsey . . . Edward . . . what shall I *do*?"

He kissed her then. His lips were soft enough, but with no firmness, and the kiss became . . . squishy. It compared very unfavorably with Ingram's magical kiss. Dorsey's hand wandered, too, down her back to her bottom and he squeezed. She jumped and gasped.

"Edward!"

"Ariadne!" He covered her mouth in another formless, wet kiss. "Marry me, my darling!"

She stifled her revulsion. "Yes, oh, yes, Edward!"

Chapter Ten

"Let me be the first to congratulate you, Mr. Dorsey!"

Dorsey started and pulled away from Ariadne. He stared uneasily at Ingram, who stood in the pool of light shed by the open French doors with Olivia Beckwith on his arm. Poor Olivia, Ariadne thought, biting her lip to keep from giggling. She looked like she would rather be anywhere than on the arm of a man she despised.

She played her part to perfection, though. A necessary part of the scheme, Olivia had the social standing to enforce Dorsey's rash moonlight promise. She stepped forward.

"Mr. Dorsey, you have attained a rare and perfect gem in Ariadne Lambert. Let me be the first to congratulate you, my dear." She stepped forward, a little too happily dropping Ingram's arm, and gave her friend a kiss on the cheek. "Now we must see about bride clothes. I know the best seamstress, and she does not cost the earth. We will let the gentlemen alone to speak of other things."

Ingram watched the two women walk away and admired the perfect, lingering, regretful glance Ariadne threw back as she said, over her shoulder, "We will talk tomorrow, Edward, dear. One o'clock. My house."

Dorsey, stunned-looking, nodded.

Ingram handed him a cigar. "Well, Dorsey, you have done well for yourself."

The other man preened. "Not too bad."

"She's a fascinating woman, is Miss Lambert."

"And rich," Dorsey said, winking, as he lit his cigar from Ingram's.

"How much?"

Dorsey shrugged. "Enough. She owns a house in Chelsea."

"Really. Did you check out the figures?"

"Her figure?"

Ingram restrained the urge to roll his eyes. Dorsey, though clever, was not intelligent. There was a subtle distinction. "No, the money. Do you have a sum? Did you ask around?"

Dorsey drew himself up. "A gentleman would never do such a thing." It was clear he had not even thought to do so. "Besides, ladies do not lie about things like that."

Ingram raised his eyebrows. "In my estimation," he said, with a silent apology to the very intelligent Miss Lambert, "women don't have any idea what money means or how much it takes to live. An enormous sum in her mind might be five hundred pounds. Better get it in writing."

Dorsey, for the first time looking unsure of himself, said, "I will do no such thing, Ingram. Only a base fortune hunter would do that."

"Mmm, yes. Wouldn't want to look like a swindler, eh?" Ingram paced around Dorsey, thinking that perhaps he had overestimated this particular rogue. Dorsey had, possibly, just been lucky in his victims before now. He tossed his dice. "I know a gentleman of whom you might ask a few questions," he murmured.

The other man frowned. "I have no need. Miss Lambert is perfectly well set. You are just jealous. I saw you buzzing about her—you are out of funds yourself, no doubt—but you should have known ladies prefer a fair face over ... well, over almost anything else, even a title."

Ingram nodded. "Perhaps you are right, Dorsey. I wish you much luck of Miss Lambert and her ... well-shrouded fortune."

He tossed his cigar down and crushed it under his heel. He moved toward the French doors, but paused and said, "But unless you are truly in love with Miss Lambert and would have her on any terms, I would make sure her nest is as well-feathered as you think before committing yourself to eternity in her bed. She appears to be a very healthy woman and will likely live to be ninety, money or no money.''

"What did he say to you?" It was the next morning, and Ariadne had walked with Ingram along the Embankment. Together they gazed out over the Thames, watching a shouting match between two boatmen who had scraped bows. The morning, from a damp start, had turned out to be unseasonably warm.

"Unfortunately our bird is very sure of your veracity as far as money is concerned," he replied. "Or seems to be. I hope I have planted the seeds of doubt."

Her hand rested lightly on Ingram's arm, but her fingers twitched with the nervousness she felt just being close to him. How could they talk like this and not discuss what had happened between them just the night before? He had kissed her, a long lingering kiss that had left her with little doubt of her feelings toward him.

He, unfortunately, was still very much a mystery to her, a delicious enigma. He was treating her now with the cool, disinterested attitude of friendship, and it made her jumpy and anxious. But how could she expect anything else? She knew so little of him, really, but what he had told her as they walked and talked these few times. If he was like most men, though, he would not be interested in a vinegary, plain spinster of intellectual bent. He would probably prefer a fiery Italian opera singer, or a Cockney shop girl, or . . . a million other women than a virtuous spinster of a certain age. And despite his unprepossessing looks, Lord Ingram was a force to be reckoned with, a powerful man many women would be drawn to, handsome or not.

They had been silent for a few minutes. They really had nothing more to talk about. When Dorsey arrived at one, it would be up to Ariadne to heighten his doubts, magnify his worries. She knew her job very well.

He stood staring out at the river, the play of thoughts and

emotions on his rugged face fascinating to her. How she
would love to watch him, touch him, know him more deeply.
He interested her in a way no man ever had before, though
she had had her share of infatuations, all of them unrequited.

His dark brows drew down over eyes the color of coal,
and he shook his head. A self-effacing smile flitted over his
lips, and he sighed. He turned and said, "I suppose we ought
to get back, Miss Lambert."

"Ari. You called me Ari once."

"Ari. Airy. Aerie. Aery." He varied the pronunciation
each time, subtly, lingering over the syllables, his deep voice
husky.

She loved the sound of his voice, melodious, with a burr.
It was like the purr of the giant cat he resembled. "What
shall I call *you*? Ingram does not seem to fit, though it is
proper, I know."

He shrugged. "My name is Lovell Melcher."

She smiled suddenly. "Shall I call you Love?"

His dark eyes widened and he seemed arrested in mid
breath. "What did you say?"

"N-nothing," she said, alarmed. "It was just a . . . a joke.
On your name . . . Lovell."

"Oh." He took her arm. "I should get you back."

"Yes. I must prepare for my piece."

They returned to her home with no further conversation,
and he departed.

Ariadne sat with her hands folded. She wore her most
hideous dress, one she had forgotten about, so desperately
unflattering it was, and her glasses, and had a hank of knitting
on her lap, something fuzzy and amorphous. She should
have borrowed a few of the scroungy cats from the livery
stable at the inn, but hadn't thought of it in time.

She had to make this convincing. It was imperative that
Dorsey be uneasy, alarmed, and to that end she must appear
worried and frightened. So she began to think of the most
difficult periods in her life; it was not hard, for her existence
had not been without turmoil.

There had been times of great pain: losing both her parents

when she was just fifteen, within months of each other, from cholera, and before that her baby sister's death from typhus. Struggling with little money, just enough to get by for a long time, until her financial affairs had been straightened out by a kind great-uncle.

She felt the leaden weight of the old pain descend. She had been just getting to know him—he had been benevolence personified, and was going to adopt her as his heir—and then he died suddenly of an apoplectic fit before any formal arrangement had been made. She had been there and help-less, just nineteen and alone again.

His sister had been the one to whom she finally turned, and there was a measure of peace in her household, at least. She had not been a warm woman, but good at heart, and grateful for Ariadne's care. Ill for many years, her death, though sad, had meant freedom for the poor woman.

And freedom and plenty for Ariadne, at last.

Dolly came to the door, her blue eyes wide and her cheeks pink. "Gentleman to see you, miss," she said breathlessly.

"Show him in."

Dolly had not reacted that way over Ingram, so this must be the fair of form and foul of mind Dorsey. Ariadne took a bit of the tender flesh on her arm and pinched, very hard. Tears welled up in her eyes.

"Miss Lambert . . . Ariadne, I am so happy . . ." Dorsey, hat in hand, advanced into the room toward her.

Ariadne raised her face to him, knowing her tear-filled eyes behind the glasses must appear huge.

"My dear," Dorsey said in melting tones. "What is wrong?" He sat in the chair by her, placing his hat on the floor underneath it.

Sniffing, Ariadne raised her voice and injected a whine into it. "M-my solicitor, beastly man, has just left. He tells me I will have to leave this house! I c-can't afford it!"

"What?" Dorsey's tone was hollow.

"And I have been so economical, only hiring one male servant, not eating beef but once a week. And no beeswax candles, only tallow!" She sobbed and took off her specta-cles, dabbing at her eyes with a scrap of a handkerchief.

"Surely just a mistake," Dorsey said. "You cannot be turned from a house you own . . ."

"But I do not own this house! I just rented it for the Season. I wanted to see what life was like in London. Oh, and it has been just a dream! First, Olivia has been so kind and gotten me invitations to all her fine functions, though I know we do not travel in the same circles at all. And then . . ." Ariadne sighed. "And then I met you, *dearest* Edward. I am so fortunate. Just as I am having to face the unpleasant truth that I shall have to go back to Thrapston . . ."

"Go back to . . . where?"

"Thrapston. My home village. I shall have to rent a tiny cottage there . . . just enough room for two!" She giggled idiotically and sighed, putting her hand over his. "You can work for the vicar, Mr. Post—he is quite elderly and needs help writing his sermons—and I can raise chickens and sell the eggs. We shall manage!" She gave her fiancé a watery smile. "Together, man and wife, forever and ever!" She sighed.

Chapter Eleven

"Ingram, may I have a word with you?"

The viscount laid down the paper he had been perusing in the reading room of his moderately priced club, Aleworthy's. He looked up at Dorsey, and nodded. "Certainly. Hope there is nothing amiss?"

"N-not at all," Dorsey stuttered. "Just need the name of that fellow you said could find out a person's worth discreetly."

"Ah, yes." Ingram leisurely stretched and put his hands behind his head. "He is a banker, but with an affection for the betting books. Always needs a little cash."

"Where can I meet him?"

"Where? He will not risk meeting you in a public place. After all, not the done thing to sell information like that. I will tell you after I speak to him. I can make an appointment for you tonight, if you are in a rush. Hope nothing has gone wrong between you and the inestimable Miss Lambert?"

"N-not a thing." Dorsey's downy upper lip was beaded with sweat and he was turning his hat around in his hands.

Ingram watched him for a moment, then signaled to one of the waiters who stood discreetly waiting for just such a summons. "Brandy, Donald, and be generous." He grabbed the papers that were piled on the chair beside him—they discouraged those who would perch and chat—and indicated it. "Have a seat, Dorsey. You look like a man who needs a drink."

"Much obliged, Ingram." Dorsey dropped into the chair and put his head in his hands, groaning.

"So, I take it from your request to see my banker friend that things are not all that you thought?"

"She talks of giving up her *leased* Chelsea house. Thought from the way she talked formerly that she owned it. And she wants me to work for the vicar in Throck-someplace-or-other. The *vicar*! Writing his deuced sermons, or some such nonsense. And she talks of keeping chickens!"

Ingram silently congratulated Ariadne on a brilliant ploy. A whiff of the cloth was more potent than anything else, when it came down to a gambling-addicted young man. And chickens? Brilliant. Nothing more prosy or boring than chickens.

"But if you are going to marry her," he drawled, "you will be dealing with her solicitor when you do the marriage agreement. Whatever she has will come to you. You will find out then what she is worth."

"I cannot wait," he said nervously, wringing his hands over and over each other. "It will be too late once the papers are being drawn up. If she is not flush, then I will need to find a way to get m'self out of it. I need money, and soon."

Ingram stared at Dorsey. He couldn't have been more than twenty-seven or twenty-eight, and yet he had already embarked on a career that was sure to see him in either Marshalsea or Newgate before long. Ingram had done his research; Dorsey's late wife had left him in possession of ten thousand pounds, an amount that should have been adequate for his sustenance for many years, if he had lived frugally. But there was nothing of that left, and the young man's creditors were becoming impatient. He had used up his credit at the hotel he had last been residing at and now had rooms at a boardinghouse in Cheapside. The young woman who acted as Dorsey's "sister" was, of course, his mistress, and lived there with him under the name of Miss Anne Dorsey.

But before she had assumed that identity, she had been called Mrs. Bonnie Chandler and had lived in the seaside town of Ilfracombe in Exmoor. Mr. Chandler, a rather burly merchant seaman, was still looking for her.

All this Ingram had culled from discreet questioning, and a tidy sum dispensed to a smart little "inquiry agent," as he called himself, a small gentleman who made his money by ferreting out secrets others would rather leave mysterious.

The brandy arrived, and was decanted generously. Dorsey drank it like it was cheap hock. He drank like a man desperate. All the better. It was going to be an interesting evening.

When the message arrived, Ariadne was struggling with phrases to describe the salubrious nature of the air in Chelsea, for a chapter of her book on the Thames. No matter what she did, the words came out dry and dull. As it stood, no one thinking clearly would read *England's Artery: The Thames and its Tributaries* except the most avid river buff. Assuming anyone would publish such rubbish.

Perhaps she was not a writer after all.

The message was a welcome respite. She threw down her quill, sending a spattering of ink over the white tablecloth, and took the paper from her lazy footman, James, who then sauntered off to do nothing somewhere else. The note was brief and to the point, in a slanting, compact hand that was typical of the writer.

The game is on; the prey has been flushed. Set the hounds to baying.

Immediately, Ariadne scribbled a note to Olivia and rushed to get ready. It was going to be an interesting evening.

In the shadows of the trees that lined the Embankment near Chelsea Old Church, Ariadne waited for the signal. Olivia, draped in black and veiled, too, hushed her companion, who was prone, it seemed, to a kind of moaning monologue that Ariadne had tired of in the first three minutes of their acquaintance.

A fog rose from the river; Ariadne wiped her glasses impatiently, and looked at the watch pinned to the bosom of her dark wool spencer.

Five minutes to midnight. Ingram had a surprisingly dramatic turn of mind when it came to setting the scene. They could have done all of this in her drawing room, but they must needs gather in the foggy gloom because Ingram said so. For a man who seemed so pragmatic on the surface, it was an interesting glimpse into his character. The timing and the setting could not have been more theatrical, with the scrape of a boat bobbing at a dock, the fog, and the sound of water rats skittering too close for comfort. And behind them, Chelsea Old Church loomed, the bell tower clear against the moonlit clouds.

Midnight tolled.

The sound of footsteps echoed, and Ariadne's heart beat faster, catching up with the impatient tattoo of booted heels. Tonight would either see the end of Dorsey's career as a scoundrel and blackmailer, or he would be turned in to the authorities. And tonight would see the end of her own association with Lord Ingram, for what could he possibly have in common with a bluestocking spinster? His kisses must have been an aberration, a strange whimsy in a man known to walk his own path with little regard for the feelings of others.

But it was no time to be thinking of Ingram's intoxicating kisses. She straightened and stood, waiting. Olivia's companion, veiled like her friend, was leaning heavily against her.

Near the church, by the wrought-iron fence that topped a low brick wall, a dark figure lingered, but Ariadne could not make out who it was; a confederate of Ingram's perhaps.

She could see the figures now looming out of the fog, of Ingram and Dorsey, Ingram with the bolder step and broader shoulder, his caped greatcoat fluttering around his booted legs as he strode forward. Dorsey, now that the time was near, appeared hesitant, sensing perhaps that he was not coming for the purpose he had been led to believe. He skittered behind Ingram.

She stepped forward, into the very faint light shed by the church gatehouse's lamp.

"Here," she said, her voice muffled in the eddying fog.

Ingram took Dorsey's arm and guided him forward. He

hung back now, like a dog unwillingly returned to a cruel master.

"What is going on, Ingram?" he said, his voice quavering.

Olivia stepped forward now, with her veiled friend. "Dorsey," she said, her voice trembling. She threw back her black veil and dramatically pointed one finger. "I accuse you of the base crime of blackmail."

Ariadne reflected that Olivia had more in common with Ingram than she would likely confess. It was like bad theater.

"What?" Dorsey's eyes widened. "I don't understand." Quivering, he took a step back, but was held firm by the viscount's iron grip. "I am not now, nor have I ever been a blackmailer."

The other woman stepped forward and pushed back her veil. She was revealed to be an older woman, with a round, handsome face. "Edward," she said, in the moaning voice Ariadne had come to despise. "Please, just give me back the letters!" She put out her gloved hands beseechingly.

"Henrietta?" Dorsey stared at her, his expression mingled relief and anger. "What are you doing here? I *told* you to leave me alone."

Ariadne frowned.

Ingram said, "Do not try to weasel out of this one, Dorsey." He had a firm hold on the younger man's arm.

"I am not trying to ... I say, what is going on here?" Dorsey began to struggle. "Miss Lambert? What are you doing here, and with ..."

Olivia said, impatiently, "Henrietta, *tell* him! Tell him that if he tries to blackmail you about those letters you will see him in Newgate, no matter what the consequences."

The rotund woman looked sheepish, and said, "I *do* want my letters back, Edward. And *you*! Oh, Edward, my love, come *back* to me!"

With that, she threw herself down at Dorsey's feet while he stared down at her in wide-eyed puzzlement.

Ingram released Dorsey's arm and pulled the woman to her feet. "Madam, do I understand this correctly?" His voice was dry and almost amused. "Dorsey never blackmailed you. You used us to corner him for you and accost him. Perhaps you even hoped to force him back into your bed.''

"I love him! I will *always* love him. He knows that. After what we have been to each other . . .''

Dorsey, looking hideously embarrassed, said, "Henrietta, I hold you in the highest esteem, but I told you it was over. You shouldn't have followed me here from Brighton.''

Olivia Beckwith, a disgusted look on her face, said, "Henrietta Godersham, I cannot believe you let me make a fool of myself like this. I am going back to my husband before he calls in my physician. I have had to conceal all of this from him, and he has been most alarmed by my behavior of late. Good-bye to all of you.'' She pulled her veil back down over her face, but then impatiently threw it back up over her hat. "Can't see a blessed thing with that on. Ari, I will see you on the morrow. My apologies to all, but I am washing my hands of this affair.'' She turned and left, her footsteps echoing in the fog until she disappeared. The distant sound of a horse's hooves came to them after a moment.

The figure that had been lingering along the church wall—Ariadne had forgotten about that loiterer in the drama of the moment—broke away from the shadows and raced over to their strange group. It was the young woman who had been posing as Dorsey's sister. "Edward, what are they doing to you?''

"Bonnie,'' he groaned. "I told you to stay home. I told you I would take care of you, and I will.''

Ingram grabbed Dorsey by the collar of his coat and said, "Well, at least you can turn over the letters to this lady, or I will send a note to this young lady's husband—this Anne who is not Anne at all, but Mrs. Bonnie Chandler—as to her whereabouts. It has come to my attention that he is looking for her, after you basely tempted her away from his protection. Unless you do what I say, I will return her to him.''

Anne/Bonnie screamed and staggered, and Ariadne found her own services as support necessary. She fanned the girl's face. "For heaven's sake, Ingram, must you be so gruff?''

Chagrined, the viscount said, "Good God, I just said I would send her back to her husband! I do not understand any of this except that Dorsey does still have this lady's letters." He indicated the weeping Henrietta Godersham.

"Please, Ingram, do not contact Chandler," Dorsey said, his hands clasped in a pleading gesture. "I will do anything. Henrietta can have back her letters; I never wanted them in the first place." He took the weeping Anne/Bonnie in his arms and held her close. "Just do not contact Chandler. He is a brute and a monster, and will kill her if she is forced to go back to him. Especially in the state she is in."

Ingram, his head in his hands, muttered, "Let me get this straight; you, Dorsey, *rescued* this girl from her husband, who beat her."

"Not my husband, sir," the girl said, sniffing. "We . . . we was never married legal-like. But he did beat me. Eddy is kind, and . . . and I love him."

"She is . . ." Dorsey took a deep breath, but even in the dim light of the gatehouse lantern, it was plain that he was pale and sickly looking. "She is carrying my child," he said. "I wanted to marry her, but I had no idea how I was going to support us, so . . ."

"How noble. So you thought you would marry me and support her on the side from my money," Ariadne said, her tone sharp, her hands on her hips. "Instead of marrying the girl and finding a job."

He shrugged, a sullen expression on his handsome face. "Don't know how to do anything but gamble and talk."

The moon disappeared from view and the Embankment grew darker. Ariadne, done with all of the nonsense, the drama having turned out to be a farce, said, "Henrietta, Mr. Dorsey will return your letters to you via Lord Ingram. Will that be agreeable?"

Dorsey nodded, and so did Henrietta. Ingram moved to join Ariadne. He took her arm in his and squeezed it.

"And Dorsey, you will marry the mother of your child," Ingram said.

In the shadowy darkness Ariadne thought that Dorsey did not look wholly enthusiastic, but Ingram's powerful personality cowed him, and he mumbled, "If you think I should, my lord."

"You should," Ingram said, grimly. "Give your child a

name, at least, Dorsey. It is all my father did for me, but it turned out well in the end. I think I will make sure you live up to your promise. We are all a witness to his promise to marry this young woman?''

''I am a witness, Lord Ingram,'' Ariadne said. ''And since the young man is about to breach his promise to me, he had better keep this one or I will see him in court.''

Dorsey was silent, but the girl burst into tears of joy; at least Ariadne hoped they were joyous tears. She was not so sure they were doing her a favor, but the stain of illegitimacy would not harm her baby, at least.

''I think this play is at an end,'' Ingram said quietly. ''Miss Lambert, may I walk you back to your home?''

She would have liked that; she would have even invited him in, though that was shocking at this time of night. She could picture them in her elegant drawing room, with the moonlight glistening off the Thames through the front window, drinking sherry and talking over the evening. His dark eyes would glitter with amusement at the way this drama had played out, and she would watch his expression, loving the sight of his broken nose and combative chin. But there were others involved.

''I think you should accompany Mrs. Godersham home, since Olivia has decamped on us,'' she whispered, glancing at the pale and weeping woman, the deserted and desolate Henrietta.

''You *would* think of that,'' he said grudgingly, following her gaze. ''I would much rather be with you.''

She felt a thrill race down her back. ''Would you?''

''I would.'' He turned back and caught her expression. His lips parted to say something, but then he thought better of it evidently, and sighed. ''May I call on you tomorrow?''

''Certainly,'' she replied. ''Good-night, Ingram.''

''Goodnight, Ari. *A demain.*''

Chapter Twelve

Ariadne sat out in the walled garden behind her house. The day had turned out fine, the warmest day of late spring so far. Olivia had been by in the morning, and over tea they had canvassed all of Henrietta's perfidy, how she had taken in her best friend, and for a weasel like Edward Dorsey.

And now she was anticipating Lord Ingram's arrival. What to expect? She had hopes. He had said he would rather be with her than Henrietta Godersham, though even Dorsey probably would have preferred her company over that of the wailing widow. It was small crumbs.

But he had kissed her and called her intelligent; for someone unused to such heady praise that was strong wine indeed. As for herself, she had come to the conclusion, after a sleepless night, that she was in love with him. He was, to her mind, her perfect match, as little needing polite Society as she, and with enough pain in his background that he would not expect every day to be sunny. She could not abide those who expected life to be one smooth road with no twists and turns. It indicated a vacant mind and a poverty of spirit.

And yet she could be building air castles from moon dreams. She counted the facts, as they stood.

He had kissed her. Well, he had probably kissed a hundred women or more, while he had been her only experience.

He had called her intelligent. But intelligence was not a

noted aphrodisiac, or the libraries would be busier and the
mantua makers idle.

He had said he liked her company. But that was in comparison to a whining, lying, foolish woman who didn't know
herself to be lucky when she so clearly was, to have escaped
from the insignificant clutches of Edward Dorsey.

She sighed and played with her glasses, turning them so
they could catch the sunlight and focus it on the newspaper.

"You will set yourself on fire," Ingram said.

Ariadne turned and gazed at him, where he stood, lounging
against the gated entrance to her garden. "You came," she
said.

"Of course. Did I not say I would? I always keep my
word. That is what Dorsey will learn at four o'clock today,
to his distress. He tried to leave London without his mistress
this morning. I have a fellow, though, who caught him. He
will not try it again."

Ariadne shivered in the sunlight. How much did she really
know of this man? Enough? Not enough? "You . . . did not
hurt him, did you?"

"Of course not, Ari. Do you think me a brute?"

She hesitated, but shook her head. No, he was not a brute,
but there was a layer of him that was far from civilized.

"I only ever beat those who thoroughly deserve it." He
quirked a half smile. "And who can defend themselves."
His expression grew serious again as he gazed at her steadily.
"We know so little of each other, really, don't we?" He
moved away from the gate and came toward her, an intent
look on his dark face.

"Yes. So very little."

"Is it enough, I wonder?" He pulled a chair close to hers,
turned her glasses over just as the paper started to smoke,
and took her bare hand in his own. He caressed it.

Enough for what?

"Enough for what?" She was not one to let her thoughts
go unsaid. She had learned that one often had only one
chance.

He smiled. "I love that you do that. Confront, challenge,
advance. What an unusual woman you are."

Ariadne was not sure, but it did not exactly sound like a

compliment. But speaking of confronting . . . "Ingram, Olivia Beckwith overheard something, something you said to someone else. I believe there is likely a rational explanation for it, but I would hear it."

One eyebrow raised, he said, "Ask away."

She told him what Olivia had overheard between him and Lord Duncannon, about money. That Ingram had better get the money to him soon, before it was "too late."

He thought for a moment and then laughed out loud. "Duncannon! That fretful old haggis. It is a little embarrassing, actually, but if you want to hear about it . . ." She nodded and he went on. "As trite as it sounds, one of his manservants impregnated one of my maids. Don't ask me how when they have so little free time, but it was managed. And the impudent fellow said he would marry her, but that there needed to be some money changing hands."

"And so you were going to pay him off?" She was a little shocked that such bad behavior was to be rewarded, and by a man like Ingram.

"Better than to leave the girl with a bastard child and her reputation in tatters, my dear. This will allow them to start life over."

"I knew it would be something like that," she said, staring into his eyes, loving the dark, gleaming depths. "I knew it would turn out to be something that showed how good you are."

He shook his head. "I am not so good, but that you think I am means a great deal to me. It may even make me a better man, eventually. I had thought never to find anyone like you," he mused, gazing down at their twined hands.

She wished hers were not so bony. She wished she was prettier. Plumper. "Like me? In what way?"

"My match. My equal. My superior. I do not mean superior in any moral sense. Most women are better than I." With his free hand he touched her cheek and gazed steadily into her eyes. "Do you like adventure, Ari?"

Off-kilter as usual in his presence, she said, immediately, "Yes, most definitely. Although I have never had one. Other than last night."

He grinned, and then laughed, his dark eyes dancing with

reflected sunlight. When he sobered, he gazed at her and said, "Ari, marry me. Marry me and your life will be an adventure, I promise you. I am not an easy man to live with. I have vast faults, one of them being an uncertain temper. But I am never cruel, nor mean. I know how to value beauty and intelligence, and you have both of those, and . . ."

"Stop!" Ari put up one hand. "Ingram, if we are to marry, I mean to make you remain honest. I am certainly not beautiful."

"I didn't think so either, at first. But I do now, and so I *am* being honest."

Ari thought for a moment. It was a lovely compliment, really, she decided. "You have not told me you love me. I should like that."

"But only if it is the truth, correct?"

She took in a shaky breath. "Yes," she said wistfully, staring into eyes dark as obsidian, dark eyes she had learned to adore. "Only if it is the truth."

He slipped off his chair and knelt before her, taking both her hands in his. "Ari, I love you. I truly do. You make me laugh, and that is not an easy thing to do. I am reckoned rather grim. And I want to show you what love can be. I have not experienced it myself, but I have a strong feeling that things I have done before will be entirely new experiences with you."

She shivered, remembering kisses in the dark. "And I love you, too, Ingram."

"Thank God." He swallowed hard, and swayed for just a second.

Alarmed, she freed one hand and put it on his bulky shoulder. "What is wrong, Ingram?"

"I was afraid you would not be able to say it. Afraid you didn't love me. *Couldn't* love me. You are too good for me, you know."

"You do not know me well enough to say that."

"But I will soon. And then I may sicken you by telling you every day that you are far too good for me. Will you marry me?"

"If you sicken me about it, I will tell you to leave off or I will crush the pedestal you have put me on."

"Will you marry me?"

"Of *course* I will. Do you think me stupid enough to say no to a man like you?"

He rose and pulled her to her feet, wrapping his arms around her. The sunlight poured through the willow and touched their faces. As one, they turned their cheeks up to the sun. Ari smiled, and he kissed first her cheek and then her lips, tenderly, then deeper and with growing passion.

"Shall we make it a huge wedding, very Society, very formal, with every lord and lady in attendance?" He put his forehead against hers as they stood, entwined, under the willow. "I can afford it, you know. I am very, *very* rich."

"Certainly. And I shall ask the Duke of Wellington to give me away and we shall see if the Princess of Wales will attend me."

His gusty laugh echoed off the walls of the garden.

"Or we can marry in two days in Olivia's home in Mayfair," she said breathlessly. "She will put up a fuss, for she does not like you, but we will bully her into it."

"Then we could begin our honeymoon immediately. I suggest a barge trip down the Thames. And a different hotel room every night. We may wear out our welcome in each one, if my instincts are right about you, Miss Lambert." He kissed her deeply, fiercely, his breathing becoming raspy. And then he said, "May I live with you while I build us a home here in Chelsea?"

"Why do we not just stay in this one forever?"

"Good idea. I shall sell my property. May we have cats? Three? Named Prinny, Maria, and Caroline?"

"As long as I may keep chickens."

Nonsense thoroughly canvassed, they stared into each other's eyes for a moment, and he said, "I never thought I would marry."

"Neither did I."

"Are we doing the right thing?"

"Absolutely." It came out rather shaky, and so she said again, voice stronger, "Absolutely. I intend to make love with you very soon, and I can only do that if we are married, as I have been very properly raised."

Ingram's laughter rang out so loudly that Ari's neighbors

poked their heads out of windows that overlooked her garden. "I love you, Ariadne Lambert, soon to be my lady, Viscountess Ingram."

"Viscountess Ingram! I never thought of that. Oh, dear, shall I have to start making social calls?"

"Not if I have anything to say."

"Good. I should be dreadful at it."

He bent his head to kiss her again, shocking the onlooking neighbors, who were wondering what the commotion was all about. "Do you know what you are getting yourself into?" he asked, finally.

"I hope so. You will remain irascible, and we will likely find out we have much to argue about. I have discovered that I am a dreadful writer, so I think I shall give it up and spend all my time hectoring you."

"Good. And I shall spend all my time shocking you with stories of my youth."

"Except at night," she said primly. "When you will be quite busy."

"Who said it would only be at night?" He glanced around, noting a couple of dumfounded gazes directed their way. "We have already shocked your neighbors. Shall we stop?"

"No, let them stop staring if it bothers them so. Kiss me again."

"Gladly." He was as good as his word, kissing her deeply and fiercely. "And then I must go and bully Dorsey into marrying that poor girl."

"Oh, dear," Ariadne said. "Should we do something for them? Find him a job? Give them some money?"

"Good God, no! I did not know you were so soft." He caressed her and gazed down into her eyes. "Maybe I will put in a good word for him at a company I have an interest in. But if he goes back to his old ways—I am not convinced he will even stay with this girl, you know, child or not— then I reserve the right to toss him out."

Ari bit her lip. "Do you think we are doing the right thing, making them marry? Should we perhaps . . ."

"Shut up!" He snickered when he saw her tight-lipped shock. "Good, that did the job. Ari, if there is one thing I have learned, it is that people must be left to stand on their own. Give them too much support and you only make them weak. That girl loves him, and her baby needs a name. It is the best we can do. Other than that, it is their own lives."

"I suppose you are right." She lifted her chin. "But don't you *ever* tell me to shut up again!"

"That's my girl. I love you, Ariadne Lambert."

"And I love you, my lord."

"That is the first time I have ever liked being called that. I think I shall insist on it, even in the bedroom. Especially in the bedroom." He put his arm around her waist and walked her toward the house. "And now, since I am going to do something shocking to you, I think we had better go inside."

Her stomach trembling, Ari understood in that moment that the world was going to be a very different place for her from this moment on. And she couldn't wait.

"Do you think you could shock the servants enough to make Dolly quit? She is truly an abysmal maid."

"I'll see what I can do," he said with a low, wicked chuckle. "I think I can probably manage it."

They entered the house and closed the door behind them.